PARADISE
BAY

Also by James Michael Pratt

Ticket Home

The Lighthouse Keeper

The Last Valentine

PARADISE BAY

James Michael Pratt

St. Martin's Press ✿ New York

Grateful acknowledgment is made for permission to reprint the following:

"Eve of Destruction." Words and Music by P.F. Sloan. © Copyright 1965 Universal—MCA MUSIC PUBLISHING, A DIVISION OF UNIVERSAL STUDIOS, INC. (ASCAP). International copyright secured. All rights reserved.

"Strangers in Paradise." Words and Music by Klaus Meine, Herman Rarebell, Jim Vallance. © Copyright UNIVERSAL—POLYGRAM INT. PUBL., INC. on behalf of POLYGRAM INT. PUBL., INC. (ASCAP). International copyright secured. All rights reserved.

"Strangers in Paradise." Words and Music by Jim Vallance, Klaus Meine, Herman Rarebell. © Copyright ALMO MUSIC CORP. on behalf of itself and TESTATYME MUSIC (ASCAP). International copyright secured. All rights reserved.

"Woolly Bully." By Domingo Samudio. Copyright © 1964 (Renewed) Three Wise Boys Music LLC (BMI) and Sony/ATV Songs LLC d/b/a Tree Publishing Co. (BMI). International copyright secured. All rights reserved. Reprinted by permission.

"Woolly Bully." Copyright 1964 (Renewed) Sony/ATV Songs LLC and Embassy Music Corp. All rights on behalf of Sony/ATV Songs LLC administered by Sony/ATV Music Publishing, 8 Music Square West, Nashville, TN, 37203. All rights reserved. Used by permission.

ISBN 0-312-26634-0

For my brothers Grant and Nick,
U.S. Army Vietnam veterans, '65–'67
and for my friend Lt. Commander Ronald Ringo, Jr.,
Chaplain USN—
God's recon men

ACKNOWLEDGMENTS

THANK YOU, JEANNE, AMY, AND MIKE FOR YOUR LOVE AND support. I couldn't be creative without you and all you do for me.

My sincere thanks to Ken Atchity, Andrea McKeown, Chi-Li Wong, and others of Atchity Entertainment International. I will always be grateful for your belief and support. Thanks also to my legal counsel, Joel McKuin, for his expert support.

Jennifer Enderlin, associate publisher and senior editor at St. Martin's Press, has again been so thoroughly enjoyable to work with and has made each of my four published novels a better work through her skilled insights and judgment. Thanks, Jen!

Dr. Neil Whitaker at Central Utah Medical Clinic, friend and personal physician, and Dr. Kevin Jenkins of the Nevada Clinic helped review medical concepts for this book. My warmest thoughts and best wishes to you for all your expertise, advice, and also treatments as I discover avenues to wholeness and physical well-being.

Leo Weidner, Mark Kastleman, and Mitch Santell, as personal friends and business associates in writing and radio production, have been huge supporters of my concepts in the genre of general and moral fiction writing. Thank you for everything, but especially the brotherhood.

Thanks to my personal friends Stephen Biddulph, major USMC (retired) and Vietnam War veteran, and Navy Chaplain Lt. Commander Ron Ringo, who served as a Marine during his younger years. Their insights into the "Corps" and proper portrayal of Marine life and military vernacular were essential to the flavor I sought for *Paradise Bay*.

I want to publicly express my joy found in the support and encouragement of many hundreds of readers. I do believe their kind thoughts and wishes for my writing became manifest in this, a story of innocence and love lost and found—*Paradise Bay*.

Alas for those who never sing and die
with all their music left in them.

—OLIVER WENDELL HOLMES

PARADISE
BAY

1

OVERTURE

JACK SANTOS HAD LONGED FOR THIS DAY HIS ENTIRE LIFE. He had always carried with him the childhood fantasy of having a dad. He had been told his father was dead. Killed in Vietnam. But here he was, standing at the hospital room door of a man in his fifties, a man in a catatonic stupor, dead to the world but alive somewhere deep inside.

He had been informed only recently of his relationship by an attorney for the sleeping man's estate. The story was as long as the time the man had been away from the world of the living. It was a thirty-year-old tale of his father's loss of consciousness during a battle in Vietnam, then an amazing awakening that lasted over four years.

The wounded man, Levi Harper, awoke as innocent as a child. Full of wonder, and the expectation that he had only been out for months at best, he found his musical talent exceeded what it had been when he left civilian life behind for the Marines in 1966.

He gradually regained his memory, and the childhood love of his life. Forty-eight months after his amazing awakening in 1998, tragedy knocked once more. The music man from a small coastal fishing town in California was losing his reason to live. The gravity of his wife's failing health due to a potentially deadly disease created more stress than he could physically handle.

Just weeks before this day, he fell to a stroke. But not before he hired an investigator to search for the son lost to him so many years before.

Jack wanted to believe. He wanted to embrace what the attorney in Los Angeles and his new uncle, Jeffrey Harper, had said.

He took a deep breath and summoned the strength to confront the sleeping man, look at his face, see if he could find himself in the slumbering countenance. Releasing the air from his lungs, he allowed the stressfulness of the moment to remain outside the room. He was determined to be open to whatever this visit would hold for him and his future.

He quietly stepped inside. A nurse busily attended Levi Harper. Her back to him, she hadn't noticed him entering the room. Silky but pitch-black, her hair was pulled into a loose braid and reached below the middle of a slender waist. She stood over Levi, stethoscope placed upon his chest. Checking his pulse, she shook her head. She continued her checklist of procedures, oblivious to Jack's presence. She poked and prodded, tapping on his hand, seeking a response.

"How long has he been like this?" Jack Santos interrupted. He almost felt guilty disturbing her deep focus.

"Oh." She jumped. "I didn't hear you enter." She turned to

greet the visitor. The motionless man stared blindly at the ceiling, then closed his eyes. "Almost three weeks now. So sad."

Jack Santos thought he would immediately find himself in the presence of the man in the bed. He was caught off guard, transfixed by the striking features of the petite and quiet-speaking Asian-American woman.

"Can he come out of it?" he ventured.

"There's always hope. He came out of it for almost four years in 1998. But the emotional trauma triggered some deeply rooted physiological mechanism that returned him to this state, as if to protect him. Maybe . . ." She paused.

"Maybe what?" Jack asked, stepping closer to her and the bed-ridden man.

"A miracle. Perhaps he has the ability to reverse this himself somehow. Medicine doesn't have all the answers, and his case is certainly unique."

Her response surprised him. "Pretty open-minded for a nurse."

"Doctor," she stated sharply.

"Sorry." Jack examined the stance of the pretty woman. Lively, sure of herself. He admired that.

She glared up at him and shook her head. "You think doctors can't believe in a power outside of science?" she asked, a confrontational edge to her voice.

"Well, something like that. It's just unusual, that's all."

"Humph." She snorted. "Well, this man has made me a believer."

The woman had stirred an immediate interest inside Jack that he hadn't been looking for. She wasn't very old. Couldn't be. Her features were early twenties at best. Very attractive, strong character, he judged. No ring on her finger, he noted. She had returned to her clipboard.

"You seem to have a personal connection with him. Did you

treat him when he was here during his thirty-year stay?" he asked, breaking the silence.

He hoped she could tell him something more. He wanted all the information he could possibly get on the man whose journals and papers he now possessed.

"Yes, I did. And I've known him all my life. I used to come here with my father when I was young. He visited twice monthly and later worked here as an attendant. My father had always been very grateful to Mr. Harper. And I was so happy about his amazing awakening."

"Your father is also Vietnamese?" he probed. "I'm sorry, I . . ." His face flushed now. *Stupid*, he chided himself.

"Yes," she replied simply. "He is deceased, but very Vietnamese. I guess if my features didn't give it away, my name tag did. I'm Lin An."

"I apologize. I don't mean to sound so forward. I have several Vietnamese friends in San Francisco. I recognized the name as being . . ." He held out his hand, seeking to rescue himself from his continuing verbal blunders. "My name is Jack Santos. I've been given the honor of finally meeting the man who was absent from my life for thirty-four years—my father." He nodded to the sleeping man.

"Mr. Harper is your father?" Lin was taken aback. "I didn't know he had any other children, except for—"

"The miracle child?" He looked directly into dark, probing eyes. There was honesty there, but vulnerability, as well. This woman was more than what she appeared on the surface—the clinical practitioner.

"Yes. Do you know how the baby is?" She studied his face, his features, questioning if this Jack Santos could indeed be Levi Harper's son.

"It was touch-and-go at first, so they tell me. Making a resounding comeback, though, from the complications with the mother's condition. Delivered two months early because of Mrs. Harper's failing health. They named her Angel. Appropriate, I guess," he smiled.

"Yes," she acknowledged. "A wonderfully fitting name for a heaven-sent child," she agreed.

"You think so?"

"Heaven-sent, you mean?"

"Yes."

"Of course. Yes, I think she was sent from God. Why would you question it?" Lin asked.

"Just curious." He pursed his lips, a signal he often unconsciously gave that he was ready to change the subject.

"And what of Mrs. Harper?" Lin was a student of human behavior. Something had bothered him about the last exchange.

"Levi's brother, Jeffrey, explained Jenna's illness to me, but I'm still a bit confused. All I know is that her growing weakness from the cancer and her desire to deliver this child put so much stress on Levi that he gave out, too."

She sighed. "It's as if her pain were his, her struggle his struggle, as though they were bound by some strange lovers' contract that stated they would never live without each other again. And now you're here," she added. "A gift from God too late."

"A philosopher once said, 'Irony is where reality becomes even more whimsical than it appeared when we first noticed it.' "

"Which philosopher said that?" Lin questioned.

Jack gestured toward the man in the bed. "I have the first of several journals he wrote."

She paused, then nodded. "When did you find out he was your father?"

"Two weeks ago. Seems he'd been searching for me. His brother, Jeffrey Harper, finally stepped in and located me when he realized Levi was consumed with his search, was not going to give up. He directed me to an attorney for the estate of Levi Harper in Los Angeles, and here I am."

Lin studied Jack's face for a moment, then smiled. "I see the resemblance now. You have Mr. Harper's compassionate eyes, and his smile. His case is astounding. You do understand what happened, don't you?"

"I know he had an adjustment to confront, a new world to get to know when he came out of the thirty-year coma several years ago."

"Four years ago," she interjected.

"Yes, four years ago. Since then, I understand his childhood sweetheart came back into his life unexpectedly, and that he wrote fabulous music and sold hundreds of thousands of CDs. Funny . . . I was a huge fan."

"He was trying to make up for a lot of things," she offered. "His awakening is one for the medical journals; there really isn't a concrete explanation for it. His case gave hope to thousands of families who'd lost loved ones to brain injuries and comas. And his musical accomplishments in so short a time were truly remarkable."

"Indeed," Jack agreed. "But you could argue he earned his musical success the hard way, over thirty years, if you consider all that he stated about the melodies that would come to him in his sleeping state."

"I hadn't looked at it that way," Lin considered. "So what will you be doing now?" she asked.

"The first assignment Levi's attorney gave me was to read his journals. I just received the first one yesterday. The others are still at his house in Paradise Bay. Levi makes a remarkable case for awareness of song and beauty, even when not physically in a conscious state."

Lin considered the surprising depth of knowledge this man possessed. She wondered if he cared as deeply as his appearance indicated, or if this was simply pretense. "So you're going there?"

"Paradise Bay?"

"Yes."

Jack nodded.

"You know, he woke up speaking in a childlike voice with a stutter," she said, looking to test him. "But then there were times when his words flowed easily, and it soon became evident that music soothed his mind. Whenever it was playing, he'd be fine."

"Hard to imagine. There was certainly no stutter in his singing voice. I've never seen anything quite like it. You know, it's weird. To go through your whole life wondering who you are, where you belong . . . then bam. It's laid out before you in an eye-blink." He diverted his gaze from Lin An to the sleeping man.

"Mr. Harper once took my father and me to visit his home, just before my father passed away," Lin went on. "Paradise Bay is a magical place. So soothing. So lovely. The sea, the quiet. Someone chose a very appropriate name for the town."

"So, you really were pretty close to Levi?" Jack asked, returning his attention to Lin.

"He and my father were. It was a strange brotherhood. A bond that conflict sometimes produces. I'm sure you'll find out how they met as you read those journals. My father loved the sea. He was a fisherman before the war."

"Here in California?"

"No, in Vietnam," she replied, a reverence in her voice.

"You lived there?"

"Yes, until the late seventies. We were among the hundreds of thousands of 'boat people' who set out to sea with dreams of freedom in America. Many died. The U.S. Navy found us two weeks after we left Vietnam. We were very lucky, I'm told, but I was too young to remember clear details of the escape."

Lin did remember, but the trauma was buried in the South China Sea now, and she intended to keep it that way. Her mother and two brothers had been killed by the sea-roaming murderers who looked for and took advantage of the boat people. Lin had been violated repeatedly, and her father had been tied up, beaten, and left for dead. Looking back only reminded her that she was different, that she had been used, and was unworthy of real love.

"So, they met in Vietnam, and your father looked up Levi after he arrived here?"

"That about sums it up. But the story becomes more strange still. I don't have the time to tell you myself, but perhaps the journals will explain."

"I hope so." Jack's interest in this pretty caregiver was piqued. Her slender frame, light Asian skin, mysterious eyes, and the hint of a smile—courteous and proper as she finished her last statement—made her look younger than she evidently was. But she had to be at least past her mid-twenties, possibly even thirty. "I'd like to get to know you," he went on. "That is, I'd like to get to know more about the connection between your family and mine. Maybe I could see you after work?"

She glanced at her watch, careful not to give any indication of interest. "I'll be here until midnight, I'm afraid. Then I'm spending the weekend with my elderly godmother in Orange County. Many Vietnamese settled there after fleeing our country. You'll be going north to Paradise Bay today, right?"

"Yes. But I plan on returning in a week or two."

"That would be fine. If you're Mr. Harper's son, then your mother must be—"

He spoke up before she could finish. "She's been gone for several years now," he lied. *No need to bring her into this. It would only make her angry.* "I've been on the move ever since." Jack pulled a pen from his pocket, quickly changing the subject. "I look forward to giving you a call, perhaps to check in on Levi's progress."

Lin An handed him a business card. "You can reach me here. If I'm not in, just leave a voice message."

"I'll do that." He smiled.

"Mr. Harper is a dear man, and I'm hoping for a second miracle," she went on.

"Me, too. Miracles do happen, I suppose."

"They do, Mr. Santos. I'd be crazy not to believe in them, after all I've seen with Levi Harper. Well, I'd better get back to my rounds. You should sit with him a while. I think he knows you're here."

"Thank you, Doctor . . ."

"Just call me Lin." She extended her hand. "Mr. Santos, what is it you do?"

"Please call me Jack," he answered, reaching for her delicate hand. "I play the piano, do arrangements, record for studios. Nothing original."

"A musician, like your father? Amazing!"

"Fitting, I guess. I've always been drawn to music, especially composing. I make a decent living. Just hoping for some breakout tunes one of these days."

In reality, Jack Santos was one of the finest solo pianists in the business. His talent was always in demand with the creators of many film and television show tunes.

"That's what I call a miracle, Jack. Mr. Harper would be very proud to know you're also a man of the piano." Lin smiled and held out a delicate hand.

Jack took her hand once again—she let hers linger in his a fraction of a second longer than she normally would have—then releasing the touch, he watched as she walked out of the room. She was dignified but carrying secrets. He could tell when a woman was hiding something, had developed the instinct after growing up as an only child under a single mother's care. He turned back to the man in the bed, the man he had grown up believing was killed in the Vietnam War. Hope had been the constant theme running through this man's story, and Jack could do no less now.

He was determined to understand how all this could really be true—that he had a father, that his father had experienced a strange awakening four years ago, then fallen back into a coma. The shared paths of music they had traveled brought him to the essence of a statement he had read in Levi's first journal. Unaware, he began reciting out loud, carefully enunciating each word.

"Reality is the perceived notion of the mind, like the elusive island of sanity we all believe we have planted our flag upon. What is reality anyway? Perception is king."

Jack followed the lines and creases of the sleeping man's face, looking for himself. For an instant he thought he detected a faint smile cross Levi Harper's lips, then realized it was his imagination after all. The man couldn't possibly have heard him, much less understood.

He drew the curtain around Levi Harper's bed and closed himself in, feeling ashamed and timid as he looked around once more. He was too old, too worldly for what he was about to do, but nostalgia and the child still inside him lowered him to his knees.

He wouldn't let emotions get the better of him; men didn't do that sort of thing. But he bowed his head and whispered the prayer he'd repeated a thousand times as a young boy, night after night.

"Please, God, give me a dad someday." He prayed as if the recitation was plausible, as if God really listened and answered the prayers of insignificant boys. The same prayer he had given thousands of times was simply a fitting way to say hello and goodbye to the sleeping man. He had given up on God and answers to prayers long ago.

He directed his next words to Levi Harper, tenderly touching the hand hooked to the IV solution. "Dad," he began, clearing his throat. "I've never been able to call someone 'Dad' before, and this is real hard. My name is Jack, and I understand that I'm your son. I'm a piano man, too."

2

LIN AN

It was late evening now. Lin An checked the monitors. Levi was taking shallow breaths with the help of oxygen. His vital signs were normal, yet he lay motionless, closed off from the rest of the world. It was doubtful that he would continue living without the help of life support. The trauma of believing that Jenna was dead was all it had taken to send him into his cocoon of despair.

"Can you hear me, Mr. Harper?" she asked. "If you can, move a finger on your right hand. Jenna is alive, and recovering. She's waiting for you."

Lin An had been a student of mind-body therapy at Harvard Medical School, and the list of medical schools now teaching it was growing. Many of her colleagues had not subscribed to the fundamentals of the inexact science, but she knew that strong *belief*, such as experienced under the influence of faith, allowed the associated meaning behind the belief the path it needed to stimulate health in the body.

And according to all the experts of the new science, the body responded to *meaning;* the meaning an individual attached to an experience or event was the cause of what some called *miracles* in the healing process.

She watched his hand closely. Nothing. Frustrated, she picked up the clipboard, filled in the appropriate information, then left. She would be back during the morning rounds.

Her mind was filled with thoughts of the previous weekend she'd spent with her godmother in Garden Grove. As she did almost every weekend, she had picked up Nguyen and taken her to the Long Beach Harbor, then out on the Catalina Express into the Pacific waters, where she could feel closer to her father.

Tran An had passed away just the year before in a fishing accident. Loaded with bonita, the boat had been just hours out of port when a sudden storm claimed it, taking him and his crew of two to a watery tomb.

The shock of losing his friend had seized Levi Harper's heart. He felt overwhelming guilt for not being able to rescue his friend a second time, as Tran had rescued him. But that was a story to fill a novel, with beginnings that went back three decades now.

Now Lin An was alone, and the loss was still too much for her to fathom. Her mother, Mai, and two siblings had been the first losses to the sea, back in 1979. They had escaped from Vietnam, only to perish along with half of the escapees. Tortured by the sea, the endless drifting on open waters, then by the modern pirates who murdered the hapless boat people, Lin's mind had closed down, repressing the images. She simply refused to believe it had happened. Recalling it now was a nightmare.

Lost without the love of family, Lin had gone to Orange County to take solace and refuge in her Vietnamese friends there, and to be reminded of her heritage.

Mother's best friend, Lin An's godmother Nguyen, talked endlessly of growing up in the '40s under Japanese occupation, then the '50s in the southern city of Hue, Vietnam—the cultural heart of the country. She sighed as she would recall to Lin An her memories of Hue's beauty, grace, and the once happy people who'd finally become so embroiled in war. Learning these things had helped Lin An cope with her loss, and the stories she told today mirrored her father's tales of the past. Repeating them kept the memories alive. Loving memories, like cleansed air after a rainstorm, refreshed and breathed new energy into her.

Lin forced herself out of the reverie that had awakened new questions in her about the relationships men and women shared. She yearned for the kind of love that her parents, and Levi and Jenna, had known.

No, she reminded herself. After one failed relationship in college, and an ugly experience with a medical doctor she had trusted, she was left feeling used and abandoned. She had decided then, "Never again." After witnessing so much loss, tragedy, and abuse, she had become cynical and jaded. *Better not to love, not to believe in someone else.*

Life produced so many questions for which she couldn't find answers, she buried herself in medicine, rarely allowing herself time to contemplate.

"Are you all right?" Dr. Jenkins asked.

"Yes, of course," Lin An replied. "I was just taking a break, but I'd better continue my rounds."

"That won't be necessary. Let's go to my office. I want to talk to you about Levi Harper. I've been doing some research, and I think you're going to find what I've learned very interesting, and also very personal."

She followed him down the polished corridor, stopping when she heard a familiar tune coming from a radio or CD player. She knew that melody; Levi Harper had often played it in the recreation center here before his release. She traced it to the nurse's station.

"May I help you?" The desk attendant smiled as Lin An walked up to her.

"I just heard that music. You're a Harper fan?"

"I just bought his first CD. I'm new here, and one of the nurses told me about him. She said Mr. Harper's the miracle patient. I can't wait to meet him," she added happily.

"Could you start it over for me?"

"Certainly." The attendant repeated the track.

Lin An closed her eyes as she listened to the sweeping piano introduction to the *In Paradise* CD, one of the first original piano pieces Levi Harper had composed after awakening more than three years ago.

"Believe in Paradise." Simple words transformed into glorious promises by the melody. Lin An hummed along with Levi's impressively clear baritone voice.

> *Where second times,*
> *Like second chance,*
> *Belief becomes our sacred dance,*
>
> *And mysteries of nursery rhyme are*
> *Always solved in Paradise time . . .*
>
> *Belief in you, belief in me,*
> *Paradise, eternity . . . believe . . .*

The music faded, leaving her mesmerized by the uncompli-
cated rhythmic sounds. So ironic, she thought. So strange.

"Kinda simple," the attendant said. "Pretty, yet simple. What's
the word I'm looking for?"

"Charming. Childlike. Innocently, deliciously, naively charming. As if the world could really offer the kind of love he de-
scribes," Lin An sighed.

"Yeah, that's it. Like the song title—'Believe in Paradise.' "

"Yes," Lin An agreed. "Well, I'd better be going. Keep playing
that CD. It's good for business."

The young woman nodded, looking confused.

"Doctor An? Are you coming?" Dr. Jenkins called from his
office door.

Lin An waved and quickly wiped away the moisture filling
her eyes. She had allowed her shield, the barrier she had erected
to protect herself, to be penetrated by Levi Harper's music. It
had been a long time since she'd had a good cry, but she couldn't
afford one now.

3

JACK SANTOS

J ACK GAZED TO HIS LEFT.

An elderly woman, the quintessential neighborhood matron of the '40s and '50s welcoming the newcomer with a plate of warm cookies, stood between her tidy 1920s bungalow and a freshly whitewashed picket fence, pruning a magnolia tree. She smiled and waved as he passed by.

He returned the gesture.

To his right, an older gentleman with a fishing pole over his shoulder was ambling along Main Street toward the crashing surf on the nearby shore. As old as most of the trees on this coastal strip of land, the man and his pole were a necessary part of the landscape.

Jack acknowledged him with a nod.

He looked around as he slowed to a stop, the first and perhaps only four-way stop in town. He had always taken pleasure in long and leisurely drives up and down the coast in his restored 1966 Ford Mustang convertible. He could think more clearly away from all the distractions of the city. He enjoyed seeing how people lived in the smaller towns, and he often found new inspiration for his tunes during road trips. He sensed that this place would offer more than new tunes, perhaps something an octave up from his usual music, even an entirely new sound.

But he had work to do here. He had just arrived after an almost five-hour drive from Los Angeles. Before entering the Harper homestead, a few blocks away, he wanted to breathe the cool sea air of Paradise Bay and explore the few streets that defined its borders.

The town was nestled on the shore behind a hill just a side road's drive off Pacific Coast Highway, also known as Highway 1. The town was now a mere ghost of its glory days. He doubted that many people outside its former inhabitants even knew it existed.

Paradise Bay, a pinprick on the California map, was miles from any substantial commerce and city life. There was no real reason to come here, except to disappear or escape reality.

In fact, no one came here by accident. Situated between San Luis Obispo on the north, and Santa Barbara on the south—a more romantic destination—Paradise Bay was many miles off Pacific Coast Highway. "No Services," the sign read as he had exited Highway 1. Not even a roadside marker with the town's name and population. Just an old handmade wooden sign, once with a background of white but now paint-chipped and weather-beaten gray, with the faded words "Road to Paradise Bay" outlined in black.

Some surfers from nearby towns knew about the point, which was a mile or two from the wharf. A few recalcitrant hippies lived here, no doubt treasuring it as their private secret. Older citizens, like the fisherman passing by at the stop sign, were simply too rooted to move. Then there were artists and a musician or two who also called this town home.

Even the railroad bypassed this turn-of-the-century creation by ten miles. Only curiosity or a purpose like Jack's would bring a person to Paradise Bay, a town that had once boasted a population of 750, now down to just over one hundred.

The cannery that had employed the town for more than half a century was closed down in the late '60s, and now was just a hollow, ramshackle building of weathered boards and broken glass. It had recently been purchased by an optimistic investor who intended to turn it into a seaside restaurant and inn.

The rest of the town stood in mute testimony to happier times, an era of innocence the world could barely recall now. An early 1950s 7-Up sign hung lazily from the window of the closed gas station. One grocery appeared to be open, and a barbershop displayed its hours, but all other commerce had abandoned Main Street.

A boarded-up church with a plain steeple, its white weathered siding peeling away with each unpainted season, seemed to invite him. But the ghosts who worshiped there would have to wait.

A cloud of dust trailed behind the car as Jack pulled up the long driveway from Dockside Road. He came to a stop at the edge of a well-manicured flower garden and a lawn that stretched out over one hundred yards to the edge of the sand dunes.

No sign of people, he thought, looking out at the sea beyond the bordering dunes that were just a jog away from the shore. Bittersweet silence in this sleepy town greeted his entrance to a place that had once been alive with the noise of living.

Loneliness was sometimes the price a songwriter had to pay for solitude. The sweet and the sad, the stuff that drove a person to create new sounds, were always drenched in the surrounding silence and coveted calm of places like this.

Claire would've liked this place, he thought. He had been crazy in love with her. Just twelve months ago, still married, he had faced the bitter reality that he was a loser in the art of *amore*.

"I don't love you anymore," she had said.

"Why?" he had asked in shocked disbelief.

"You love your music. You spend more time touching piano keys than me. You don't know how to love a woman, and I've found someone who does."

Just like that, after three years.

It had been a year since Claire left him, and those words still haunted his every waking hour. He couldn't hate her, though. He would do anything for a second chance. But he knew it was too late.

Memories are a burden sometimes, he considered. Lines from Levi Harper's first journal.

A deep breath of salty air and the feeling that he had arrived home carried him to the spacious wraparound porch. He approached the windows, baked by the afternoon sun, and peered inside. He could make out a stack of boxes here, another there. The only sound disturbing the pleasant isolation was the occasional roll of a wave, the coastal surf pounding just beyond the dunes. A car passing by in the distance added a faint rumble to the air, but it quickly faded.

This Victorian by the sea had been Levi Harper's home. A family had enjoyed decades of Pacific Ocean sunsets here. This was where his story had really begun; the repository of a history that had been kept from Jack Santos for his entire life.

4

SILENT SONG

He walked the distance of the surround-porch, coming to the entrance of the office, a double-entry Coke-bottle glass door. A vintage restoration, this door to the century-old home had originally been the front entrance to the parlor.

It opened easily. The house seemed to welcome him in at the mere touch of his hand on the diamond-cut glass doorknob. The studio office filled with western sunlight as he stepped inside. Spring air wafted in behind him, breathing the freshness of the ocean into the stale room.

Silent songs sung here. Phantoms. Jack almost sensed a presence whispering to him.

Welcome home, son. Take a seat. Don't be frightened.

"Okay," he said out loud, then released his remaining apprehension with a sigh. He felt like a child today, a child on the most profound adventure of his life.

This was a dream that could happen just once in a lifetime. To be handed the missing pieces to the puzzle of his thirty-four years had been an unexpected shock, yet fit as easily into his mature world as a well-worn glove fit its owner's hand. He would spend several days with the boxes of secrets bequeathed to him.

His head throbbed with questions. He never really had a father figure in his life. His mother had married three times, but only one man had tried to act like a father. And he had left within a year and a half, before Jack had allowed himself to trust the stranger.

He had always fantasized that his real father would walk up the driveway one day and hold out his arms, and then Jack would know, right then and there, what it was like to have a dad. Of course, his mother had told him his father had died in the war, but his heart told him it was permissible to hope. Now the documents, the fruit of his dreams, were laid out neatly before him on the private desk.

Musical scores. Journals. The stuff of a life filled with belief. Like the warmth left on a stone after the sun sinks under the horizon, they invited him to linger, to touch them.

His rational mind told him no one could be watching, yet the essence of the man remained, as if eyes were upon him, expectant eyes.

His newfound relatives had told him to go through the journals on the desk first, that he would understand the materials stacked in boxes and lining one wall of the office if he read these at the outset.

He positioned the first stack of leather-bound, handwritten journals squarely in the center of the desktop, then opened an old tin box, at least forty years old, that had once held cookies. He smiled. Oreos were his favorite.

Thrill mixed with melancholy gripped him as he searched through the decades-old treasures inside. He found a photo of a youthful Levi wearing a striped T-shirt and cutoffs, holding a string of fish up next to a small skiff or boat.

There was also a black-and-white photo of him with a little girl—Jenna, he thought—which was clipped to one with a teen-age girl, his mother, Carol Santos. Another with his father wearing Marine dress blues, standing arm in arm with his teenage mother. They were both smiling. *What had happened?*

In a group photo, Levi was sitting at the piano with a guitarist and drummer. They were all wearing the ancient clothing and hairstyles of the "groovier" 1960s. A photo of a boy was clipped to another of the same person as a man dressed in combat fa-tigues. The name on the back identified him as Al Tenny, No-vember 1967, Republic of Vietnam.

Jack smiled as he continued working his way through the tin, finding the musical scores written by the man he had seen in concert, the original rough drafts of "Believe in Paradise," which had been neatly folded and placed near the bottom.

Anger rose up inside him at the thought that his mother, now a reformed hippie living a reclusive artist's life behind a gallery in San Francisco, had kept this information hidden from him all of his life. He just as quickly pushed it aside. She'd done her best, he reasoned. He didn't have time for a debate over the right or wrong of his mother's actions.

This was the time to find out who Levi Harper was, what made him tick. Claim the heritage and legacy concealed from him until now. Find out who Jack Santos really was.

He put the photos and musical scores back inside the con-tainer and looked out the wide airy window toward the sea, just over the crest of the closest dune where it met the sky. Perhaps

Levi had gazed out this same window and wondered about his son, how to go about finding him.

I wish I could ask him some personal questions. How had he lived? What did he think about after he awoke from his thirty-year coma? What magic had made him so musically prolific over such a short span of time, the four years before he slipped back into a comatose state? And after losing so much time, so much understanding of the world, what was he doing here? He could have been in therapy, retraining himself, asking professionals for their help.

Jack felt certain he could find a big part of himself if he could talk to Levi, see through his eyes. He finally surrendered to the only course that could give him the answers. He opened the first journal.

After a fitful night's sleep and the long drive up the coast, Jack should have been exhausted. But as he began reading the first page, an energy he had rarely known possessed him.

5

SLOW TIME

Paradise Bay, Spring of 1998

I'VE BEEN INSTRUCTED BY MY PHYSICIAN TO WRITE, TO record on paper my life, my feelings, what it means to wake up after a sleep of thirty years. To be a 21-year-old in a 51-year-old's body has a meaning I must discover if I'm going to survive in this world of 1998 and beyond.

I feel very lucky for getting a second chance at life, and to make all the music I was destined to play. And not least of all, the good fortune and gift from God to love again, to be with Jenna for whatever brief time remains.

As I think back, if my childhood and the 1950s are still part of who I really am, then those years deserve a fair retelling. And as I recall them, they all seem to start with finding Jenna and those slower times here at the bay. Perhaps general memories of the times leading up to my first meeting her would help to set the tone and be an appropriate beginning.

Even though she wore Mickey Mouse ears on her head, Annette Funicello captured every schoolboy's heart in 1956. It's hard to describe the wonder of that simpler time, with today's never-ending technological growth and its ability to re-create itself each year.

Back then, the marvel of television going from black-and-white to color was amazing enough. A transistor radio that you could hold up to your ear to hear music being played by a local radio station was on the frontier of ever-expanding scientific possibilities.

Going to Disneyland, being swallowed by the whale on Pinocchio's ride, paddling a canoe past burning villages at Frontier Land, or enjoying the magic of Mister Toad's Wild Ride, were awe-inspiring. They were magical times in every way.

Prosperity soared in the ten years following the big war. There had been two solid decades of austerity and scarcity by the time my parents reached their thirties. Barely getting by and doing without was all they could recall. Making a dollar stretch had literal meaning to their generation. Making do with what you had, or doing without, were American virtues.

I'll always remember the day in '56 when my dad brought home a check from the cannery for $92.67 and proudly handed it to my mother, as if he'd won a sweepstakes. They had arrived, and they knew it.

I swore that if I ever made that much in a single week, I'd know there was a heaven; $92.67 bought a lot of stuff back then. A Hoola Hoop cost just under $2 when it became a must-have for every family with children in '58, and an LP record cost less than that. Gasoline was under 25 cents a gallon, and food . . . well, $10 worth provided days and days of casseroles.

TV dinners on trays transformed how and where families ate meals together. We didn't have to miss *I Love Lucy, The Honey-*

mooners, The Ed Sullivan Show, or the westerns, *Wagon Train* and *Gunsmoke.*

James Dean was the hottest box office draw in 1955, and he became even more popular after his tragic death. *Walt Disney* and *Captain Kangaroo* lasted many years and were the hottest television shows by far for youngsters.

Dr. Jonas Salk invented the polio vaccine in '53, and in '54 it began wiping out the annual winter scourge that had been inspiring fear in everyone for centuries. Back then, someone in every town either died or ended up paralyzed from it, but now a whole class of disease was being virtually eradicated. Miracles were happening, and more were just around the corner. Everything and anything seemed possible.

I roamed the wide-open spaces and the shoreline of Paradise Bay, when time stood still. They were the golden days of my youth, even more golden in the summer, if that could be possible.

The nights were cool and pleasant on our land, a gentle rise above the cove. An ageless gray owl always perched on the branches of the date palm out back, adding mystery to the hours after sunset. Knowing all, seeing all, it reminded me that ghosts from the past only care about two things: letting you know that they were once alive, and that they intended to remain until you finally believed in them. The owl and a sense of the supernatural mixed nicely with the modernizing of our town, as if old hands were shaking the new, passing on a heritage to guard and keep.

In school, we believed in country, progress, and team playing. In church, we believed in God, family, and succeeding by faith. Televison and big-screen heroes never let you down; they always conquered evil and believed that a just cause, a moral cause, was all it took to win.

The magic in the air of progressive post-war California was

considerable. "Booming" would be a good word to describe it. Folks from all over the country were moving here to help build bigger bombs, planes, cars, homes, ships, and, of course, better entertainment.

And as the ground was being cleared to build Disney's Magic Kingdom, the orange, lemon, and walnut groves planted ten, twenty, and thirty years before were also being cleared to make way for the new, small, three-bedroom, two-bath square houses with stucco exteriors and window shutters that didn't actually shut. New folks were arriving every day, it seemed. And if something big could get bigger, then those were the days it happened in California.

Even though big things were happening all around us, Paradise Bay remained an island of simple events. For me, 1956 was a year so full of awareness that my mind naturally drifts back to those days of carefree, easy living. But I guess I remember it best for one singular event: finding Jenna. It was the year she stole my heart.

"This is 1956, for crying out loud. We got a television set, a transistor radio each, and we're about to set a record for the crosstown scooter race on Cabrillo Hill Road, if you'll just give up those skates and let me put them on the two-by-four. I'll buy you a new set with the money we win. Right, Jeff?"

"Right, Levi," the younger brother agreed. "I'll throw in my Joe Bazooka bubble-gum wrappers. You can get a real neat top that whistles when it spins, or a glowing yo-yo with just a hundred and fifty more," he added.

Karen Sue wrinkled her nose and held on tight. She wasn't convinced that her two older brothers would really come through. "Why do you need my skates? Why not use yours?"

"Yours have new ball bearings. They're really fast. Too fast for a little girl, anyway."

"I don't know . . ." She held on tighter to her new shiny skates.

"Tell you what, Karen Sue. Just hand over those skates and the key around your neck, and let me use them. If we win, we'll go right over to Ben Franklin's Five and Dime and order an even better pair." Levi held out his hand.

"Promise?"

"Cub Scout's honor."

"Oh, okay." She handed Levi the chrome set of attachable skates, the kind that adjusted to foot size and clamped onto street shoes, then the key that loosened the front from the back wheels. "But you better keep your promise, or I'm telling Daddy. And you know where Daddy says liars go."

"Straight to H-E-double-L," Jeff roared.

"You said the H word! I'm telling! You're in trouble now!"

"You tell, and there won't be any Joe Bazooka wrappers. That means no glowing yo-yo."

"Come on, Jeff. She won't say anything. We got work to do." Levi pulled his brother by the arm. They ran behind the turn-of-the-century Victorian and headed for the work shed.

"Where's that two-by-four?" Levi asked as he flipped the light on. "I saw it just yesterday."

"The chicken coop."

"What?"

"I think Dad used it on the chicken coop," Jeff answered.

They hurried out to the coop on the shady side of the shed. "I gotta have that two-by-four," Levi went on. "Looks like Dad used it to hold down the roof. He's got some hens locked in there with the rooster. Poor hens."

"Dandy's been a real pest lately. Gus up at the feed store says if he sees Dandy getting into his feed one more time he's gonna cook his goose . . . he should cook Dandy, though," Jeff added seriously.

"Dandy is just gonna have to pay attention to the hens for awhile. We gotta have a two-by-four to tack the crate onto the front of the skateboard. It's not allowed in the race without the box on the front."

"We'll just borrow it for the day. Right?" Jeff sounded uncertain.

"Yeah." Levi grabbed it without hesitation. "That old rooster ain't goin' anywhere. He does his stupid stuff at night."

"All chickens are stupid. You should've seen 'em flyin' around stuck together. Don't they know it's easier to fly alone?"

Levi nodded. "You should've been there the other day, when Dad chopped the heads off them two so we could have that big Sunday picnic down at the church. Too bad you had to go with Mom. Those two hens flew up into the pecan tree, with no heads! It took Dad ten minutes to get 'em down. Until we got these chickens this year, I thought it was all talk about chickens running around with their heads off. But it's a fact."

"Man, I can't wait until the next picnic." Jeff grinned.

"Those chickens deserved to be eaten. If they were smart, they would've flown up there while they still had their heads." Levi started back toward the shed, carrying the board. "Where's those skates? Get some nails out of that jar, Jeff."

The weather was pleasant, and it was the first day of summer vacation. But all days in the temperate coastal climate of central California were pleasant, and the boys were shirtless, dressed in cutoff shorts. Soon, they were ready to test the scooter on the hill that connected Cabrillo Hill Road to Dockside Road, the street their home stood on. The downhill race would lead almost directly into the vacant Smith house on Cabrillo Hill Road, which was where they planned to stop.

"Okay, Jeff. You sit up front in the box, and I'll steer. Here goes."

They pushed off, heading out into the street, and soon found themselves sailing down the asphalt road with Karen Sue's new skates attached to the bottom of the two-by-four.

"Whoo-hoo!" Levi hollered, unaware of the '55 Chevy sedan that was about to disrupt their planned jumping-off point.

"Hey! Oh, no!" Levi shouted as it pulled into the driveway they were headed toward. "Whoa! Hold on, Jeff!"

Levi quickly maneuvered the scooter to the right and steered onto the grass. The back door of the car opened and a pretty freckle-faced girl, her tawny gold hair pulled up into a ponytail, stepped out.

"Watch out! Get out of the way!" Levi yelled.

"Mom!" the girl cried as her parents emerged from the car. She pointed to the out-of-control scooter.

The scooter crashed onto the water-deprived lawn, sending Levi and Jeff tumbling across it.

"That was close," Levi said, finally catching his breath.

"Owee!" his younger brother whined, seeing the blood trickling from his knee. The dry grass was like fine sandpaper against soft skin.

"You boys okay?" the girl's father called out. He ran to the two boys sprawled out on the yellowed turf.

"I think so," Levi replied, standing slowly. "You okay, Jeff?"

"Yeah, but my knee hurts."

Levi ignored his bleeding elbow and scratched knees. His gaze was steadfast, fixed upon the new girl. She turned away. His eyes followed.

"Oh, dear," the woman said as she joined her husband. She turned to her daughter. "Honey? Get the first-aid kit from the glove box."

When the girl returned, her mother prepared to apply some iodine and a bandage to Jeff's cut. "Now hold still. This is going to sting a little."

Jeff bit his lower lip, and tears sprang to his eyes.

"All done now," the nice lady said, patting Jeff on the leg as she finished. "You'll be just fine. Your turn, young man," she said, motioning to Levi.

Levi shook loose from his trance and obeyed. He had never had this happen in his young life before. No girl in Paradise Bay ever caught his attention like this.

"You boys ought to know better than to head down a steep hill in that contraption. What got into you?" the man scolded. "One or two seconds sooner, and I might have run you over."

Levi had no answer. He just looked over at the mangled scooter and bent skates, unwilling to admit that he had done something stupid.

At least not in front of the pretty girl.

Worse, now there was no way to win the race and pay Karen Sue back. And his dad would be mad as H-E-double-L, too.

"Hey, now," the man said kindly, noticing Levi's downcast expression. "We can fix this. Here comes the moving van with my tools."

"You're moving in here?" Levi asked, surprised.

"Yep," the girl said. "I'm Jenna. We came all the way from Utah. And I'm going to get to go to the beach every day," she added happily. "Bet you didn't know we have seagulls in Utah, too."

"Nope."

"Bet you also didn't know that the Great Salt Lake was once an ocean."

"Nope."

"I'm going to like being near the real ocean," she went on. "Hey, what's your name anyway?"

"Levi. And this is my brother Jeff."

"Well, Levi and Jeff," the girl's father interjected. "Let's move out of the way and make room for the moving van. Take that scooter out back to the garage. I'll see if we can straighten those wheels out and reattach that box."

"That's my dad," the girl explained. "His name is Bill. He's the new manager of the highway crews from here to some town way up near San Francisco called Santa Cruz. And my mom is Jan. She says we're going to be really good neighbors."

Levi nodded. The girl had a sparkle to her that left him temporarily speechless.

"You're really tan. Don't people wear shirts around here?" she went on.

"Well, uh . . . not in the summer," he replied self-consciously. A girl shouldn't be talking about that kind of stuff, he thought.

"Jenna, honey," her mother called out, waving from the porch. "Don't you want to see the house?"

"I'm coming," she called back. "Well, guess I gotta go. 'Bye."

"Yeah. 'Bye," Levi said.

"Come on, boys." Bill was standing by the garage, a toolbox in his hand. "Bring that rig over here and let's fix her up. Then I've got to get to work."

"Yes, sir," Levi called back. "Come on, Jeff."

"She likes you," Jeff teased as they picked up the skateboard and box and limped toward the garage.

"Ah, shut your trap."

"We'd better go see if Dandy stayed with the hens as soon as we get home," Jeff went on, growing serious.

"Chickens are stupid, remember? He won't leave them hens for food until he gets real hungry," Levi reassured.

"Dandy's a rooster. Dad says there's a difference."

"Yeah. A different kind of stupid. Now come on."

6

VICTORIAN AND THE SEA

Summer 1998

THOSE DAYS WERE CAREFREE AND SLOW, AN ENDLESS summer to a boy growing older in Paradise Bay during the 1950s. Those simple days of imitating the hottest television heroes, like the Lone Ranger and Superman, proved that, next to his dog, imagination was still a boy's best friend.

A movie at the Holiday Theater was a quarter, and popcorn was fifteen cents. Root beer was a dime, except on Mondays; then it was a nickel. They were times of black-and-white, good versus evil, and discovering new music on the teen television show *American Bandstand* with Dick Clark.

Superman was responsible for leading more than one kid to believe he could fly. He actually hurt more kids in the '50s than he saved. At least, looking back it seems so.

The bath towel I'd drape around my neck never worked very

well, no matter how high I climbed. I'd jump from the trellis or the pecan tree out behind the house. Mom tried to put a stop to it, so I'd just change locations.

But I was a believer. If a boy climbed just high enough and stretched just far enough, maybe he could fly. It sure hurt trying, though. I finally gave that up for parachuting with pillowcases after watching a World War II movie. You still had to climb real high, and the air that filled the pillowcase when you jumped should've slowed you down more than a towel behind your neck, but I always hit the ground just as hard.

Compared to the others before us, we were a generation of excess. Our parents spoiled us with each new Mattel or Whammo toy that came on the market.

"If it's Mattel, it's swell," the slogan went. The toy industry had its leaders in sales, and every parent who could made sure the family had at least one set of something new. Part of it was just to keep up with the Joneses, and another part of it was to make up, in some strange balancing of life's accounting ledger, for what they'd never had.

Even so, the venerable pea-shooters, slingshots made from tree branches—with thin strips of rubber tire for propulsion— rubberband guns, and water pistols were our weapons of choice in the war games we played. Imitating the plethora of movies glorifying World War II and Korean War military adventures, we made the beach our Iwo Jima and Normandy.

Even though we lived within earshot of the crashing waves, we had a feel for the land. Most people thought our lives re- volved around harvesting seafood and eating it. But Dad wanted to make sure we experienced what it was like to care for animals and grow our own food, along with making a living from the sea. Unlike today's children, we knew where eggs, milk, and butter came from.

My big awakening to music came in 1956. Rock was young, and I was impressionable. And there was also someone to impress.

Turns out, I learned a lesson from Dandy's final adventure, and it stuck with me for a good purpose. In fact, if it hadn't been for Dandy, I might never have met Jenna the way I did.

"Dandy left the hens alone and made his way to the feed store," Jeff moaned. "We've had it now."

"Stupid chicken. Let's go get him before Gus sees him," Levi said.

"Levi's got a girlfriend," Jeff chanted as they ran across the open field to Gus Cook's feed store.

"Knock it off!"

"I saw the way you were looking at her," Jeff persisted.

"Who?" It had been less than an hour ago, but Levi's heart was still racing from the thought of the pretty girl.

"You know who. Jenna. The girl you almost ran over with the scooter."

Levi didn't respond. It was a beautiful day for just about anything. The sun was hot, the breeze down. The surf would be mild. He'd already decided that once they got Dandy back in the coop he'd go out to the pier and take the small launch for a spin just beyond the breakers.

"Looky there, Levi," Jeff pointed, mouth hanging open.

"Is that Gus's dog?"

"Uh-huh."

"Uh-oh." The dog began growling as Levi approached. "Nice doggy. Put Dandy down. Come on, doggy. Here, I got something for you." Levi put a hand behind his back as if hiding something. The dog snarled, holding the struggling bird in its teeth.

"Dandy quit moving," Jeff whispered.

"Maybe he's smarter than we think. Faking it."

"His head's just kind of dangling, Levi. Uh-oh. I think it's gonna fall off." The dog began snarling more viciously as the boys crept closer. "I don't think he's faking it."

"Me either. Come on." Levi turned abruptly and started walking away.

"Where we going?"

"Over to the church."

"To pray?"

"No, stupid."

"But Dad's there. What are we gonna tell him?"

"Nothing yet. He'll figure out what happened if he sees that the two-by-four's gone. But he's got some more wood behind the junk out back, so all we gotta do is find a piece and take it back over to the coop. Then nobody can blame us for Dandy's miraculous escape."

The boys sprinted to the south side of town to check on their part-time minister father, hoping mercy would outweigh justice. Taking cover behind the woodpile by the walnut grove that bordered the small white church, they began the search.

"We gotta lay low," Levi whispered, sorting through the wood scraps. "Dad's around here somewhere." He found what he was looking for. "This looks just like the one we used. Let's go."

Rex Harper was watching from his vantage on the roof, where he was replacing worn shingles. He was happy to see his sons playing so well together, and he grinned as they ran off with the two-by-four. *For the scooter.* He smiled with satisfaction.

Life is good, he told himself, looking out over the ocean. God had allowed him to return from the war in the Pacific ten years ago. The battles he had seen seemed distant now, except for the flashbacks he suffered during nightmarish bouts with malaria.

Almost every man in his platoon on Guadalcanal—those who survived—had contracted malaria.

He hoped his sons would never see war, and he didn't like it when they played war with the other boys in the neighborhood. But at least they had gentle hearts, and knew how to use their imaginations.

Levi finished with the handsaw. He had cut a piece of wood about the same length he'd taken from the lid of the coop.

"Dad's gonna ask us if we know anything about this," Jeff said as Levi tossed the two-by-four on top of the coop.

"Yeah, and we can't lie. Dad always finds out anyway. But it isn't a lie to say we don't know how Dandy got out, since we didn't actually see him leave the coop. And anyway, Dandy would've flown the coop sooner or later. He was stupid, and that's all there is to it."

"Yeah," Jeff agreed.

Levi put the handsaw back into the shed and wiped the dust off the workbench. "Let's go try—"

"Hi, boys. What's up?" Rex said. The two boys turned to find their father standing in the doorway. "I saw you out back behind the church. Making something?"

"Uh, yeah," Levi murmured. Jeff stared at the concrete floor.

"Well, show me." Rex smiled.

"Dad, before you say anything, I just want to say we made a deal with Karen Sue for her skates. We're going to get her an even better pair. Right, Jeff?"

"Right."

"And we needed some wood for the scooter, so we used some that we scrounged up."

"From the woodpile?"

"Well, sort of. We got a race tomorrow, and we just want to win, is all. Can we go now?"

"What about your chores?"

"Can we do them later?"

"Sun's gonna be going down in a couple of hours. Don't you want to get a good start on that race tomorrow? Be a shame to miss it because you had to mow the lawn, clean out the chicken coop, and water the garden."

Jeff looked at his brother. Levi always seemed to find a way out when he needed one. But no one was going to get by Gus, who was now looming large in the background. Rex Harper turned to greet him.

"Sorry about your rooster, Rex," Gus said, tossing a very dead Dandy onto the ground in front of him. "Seems the old rooster cared more for the seed than the hens. My dog didn't seem to take too kindly to him, though. Real shame."

Levi and Jeff slunk off to the back of the shed.

"We'd better hightail it, Levi," Jeff whispered.

"Yeah."

Rex walked over to the chicken coop, picked up the two-by-four and examined it, then walked back over to Gus, acting as if his boys were invisible.

"What do I owe you for the seed, Gus?"

"A dollar will do."

Rex reached into the pocket of his trousers and pulled out a handful of change. "Here's a dollar-ten. Keep the change. Sorry for the bother."

"Thanks, Rex. See you around." Gus tipped his hat, then turned and walked away.

Levi and Jeff were across the field by then, up toward Cabrillo Hill Road and the new girl's house.

Rex shook his head as he studied the weathered piece of wood and spotted the fresh saw marks.

Levi looked back at his father, a distant figure now, and knew they hadn't fooled him. You never could get around Rex Harper—not really. He loved his father for his gentle sternness, which made him all the more willing to do whatever his father asked. But he wanted this race badly, and he needed to impress the new girl. He'd make it up to his dad somehow, volunteer to do something around the church.

He didn't feel too bad about Dandy. But he had learned a lesson from the rooster. Wanting to have more, becoming like the feed store chicken, meant you had to risk your neck, stick it out where some dog could get hold of it. If you were going to have more and take the risks, you had to make sure the dog was asleep. And if he woke up, you needed to make sure you had a backup plan. Just in case.

7

BRAVISSIMO

Fall 1998

MY FATHER WAS A FAIR MAN. I APPRECIATED THAT. HE had his rules, and he applied them without force or coercion. He did withhold, though. He attached meaning and a reward to everything, it seemed. Back then, I had no idea this concept was sinking into a part of my brain for retrieval later in life—for now, as I write these memoirs.

But life, Dad would say, doesn't ask what is fair or what isn't. It rewards or holds back, depending on our performance and choices. So I lived with the consequences of my choices.

One choice that made all the difference, and comforts me now, was finding a love for making music. It meant I could count on my new ability to impress the girls, and it was also an outlet for the male energies beginning to emerge in me.

I suppose all adolescent boys must find some way to direct

the strange sensations growing inside them. No matter what any-one says, no matter what preparation is given, no boy is fully prepared to become so thoroughly distracted by a girl once the chemistry kicks in.

I had Jenna on the brain from that year on. I was determined to see her as often as possible and have her notice me. Between music and an understanding of the ocean, I had the upper hand in Paradise Bay over the other boys interested in the new girl. Some said I was showing off. I called it my "backup plan."

"I'm just about finished, Mr. Santos," Levi said, stacking the last of the soda bottles for the grocer.

"What you say?" the portly Italian from New York called back.

"I said I'm just about finished. I want to ask you something. I want to know something about that music you always play."

"Opera?"

"Yeah. What makes the music work? I mean, Mrs. Santos re-ally seems to dig it. And so do you. But women seem to like it more than men. You know, the tenors singing all that romantic stuff about love. Is it just an Italian thing, or do all women like that mushy stuff?"

The grocer laughed. "You're a funny boy," he said, tussling Levi's hair. He walked over to the tired-looking RCA record player in the corner of the small space he used as an office. "Lis-ten to this, and you tell me." He smiled.

A slight scratching sound provided background noise to the rich baritone voice accompanied by an orchestra. Levi tried to appreciate it as Mr. Santos closed his eyes and quietly mouthed the Italian lyrics.

"This," Mr. Santos said, "is real music." He sang with the baritone on the second aria, adding distinctive gestures and emotions to his performance.

"Bravo, Mr. Santos!" Levi applauded.

"Bravissimo, Mr. Santos," a voice added from the open door to Main Street.

"You like opera, Mr. Harper?"

"I love those deep baritones. How do they do it? And the exquisite high notes the Italian tenors hit . . . it does something to me."

"Right here, no?" Santos patted the center of his chest.

"I can't understand a word of Italian, but it sure does sing to the heart. Never really thought about why I liked it," Rex said, then turned to his son. "Time for supper, Levi."

"You see, young Mr. Harper? That is your answer. The *signorinas*"—he smiled—"they love it. You got a special girl, and you want to win her some day, you just sing love songs to her heart. Italian love songs, even better."

"Thanks, Mr. Santos," Levi said as he stepped out the door. "See you Saturday."

"A happy man," Rex said to his son as they started home, putting an arm around Levi's shoulder.

"Yep."

"Well, Dandy's just about paid for now," Rex reminded him. He had come directly from the cannery, lunch pail in hand. "What do you think about that?"

"Can I go out on the skiff?"

"The sun goes down in two hours. But it's not about time. I don't like you out there once it hits that horizon. Understand?"

"Yeah. I head in when the sun hits the water."

"And what else?"

"Ah, Dad, life jackets are for sissies," Levi grumbled.

"Do I look like a sissy to you?"

"No, but that's different."

"No, son. It might've been war, but it wasn't different. The struggle to survive is a struggle, no matter how or where it happens. Life jacket," he repeated firmly.

"Yes, sir."

"And no diving for abalone without me as your partner. And, then only—"

"Inside the coves," Levi finished.

"Right." Rex nodded. "Have fun and be careful."

"A bunch of the kids said they'd be down on the beach. What if they ask for a ride?"

"Tell them to have their parents call me. That's final." They walked along quietly for a minute, then Rex added, "I don't guess I should go along, huh?"

Levi shrugged his shoulders.

"Someone special?"

"Just a friend."

"Oh." Rex nodded knowingly.

"I'll just take Jeff today. Is that all right?"

"Just keep the rules. I don't want your new freedom with the skiff to backfire on you. It took some doing to get your mother to agree. I want you to realize how serious this is, that you have other lives in your hands. Understand?"

"I got it, Dad."

"What about the music lessons?"

"Fridays at ten until summer's over, then at five."

"No slipping up on that music. Your mother expects some culture in this family."

"No problem. I don't really want my friends to know, but I kind of like the piano."

"I've been listening, son. You're really very good."

"Think so?" Levi beamed.

"Sure do." Rex pulled Levi closer to him. *Levi will grow up all too soon, and heaven forbid, be asked to do what I had to do out there.*

He had named his son for the man who died saving him. It had been a day just like today. A clear day. A deadly day on a small Pacific island atoll, where his friend had sacrificed his life to bring him out from the open, under heavy gunfire. Rex had turned his life to God that day, vowed to honor the name of Levi Young the rest of his life.

Levi looked up and noticed the moisture in his father's eyes. "You okay, Dad?"

"Yeah," he replied with a catch in his throat. "Just a little something in my eye."

8

CANTATA

Winter 1999

As SUMMER GAVE WAY TO AUTUMN, THE ROWDY OUTSIDE
activities turned me to the Kimball piano inside. I was getting
bored with everything about Paradise Bay, except watching out
for Jenna and plunking around on any piano I came close to.

By late 1956, I was getting free lessons from Mrs. Murphy
after school, in exchange for instructing beginners. Secretly, I
loved it, but I gave off an air of disdain when challenged by the
boys around town.

When my friends would call for me to play with them, I'd
have an answer that fought off the sissy image Mark Mayfield
tried to label me with. "Nah, I gotta go to piano lessons," I'd
sigh, blaming my mother.

Music was appealing, but so was the fact that the stars of
rhythm and blues and the new rock and roll were all adored by

the girls. I thought that was pretty neat. A good reason to keep playing and practicing was, in fact, that I wanted to impress Jenna and her friends, and compete with a new phenomenon from Tennessee—Elvis Presley.

When I saw how they would react to this new sound, his movements, and that pop music was not only his but every other heartthrob's key to success, I was sold.

Like cantatas, stories sung but not acted out, I found music a medium to create my own world. My life story became fused with the piano, a voice I found I could use on key, and a cause—a mission—to get noticed by Jenna and to make other people smile.

Along with Jenna, a new boy from Idaho came into my life that year, a boy who would one day save my life and give me reason to believe in a power beyond the mortal veil.

"Albert Tenny's the name," the round-faced boy announced. "I'm from Idaho. Ever been to Idaho?" It was the first day of the school year.

"Nope," an awkward and delicate new boy replied.

"How 'bout you, Levi? Ever been to Idaho?"

"Haven't been anywhere but here." Albert had asked Levi the same question a day before at Santos Grocery.

"Too bad," Albert said. "Ever eat German Browns?"

"What's a German Brown?" the shy boy replied.

"It's a trout! Huge fella! The last one I caught was this big." He held out his arms, two feet apart. "Say, what do you fellas fish for around here? They got any sea trout? Salmon, maybe?" The quiet boy shrugged. He turned to Levi.

"Shark mostly. Caught one with my bare hands once. This big." Levi held his arms out as far as they would stretch. He knew Albert, fearing the unknown, had been afraid to get into the ocean since arriving to town. "Had to save my little brother Jeff. Got a picture of it at home."

"No way! You're lying. Nobody catches sharks. Sharks eat people. I might be from Idaho, but I know that much."

"You can come over after school and see the photo if you want," Levi said. "I'm standing there, and the shark's laying right by me on the pier. Happened last summer."

"Then how'd you catch him without him biting your head off?" Albert asked, laughing uncertainly. "It's hard enough to hold a slimy brown trout just off the hook."

"I just did."

"Bet ya didn't."

"Did so."

"Did not."

"Okay, how about we go for a swim out in the bay today, and I'll show you how I did it?" Levi challenged him.

Albert's eyes widened somewhere between the size of a nickel and a quarter. "I'd like to," he stammered. "But I don't swim in the ocean . . . not yet anyway."

"What's the matter? Chicken?"

"No."

"Are so."

"Am not."

"Are so. You're a chicken. And sharks like chickens."

"Yeah, well you never rafted down the Snake River in white-water rapids."

"You never surfed. I've surfed. Waves that could knock a train off the tracks. Under the lighthouse. Out there at the point," he demonstrated with his hands.

"Ah, get out of here. You sure got some big stories. California sissy boys are all you are around here."

"And I guess you know all about it."

"Know what they say about folks like you where I come from? 'Liar, liar, pants on fire . . .' " Albert smiled smugly, sure he had Levi on the ropes now.

"You know what we say here in Paradise Bay? 'You lie like a rug on the floor!' "

"My dad was in World War Two. Killed so many Germans, they started surrendering by the thousands," Albert boasted. "He was at Normandy on D-Day and the Battle of the Bulge," he proclaimed proudly.

"Yeah? Well, on Guadalcanal my dad did something your dad didn't."

"Oh, yeah? What?"

Levi was enjoying himself. Albert riled easily. "He killed the entire company of Japs doing a banzai charge after all the other men in his squad were wounded. He was the last man standing. The Germans never did a banzai charge. Then he patched up all the wounded men in his squad. He got the Silver Star for that."

"So?" Albert said, failing to find a better response.

The bell rang, signaling that class was about to begin. Jenna appeared just as the boys were lining up near the door.

"Hi, Albert." She smiled.

"Hi, Jenna," he replied happily. "First day for you, too?"

"Yep."

"Hey," Levi interjected, jealous of the attention Jenna was giving the new boy. "Where do you know him from?"

"Sunday School," she explained. "Albert and I go to the same one. His dad works for my dad. Right, Albert?"

"Right. Best highway men in Utah and Idaho. Sent down here to make the highways straight."

"Well," Levi began, forcing a smile, "would you like to go for a ride on my boat later today?"

"Sure would! Really?"

"Sure. Just ask your folks."

"Me, too?" Jenna asked, suddenly shy.

"Sure, why not." Levi had worked the magic of a local on the pair, and had gotten the focus back where he wanted it. On himself.

9

MAYFIELD

Spring 2000

I FELL FOR JENNA COMPLETELY BY THE FALL OF 1956. SHE was allowed to come with me on the skiff, as long as we wore life preservers and scooted around the calm waters of the inlet between the pier and the breakwaters.

It usually ended up a threesome, with Albert Tenny at the bow, and Jenna and me on the seat closest to the outboard motor to compensate for Albert's weight.

Albert was always preoccupied with searching for sharks and schools of fish. He and I soon became fishing partners, another opportunity for me to show off on Saturdays after Jenna had been safely deposited back on shore with her family.

But I found that I wasn't very interested in fishing anymore, now that Jenna was in Paradise Bay. I cast my line, hoping for looks from her, admiration, anything I could hook in her. I wanted her heart, even though I didn't really understand why I felt the way I did.

School was different forty years ago. We talked about God, family, and country. We'd put our hands over our hearts every morning to recite a pledge in unison: *I pledge allegiance to the flag of the United States of America, and to the Republic for which it stands; one nation, under God, indivisible, with liberty and justice for all.*

Albert Tenny bowed his head reverently each time it ended. His family was religious, and very patriotic. Kids giggled and laughed, but I secretly respected his devotion.

Without a doubt, school suddenly became more pleasant for me the year Jenna arrived. There was something in the bounce of her step when she jumped rope, skipped along with friends, or played hopscotch. What God had done to make her so interesting I just couldn't understand; until Jenna showed up, no other girls had ever captured my attention.

"See that girl over there?" Mark Mayfield asked. "Jenna Bradley?"

"Yeah, what of it?" Levi replied, eyeing the playground bully suspiciously.

"I think she likes me," Mark grinned. "She keeps looking over this way. I think I'll make her my girlfriend."

"What makes you so sure she's looking at you?"

"Well, she wouldn't be looking at you, stupid." Mark laughed.

"Maybe 'cause I know her, S-T-U-P-I-D," Levi shot back.

"Hey, watch who you're calling stupid, Harper! I'll take that bony arm of yours and twist it into a pretzel." Mayfield grabbed Levi's arm with both hands and twisted in opposite directions.

"Fight!" someone yelled. "Mayfield's beating up Harper!"

"Get him, Levi!" another called. A ring of boys and girls had formed around the two boys, who were now wrestling on the grass.

"Grab his leg, Levi!"

"Hit him in the stomach!"

"Go for his throat!"

"Punch him!"

"Let that shrimp have it, Mark!" one of the bully's allies cried out.

Levi was sure Jenna was watching now, and he agilely avoided Mark's wild swings by ducking and rolling. Mark lunged, giving Levi a clear shot with his fist, stunning the bigger boy as they both fell to the ground.

"Thatta boy!" Albert screamed. "Kick him in the you-know-what!"

A whistle sounded. Mr. Dickerson, the fifth-grade teacher, was running toward them.

Mayfield swung at Levi's face one more time. Levi ducked, then glanced behind him as he felt someone tugging on his shirt. It was Jenna, begging him to stop fighting. Mark missed Levi, but Jenna's eyebrow was cut, and tears ran down her face from the pain of the unexpected blow.

"I . . . geez, I'm sorry," Mayfield stammered.

Mr. Dickerson pushed his way between the boys and pulled them apart.

Levi pulled a handkerchief from his pocket and knelt down beside Jenna.

"Are you okay?"

"Why did you fight him, Levi? It isn't like you. You're nicer than that." She was still crying.

"He called me stupid because I liked you, then he pushed me. I couldn't let him just push me around."

"I don't care. I don't like boys who fight. They're stupid!"

"What was this about?" Mr. Dickerson demanded.

"He started it!" Mayfield said.

"I did not," Levi growled back.

Mr. Dickerson knelt down and put his arm around Jenna. "How did this happen?" he asked, examining her forehead.

"Mark hit her," Albert Tenny volunteered.

"I didn't mean to," Mark protested.

"You're a liar, Mark," Levi shouted, enraged.

"Why you . . ." Mayfield hissed. "I'll get you."

"Yeah, only if there aren't any girls around to punch first, you big dope!"

"That's enough! Both of you boys to the principal's office. Right now. And don't say a word to each other." The teacher turned to Jenna. "Come here, sweetheart. Let's get you over to see the school nurse."

"I'm gonna get you, Levi. Better watch your back!"

"Yeah. That's right, Mayfield, you coward. You'll have to come up behind me. You don't scare me."

"Anytime, anywhere, sissy boy," Mayfield threatened. "When you don't have a girl around to protect you."

"You two just shut your mouths and keep walking," Mr. Dickerson shouted.

The boys finally gave it up. Besides, they had just reached the door to the principal's office, where Mr. Rose was waiting for them.

"Which one of you is first?"

Levi shrugged. Mark lowered his head.

"Mark, what did I say the last time you were here?"

"The paddle," Mayfield murmured.

"That's right. Come on in, and let's get it over with." Mr. Rose turned to Levi. "Then it's your turn. I can't believe it. Levi Harper. I'm sorely disappointed."

Levi had already been rebuked enough by Jenna, and now Mr. Rose's image of him was spoiled. He imagined he could hear his hard-earned halo hitting the floor with a thud. All the way to fifth grade without ever being threatened with the paddle.

Levi waited outside the closed office door while Mark got his paddling, wincing every time he heard the board smacking Mark's rump.

"Ow! I promise, I won't fight no more!"

"There will be no fighting at Paradise School. Understood, Mr. Mayfield? Next time, you'll be expelled."

Mark Mayfield came out of the office, trying to look tough. Tears filled his eyes.

"Next." Mr. Rose motioned Levi into his office.

Levi's heart was racing. Mark really was pretty tough, and to see him cry meant the swats had been hard.

"I'm disappointed in you, Levi. You've never been in trouble before. Care to explain yourself?"

"Mark shoved me and called me stupid. So I shoved him back and said he was stupid. Then it just got worse. That's all."

"What did Jenna Bradley have to do with it?"

"Nothing."

"She must have had something to do with it. She got hurt."

"She tried to stop me and got in the way. Mark hit her by accident."

"Were you fighting over her?"

"Not exactly," Levi muttered.

"Well, then. Shall we get this over with?"

"Guess so." Levi bent over, grabbed his ankles, and closed his eyes.

"I'm not going to swat you, Levi. You're getting a warning this time. But if there's a next time, you'll get a severe paddling. Understand?"

"Yes, sir, Mr. Rose," Levi replied, ecstatic with relief. "Thank you, Mr. Rose."

Levi walked out, thanking his lucky stars as he started down the corridor. Mrs. Bradley arrived, running over to her injured daughter, who was sitting outside the nurse's office. Levi tried to catch Jenna's eyes.

Girls just aren't worth the trouble, he decided. He turned around and walked the other way.

As Jenna snuggled into the comfort of her mother's arms she watched Levi walk out the door. She admired Levi for his courage and knew he'd been sticking up for her, but she wasn't going to let him know it just yet. She'd make him earn it.

10

AMORE

———
1959
———

I WISH YOU COULD JUST STAY," LEVI COMPLAINED. HE AND
Jenna were walking home, and he was carrying her books.

"Dad says the studios have offered him a job he can't turn
down. Anaheim seems so far away. But maybe you could visit,"
she added, brightening somewhat.

"I don't think my parents would let me go stay at a girl's
house."

"Guess not," she agreed. "Hey, guess what! I'm taking singing
lessons!"

"Really? Gee, that's neat. What stuff are you singing?"

"Mom says I have to stick to church choir, but I was kinda
thinking about something else. You know the Disney group? The
kids?" she asked, embarrassed.

"You want to be a Mouseketeer?" He laughed. "Wear Mickey
Mouse ears?"

"What's wrong with that?" Jenna's face reddened.

"Nothing. It'd be swell, but—"

"But what? I can try out, and I will. Sometimes you make me so mad, Levi!" She grabbed her books out of his hands and stomped off toward home.

"Girls," he moaned as he headed for the Santos Grocery.

Nobody knew about his feelings for Jenna. Except Jeff, but he didn't count. If Albert knew, and he probably did, he never let on. Anyone else would make fun of him, call it "puppy love." But Levi had it bad for her. He imagined that he and Jenna would grow up together, finish school together, even marry one day.

He hadn't kissed her yet. He didn't even know how.

He liked to go down to the Saturday matinee at the Holiday Theater on Wharf Street. For a quarter, he could watch Humphrey Bogart, Marlon Brando, Frank Sinatra, and his favorite, John Wayne. They always grabbed the girl by the arms and held them tight when they kissed them.

The leading actress would say something like, "What are you thinking?" then, with a yank, the actor would pull her close to his face and say something like, "This is what I think, baby!" The woman would put up a bit of a struggle, then surrender and, finally, frantically embrace the man. *Is that how to kiss a girl?* He'd seen his dad kiss his mom, but they were always giggling. He'd just have to figure it out somehow before Jenna moved away.

"Hi, Mr. Santos. Got any soda bottles for me to stack today?" he said.

"How much time you got, Levi?" Mr. Santos asked from behind the meat counter. He was chopping fresh cuts of sirloin and stacking the catch of the day in the ice cooler.

"I can work an hour. Then I got homework and piano lessons. Same old stuff."

"Isn't school letting out soon?" The grocer finished arranging meats and slid the tray into the display case.

"Yeah, one week." Levi was fingering a cold 7-Up in the ice chest.

"Go ahead. On the house."

"No, I got a dime," Levi said, digging in his pockets for the coin.

Mr. Santos wiped his hands on his soiled apron and pulled out a Bubble-Up, popped the cap with the counter bottle opener, and handed it to Levi. "Here, try this. Just came in. Supposed to be as good as 7-Up."

"Thanks, Mr. Santos," Levi smiled. He took a thirsty swig from the long-necked green bottle, then belched. "Oops."

"Atta boy." Mr. Santos laughed heartily.

"How can you be so happy all the time?" Levi asked, turning serious. "My mom says all Italians are alike, always laughing and eating." He took another long swig from the soda bottle.

"What's a man to do—frown? Live life with a lemon wedged between his lips?"

"No, I just mean . . . It's just that you like everybody. You smile all the time. Doesn't anything get you down?"

"No, nothin' ever gets me down. Not for long, anyway. Say, why you suddenly so intense? You studyin' to be a junior shrink or somethin'?"

"No, just thinking." Levi took the last swig from his Bubble-Up.

"Go ahead. Let it out. A nice long one. It'll make you feel better," the big Italian chuckled.

"If you say so." Levi grinned, then let out another loud belch.

"Hello, Mrs. Bradley. What can I get you today?" Mr. Santos was still laughing as the woman walked into the store. His young friend scurried for cover in the back room.

She frowned, clearly not amused. "Pastrami," she said sharply.

"Some bologna, and a pound of that lean pot roast, too." She pointed to the meat case.

"You got it." Santos smiled. "How much bologna?"

"Two pounds, please."

"That's a lotta bologna."

"Yes it is," Mrs. Bradley agreed. She gave Santos a knowing smile. "But this might be my last visit to your store."

"Not so!" he said excitedly, realizing she had a secret to share.

"Yes, that's right. My husband was offered a position with Disney in Anaheim. He's an artist, you know."

"I thought he paved highways."

"That was just temporary. He's been working on his art in the evenings, and it's finally paid off. He's going to be working in animation, and studying motion pictures, too." Her face was beaming with pride.

"Hey, hear that, Levi? The Bradleys are gonna be famous. Work at that Mickey Mouse place."

"Disney," she repeated.

"Ain't there a park there or something?" Santos asked as he wrapped her meat in butcher paper. "The place they wouldn't let that Russian commie dictator go to—Khrushchev?"

"Disneyland, Mr. Santos."

"Yeah, that's it! Well, how about them apples. Your husband's gonna work with the famous Mr. Disney. Boy, what I'd give to see that place someday."

"Maybe you will, Mr. Santos." Mrs. Bradley pulled a five-dollar bill out of her purse as he rang up her purchases. "Here you go."

"And here's your change," he said, counting thirty-one cents into her hand.

"Good day, Mr. Santos. Hope to see you again." She started toward the door, then turned around and smiled at Levi, who was still standing in the back of the store. "And good day to you, too," she added.

"See ya, Mrs. Bradley," Levi answered.

"That's one classy dame," Mr. Santos said, then noticed that Levi suddenly looked unhappy. "What's troubling you, son?"

"It's just that . . . I have this girlfriend, see. And now I don't know what to do."

"What do you mean, 'now'?" Mr. Santos asked, then put it together. "Oh, I see. It's the little Miss Bradley, is it? That's okay. Don't worry about it. Things will work out. I met Mrs. Santos when I was a young boy, too, and I loved her all my life."

"Really? But were you ever separated?"

"Nah, we both grew up in Brooklyn. We were practically cousins. But I loved that dark-haired, olive-eyed girl from the first time I saw her. Boys are born suckers. Nothin' to worry about, Levi. And nothin' you can do about it, neither."

"Well, I'd better be going," Levi said, still uncertain. "Maybe I'll come back later and help out some more."

"Sure thing, Levi. You do that. And I got a feelin' everything's gonna go just swell for you. Just remember one piece of advice."

"What's that?"

"Women like to know they're appreciated. You tell her how pretty she is, give her something to remember you by, and she'll never forget you. Ever kiss her?"

Levi felt his face flush with embarrassment. "Uh . . . no, not exactly."

"Either you did or you didn't. Now which is it?" Santos pressed, grinning.

"I don't know how," Levi replied, looking down at the floor.

"Nothin' to it, kid. Don't be too anxious, and kiss her real gentle. Real soft. Not like that stuff you see in the movies. She'll never forget it."

"Uh, yeah. Thanks, Mr. Santos." *How did he know?*

11

JUST BELIEVE

I BOUGHT THIS FOR YOU," JENNA SAID, HANDING THE YO-YO
to Levi. "It whistles when it spins."

"Gee, it's swell, Jenna. Thanks." Levi looped the string around
his finger and held his arm out. "Watch this. It's called 'walking
the dog.'" He released the yo-yo, holding it low as it scooted
along the ground. "And this one's called 'around the world.'"

Jenna clapped in appreciation, delighted to see Levi so
pleased with her parting gift.

"I bought this for you." Levi pulled a small box out of his
pocket. "It's not much, but it was all I could afford. I got it down
at Ben Franklin's." He handed it to her, still feeling the need to
explain. "It cost three-ninety-five. Had to mow five lawns and
sell my Willie Mays card for it."

Jenna opened the box to find a delicate imitation pearl necklace inside. She threw her slender arms around Levi's neck and hugged him. "I love you, Levi. I'm really going to miss you."

"Me, too," he mumbled.

"But we can write each other, can't we?"

He simply offered a nod of the head and a sad expression.

He reached up to help her clasp the necklace, but she stopped him.

"Here," she said, holding the pearls out in the palm of her hand. "If you believe, anything can come true. And I believe I'm going to marry you someday. Put your hand on these pearls and make a wish, and I'll make one, too. Close your eyes real tight."

Levi did as she asked, closing his fist around her hand. *Hope no one's watching this*, he thought.

"Just believe. Say it with me, Levi," she urged him.

"Just believe," he repeated obediently.

"Now, think about us. Think about us seeing each other again and getting married someday," she went on.

Levi imagined it with all his might.

"There," Jenna said, smiling with satisfaction. "Now, all I have to do is look at it any time I want to remember you."

Levi's heart was beating so loudly, he was sure she could hear it. "Jenna, I'm gonna miss you real bad. I even wrote a song for you."

"Gosh, Levi. I'd love to hear it."

"Then come on."

He led her to the school auditorium, pointing to the piano as he opened the door and walked in. He sat down on the bench and patted the space beside him. Once she'd joined him, he lifted the cover from the keys and began playing.

Jenna looked over at Levi in surprise as the melody wafted into the air, like a tiny down feather drifting effortlessly on the breeze. He didn't seem like the same boy. She closed her eyes and listened, face flushing as he sang her name.

Levi let his emotions carry him into the rhapsody he'd written for her, like a concert pianist performing for a packed house. Under the touch of his fingers, the keys seemed to be playing him more than he was playing them. He didn't notice that people had begun trickling in from the nearby offices and classrooms, drawn by the sound. He was lost in his music, rearranging the tune as it moved him, changing octaves and adding chords.

" 'She danced to music mild and sweet, breath of wind beneath her feet. Pretty Paradise girl . . .' " he finished. "It's called 'Jenna's Theme,' " he added, almost in a whisper.

A pair of hands clapped, then two, until more than twenty adults and children were applauding him.

"Where did you learn to play like that, Levi?" Mr. Rose asked, awestruck.

"I take piano lessons, and I made this up when I was practicing at home," he replied. "I just heard it in my mind." Levi was basking in the moment. Music was the only thing that mattered to him as much as Jenna.

"Very unusual," Mr. Rose said. "I'd like you to come see me in my office tomorrow, Levi. Would you do that?"

"Sure thing, Mr. Rose."

"Good. I'll send for you during first hour, before recess. Keep up the good work, Mr. Harper. You'll go places with a touch like that."

The crowd dispersed, leaving Levi and Jenna alone again. *Now or never*, he decided, trying to remember what Mr. Santos had said. *Real gentle.*

"Jenna?" he said, swallowing hard.

"Yes?" Jenna looked at him expectantly.

He couldn't do it like his parents did, and he couldn't do it like John Wayne or Robert Mitchum. He lowered his face toward her slowly. She didn't move away.

"I think I . . ." He couldn't say the word. He leaned closer, made a smacking sound with his lips, but missed her mouth entirely.

"Like this," Jenna said, and kissed him softly on the lips.

"Yeah. Uh . . . I guess we'd better go." A rush, a sensation filled him, a new world, one he had never known, opened. His eyes wide, and nervous, he stood outside at the curb, awkwardly holding hands with Jenna as they waited for her mother.

"I'm going to learn to sing," Jenna spoke up. "Then, when we see each other, you can play and I'll sing. We'll make a record. What do you think?"

"That'd be great," he replied, feigning enthusiasm. Without her here in Paradise Bay, nothing seemed to matter. "I'm real sorry about the other day . . . you know, when I made fun of you about the Mickey Mouse Club. I was just jealous. I wish I could go with you."

"Me, too," Jenna said as her mother's car came around the corner. "There's my mom," she added.

"Well, I guess this is it." Levi sighed.

"Remember, Levi. Remember that you just have to believe. Don't forget the pearls." Jenna pulled the necklace out of her pocket. "I'll wish on these every day."

"I'll remember, Jenna," he promised.

As Levi stood watching the Chevy sedan pull away, Jenna turned around and held the pearls up for him to see.

12

THIRTY SECONDS

Summer 2000

T HE SUMMERS CAME, FIRST 1960, THEN 1961, AND THE Bradleys returned to Paradise Bay for a week of vacation each June. Our parents had taken note of the letter-writing between us and had accepted the fact that something serious was developing.

A pleasant summer holiday of chaperoning was the Bradleys' way of showing Jenna they cared. Mr. Bradley was doing so well at the Disney Studios that they'd decided to camp out on the beach in their new Airstream trailer hitched to a new 1960 Chevy wagon.

As the adults sat around the bonfire at night, telling stories from the big war, talking about interest rates and what the latest S&H Green Stamps would buy, the neighborhood kids played tag, a version of hide-and-seek. Of course, Albert Tenny was the biggest sucker of all, always falling for some ruse and getting tagged. Then he'd come looking for us.

Jenna and I often found ourselves hiding together behind a sand dune somewhere, holding hands in the dark. A tiny peck on the lips and the thrill of holding her hand were enough magic for me.

The first kiss of the summer, I reasoned, was always the best anyway. No matter how many kisses followed, nothing rivaled the sparks flying in the first kiss. I didn't understand then, but I would learn soon enough that a kiss seemed to be an ingenious plot created by nature to stimulate the mind of a man to utter numbness.

"You have to learn control," my father counseled. "All those hormones and, well . . ." he'd say, then give me the birds-and-bees talk. I certainly didn't want to hear it, but he was dog-determined to make sure I understood how boys and girls changed and grew. How they needed to avoid things like "lying down together" and "kissing more than thirty seconds," then "only saying good night at the door," and "no touching a girl except to hold hands," et cetera.

So I followed the thirty-second rule. One kiss at a time.

Albert could shout, "Come out, come out, wherever you are!" all night long, and it would have no effect.

Levi grabbed Jenna's hand as they ran toward the jetty. It was outside the predetermined boundaries for hide-and-seek, but not far enough for them to be accused of cheating.

"I have something for you," Levi said, as they fell into the sand laughing. "I bought a black pearl that's bigger than the others," he explained, digging in his pocket, "in Pismo Beach at a small shop that cultures them in seawater tanks. I want to add it to the necklace."

Jenna took the necklace off and handed it to him. He worked the fake pearls off the chain one by one, then put the black one in the center and replaced them. Jenna moved closer so he could clasp it around her neck once more. Levi took his time accomplishing the task.

"This might sound corny, but I promise I'll always be true," he said.

Jenna had closed her eyes as he put his arms around her neck. "Me, too. I told you to believe when I moved away, and here we are."

Levi leaned toward her. They kissed.

"That was nice," she whispered. "Do it again."

Just as he leaned over to kiss her again, he spotted his father walking across the stage of an otherwise very occupied mind. *No more than thirty seconds.* Levi put his arms around Jenna and kissed her, then quickly broke away; things were happening inside his body that only made it worse. "We should get back," he said.

"Okay," she breathed. "But can we hold hands?"

"Just until we get back to where the others can see us. I don't want them teasing you—or me."

"Ollie-ollie-oxen-free!" Albert shouted.

13

CHANGE IN TIME

Fall 2000

THE CHANGES IN PARADISE BAY AND ACROSS THE COUN-try became apparent in 1962. The '50s just couldn't be dragged any further into this new decade.

Albert Tenny's father took a job running the interstate road crews out in Kentucky and Tennessee. He invited Mr. Bradley to follow after he was laid off by Disney.

I lost both my best friend and the girl that was driving me wild to the hand of fate supplied by the economic recession of '62.

Popular music still had the romantic charm of voices like Ricky Nelson's and Pat Boone's. But the opening of the new decade offered more choices in sounds, styles, technology, and the sense that the very cold war with Communism was destined to become hot.

We practiced duck-and-cover drills once a month at school, pretending our desks could shield us from the effects of a nuclear blast. Everyone assumed, and our parents feared, that with so many thousands of missiles and tanks poised in Europe and Red China, we would soon be fighting the Communists.

When John F. Kennedy was elected president, a new day of "service" to country was promised, and the vigor and optimism of youth drew blinders over our eyes to the dangers lurking across the seas. The Peace Corps was created to assist countries in need; the very sound of the government program belied any militaristic adventures we might become embroiled in.

Foreign powers were causing foreign wars, and the Kennedy brothers had pledged to stop the crime of aggression across the oceans in far-off lands, and to stop the crimes against society in our own.

Before we knew it, we had a near invasion of Cuba—the Bay of Pigs. Our forces weren't committed to it, but the patriotic Cubans based in the United States were. They were either slaughtered or captured, embarrassing our president.

With that hand played out, Soviet Chairman Nikita Khrushchev thought he could sneak some nuclear weapons into Cuba, mere miles from our shores. That's when President Kennedy decided it was time to play hardball, and the Cuban Missile Crisis of October 1962 had all of us counting our last days on earth, afraid that World War III was about to erupt.

Kennedy ordered a sea-and-air blockade of the Communist-run island. Russia blinked, finally backed down against America's resolve and determination, and Kennedy's reputation for firm military response, which he'd lost after the earlier fiasco at the Bay of Pigs, was restored.

We learned of something called "civil rights" during those days of change. Until then, we'd thought that a "race issue" had to do with a track and field event. But now we had to adjust our parochial Paradise Bay views and face the facts that a world outside our town, that seemed so distant to us, had an immediate impact on us, as well.

Any major event happening in our country in those days had a ripple effect, like a wave gaining momentum and height as it rolls toward shore. We just didn't realize how many waves would be coming our way.

A small country no one had ever heard of asked for our military assistance against Communist aggression in 1962, and by 1964 we were actually sending troops to this nowhere land in Southeast Asia called Vietnam.

Even though the menacing realities of adulthood loomed, and the vagaries of the turmoil in the U.S. and across the seas were broadcast daily, Paradise Bay stayed the same—a beat off the rhythm of the rest of the world. And life, while it had a quicker pace than in the '50s, still retained its slow and magical charm to those of us too senseless to know any better.

"A Dr. Pepper and one of those Butterfinger bars," Levi said, trying to act as though he hadn't noticed the interest Carol Santos was paying him.

"Eighteen cents for the Dr. Pepper, ten for the Butterfinger," she smiled.

"Whew! Mr. Santos and his family must really be making a fortune at these prices," Levi complained, handing over the coins in exchange for the drink and candy. "You've been away for the summer. Back east with Grandma Santos or something?"

"Yeah, why? Notice something different?" She bent down, elbows on the counter, allowing Levi more of a view than he'd be willing to tell anyone.

"Uh, yeah. You look and act older. What grade are you going to be in next year?"

"I'll be in ninth, and you'll be in eleventh. So when are you going to figure out that there's only two years' difference in our age, and that I'm not some little girl tagging behind her mommy's skirt at the Santos Grocery?" She abruptly changed the subject. "Going to the beach tonight?"

"Yeah. Maybe. Practicing some music with a few of the boys."

"Great. I'll be there. Maybe I can show you a few things with that guitar of yours." She smiled again.

"You play the guitar?"

"Learned this summer. Just a few chords, but it wasn't that hard. Bet you won't let me play it, though."

"Sure I will. I'll bring mine, you bring yours, and we'll jam a little. See you there," he added, then turned to leave and nearly ran into the closed door.

She stifled a laugh. She knew she had him.

14

DIFFERENT DRUMS

June 1965

Hᴏᴡ'ꜱ ᴊᴇɴɴᴀ ᴅᴏɪɴɢ?" ʟᴇᴠɪ ᴀꜱᴋᴇᴅ, ɪᴅʟʏ ᴛᴏꜱꜱɪɴɢ ᴀ stone into the incoming foam.

"Fine, I guess. They live in another part of town, outside Louisville, actually. Hardly ever see her, except when her folks invite us to some big church event."

"Does she look good?"

"Always."

Levi sighed, thinking he'd finally replaced the image of the toothy grin, dimples made to order, azure eyes—the too-good-to-be-true California blonde—with the pretty Italian girl who'd grown up suddenly last summer.

"I'd sure like to see her, but I don't see how that's possible. She still has a year of high school left," Levi grumbled. "Besides, I'm hooked up with Carol now."

"Skinny Carol Santos from the store?" Albert asked, incredulous.

"You ought to see her now. She's a looker, my friend. Lost those cat eyeglasses to contacts. Anyway, it gets lonely here in nowhere land. I gotta get out of this place. At least you've seen some of the world."

"If you call Idaho, Utah, and Kentucky the world," Albert replied. "You don't appreciate how good this place is, Levi, until you go somewhere else. As great as those trout streams in the Rockies are, and as nice as the folks in Kentucky are, this place is a dream come true. This is the kind of place a man decides to fight and die for."

"What you talking about?"

"The Marines. I came up here to ask you to join up with me. You either go to school or enlist with me. Let's face it—you'll just get drafted anyway, and we'd make a great team."

"Nah. Not in the cards. I'm gonna have to take my chances. Too much music, and too little time."

"Music's been around since man started this whole mess. You could bring your guitar along," Albert pressed.

"It isn't the same as the piano. Besides, I've got some gigs lined up in Los Angeles, and some in Santa Barbara, too. All it takes is the right person to hear my songs, the right station to play one, and I'll be on the road to fame, Al."

"Ah, Levi, you'll be wasting time when you could've gotten the GI Bill money for college by signing up. And what'll you do if you don't get that big break?"

"Make the world a better place one song at a time," Levi replied matter-of-factly as he skimmed another smooth stone across the surface of the water. "Make sure my music's something every music lover can relate to."

"Some like pop-rock. Some like blues, jazz, country. How you gonna please everyone?"

"The keyboard's the equalizer. Lyrics, too. Maybe I'll just say what I feel. Look at all the groups out there making history. They all started out like me, taking gigs in bars and school dances. Besides, I'd be letting the other boys in the band down, and I'm not as gung ho about this war as you are. The Commies are a world away."

"See, that's the trouble with you, Levi. The Japanese attacked Pearl Harbor right out there." Albert jabbed a finger in the air. "The Communists almost took over Korea in 1950, and now it's Vietnam. Then it'll be Cambodia, Laos, Thailand, and India. Did you know, my friend, that almost half the world's under Communist socialism as we speak?"

"Hadn't given it much thought."

"Well, you should. While guys like me are fighting the Communists in Vietnam, guys like you will be kicking back, getting the benefits of freedom. *Free*-dom, Levi. That's what this is all about!"

"Look, I admire your enthusiasm for the war, Al, but we got bigger weapons than one more Marine firing a machine gun into the screaming Commie menace."

"And what's that?"

"Music."

"You've gotta be joking. You think those guys care about music?"

"They're human. And if they're human, they care about music. Music touches everyone. It soothes the soul and levels the emotions. What if I could make the kind of music that gets people to stop, think, and feel?"

"Feel what?"

"Their souls, Al!"

"Geez, Levi. You sound like one of those freak pacifists. This is 1965, and those Commies are about to do exactly what I said—take over one country at a time. They've already got Cuba, and they've got guerillas in Central and South America. We'll have to fight there if we don't stop them somewhere else. What happened to the patriotic kid that used to play war games on the beach with me?" Albert's tone sounded disappointed and frustrated now.

"I believe in peace and music. War makes war, peace makes peace. We haven't given anything but war a chance in this century. Every fifteen to twenty years, we get into some war, and who's dying? Guys that should be raising families and enjoying their lives." Levi paused, then looked his friend directly in the eye. "I sure would hate to see you go off and get yourself killed."

"I'd gladly give my life for my country, if that's what it takes," Al shot back, refusing to back off the argument.

"And if those Communists attack my country, I will, too. But they haven't yet, and I'm not going unless I get drafted. I think I'll take the college deferment and scholarship to UCSB. I'll make music. Look around. See anybody losing sleep over the Vietnam War ten thousand miles away?"

Albert stood up. "I'm sorry you feel that way, Levi. I've gotta go. My folks are throwing a going-away party at my uncle's place down in San Diego tomorrow night. I told them I needed to see my buddy."

"Aren't you staying the night?"

"Well, if you want me to. But . . ."

"No 'buts.' You're staying."

"Thanks for putting up with me, Levi. I've missed this place. With the right girl, I'd like to make a place like this home."

Albert thought the invitation to Levi was worth one more try. "Levi"—he hesitated—"if you'd join up with me, we could come back and start a fishing business together. What do you say?"

"I'm gonna miss you, Al," Levi replied with a smile. "You're a good friend."

"I'm heading down on the Greyhound tomorrow. I already have my enlistment papers. If you change your mind . . ." Albert bit his lip, resisting the urge to push it any further.

The two young men shook hands, then embraced.

"I'll be praying for you, Al," Levi said, clapping his friend on the back.

"So . . . how do we kill the rest of the day?" Albert said, taking in a deep breath of the coastal air. "Sure would like to go fishin' one last time." He looked hopefully to Levi.

"Sure, why not." Levi laughed. "Let's get the skiff. A couple hours and then I've got a surprise for you."

He had invited their old friends from Paradise School, recent grads included. There would be a grunion run tonight, a bonfire down on the beach, probably some Beach Boys music for atmosphere. Of course, there'd be Carol, too.

"What kind of surprise?" Al asked as they brushed the sand off their trousers and began walking up the dunes to retrieve the fishing gear from the garage.

"Tag, you're it." Levi laughed. "Come on."

15

THE BOOT

W inter 2001

I TRADED IN MY PIANO FOR A RIFLE IN LATE 1966, NOT BY choice but by default. I had left school to focus on music. College was a way to a draft deferment, but that was all. I had no real interest in a degree and didn't see how the nights in the campus library at the University of California at Santa Barbara were furthering my musical career.

I had lost track of Jenna by this time and wondered where she might be, but Carol was becoming more and more interested in making music with me and my band. Feeling as warm as I did toward Mr. and Mrs. Santos made it considerably easier to push Jenna to the back of my mind.

I made my share of mistakes that year, all of which led to my becoming a draftee for the United States Marine Corps, a Boot at the San Diego Marine Recruit Depot.

• • •

"Go! Go! Go!" the drill sergeant yelled into Levi's ear as the draftee struggled to do a hundred push-ups with his rifle balanced on top of his hands. "Don't let me see that rifle even touch the ground!" The big man wearing the Smokey the Bear drill instructor's hat seemed to want to make certain that the others in the platoon, who were making laps around the parade ground, could hear him. "I can't hear you, maggot! Start over. All hundred! And let me hear you this time!"

"This is my rifle," Levi grunted as he began the new set, which the drill instructor counted out loud for the benefit of the rest of the Boots now returned from the run and in formation. "There are many like it," Levi went on, "but this one is mine. My rifle is my best friend. It's my life. I must master it as I must master my life," he recited as loudly as he could. "My rifle is useless without me. I am useless without my rifle. I must fire my rifle true. I must shoot straighter than the enemy who is trying to kill me. I must shoot him before he shoots me. I will—"

"Fifty! Halt, you scum! I said halt! In Marine jargon, that means stop, you worm!" he screamed. "Or are you enjoying this little exercise so much that you'd like to start over?"

"No, Drill Sergeant, sir!" Levi froze in push-up position, his arms quivering.

"Now, the rest of you fairies, whose dainty feet ain't fit to walk upon the same hallowed ground as a real Marine, will motivate this quivering Boot to give us his very best by repeating after each of the remaining fifty push-ups. You sorry excuses for mentally deficient, weak, two-legged mules—which most good farmers would put out of their misery—will repeat the number after me along with this rifle-dropping vermin. And if any of you ever drop one of my rifles like Harper did, you'll be doing push-ups all night, or until you're dead, whichever comes first! Do I make myself clear?"

"Yes, Drill Sergeant, sir!" the platoon of recruits and draftees replied in unison.

"You ready, maggot?" the drill instructor asked in a patronizing voice.

"Yes, Drill Sergeant, sir!" Perspiration was streaming down Levi's face.

"Now, the rest of you lowlifes, unworthy to wear the uniform of the United States Marine Corps, will follow as I demonstrate. I will call 'fifty-one,' upon which Harper will come up from his push-up and continue his memorized recitation of the United States Marine Rifle Creed. You will then repeat, 'Fifty-one, maggot,' and so on until Harper succeeds with his assignment. Do you understand?"

"Yes, Drill Sergeant, sir!" all forty-eight recruits yelled.

Levi was in agony, but he knew there would be only more push-ups if he failed to get through this torturous session.

"Are you ready, you disrespectful sissy boy?"

"Yes, Drill Sergeant, sir!" Levi could barely talk through his dry, cracked lips. His tongue felt sticky, like he had cotton wadded between it and the roof of his mouth. He'd collapse if he didn't get water soon.

"You ever gonna drop one of my rifles again?"

"No, Drill Sergeant, sir!" he struggled.

"It appears that this crawling worm down here is thirsty," the D.I. observed mercilessly. "For the benefit of the rest of you fools, Mr. Charles Cong in Vietnam don't give a damn if you're thirsty! The only thing between you and Mr. Victor Charles, also affectionately known as V. C. or Viet Cong, is this rifle that Harper dropped during our run. And you know what? Harper would be dead right now! Mr. V. C. won't give this dirtbag the luxury of a hundred push-ups to clear his name, to regain his dignity as a United States Marine, if he should live so long to be so honored! Do I make myself clear?"

"Yes, Drill Sergeant, sir!" the platoon called back again.

"Ready, down!" The count began, and Levi resumed his recitation of the United States Marine Rifle Creed:

"My rifle and myself know that what counts in this war is not the rounds we fire, the noise of our burst, or the smoke we make. It's the hits that count. I will hit . . ." he droned. "My rifle is human, even as I, because it is my life. Thus, I will learn it as a brother." Levi heard the count reach sixty-nine, and his voice gained strength. "I will learn its weaknesses, its strengths, its parts, its accessories, its sights, and its barrel." He had now accomplished eighty push-ups. "I will ever guard it against the ravages of weather and damage as I guard my legs, my arms, my eyes, and my heart. I will keep my rifle clean and ready. We will become part of each other. We will . . ."

"Ninety-one, maggot," the D.I. barked.

"Before God . . ." Levi gasped, "I swear . . . this creed. My rifle and myself are the defenders of my country. We are the masters . . . of our enemy. We are the saviors of my life."

"Keep goin', you sorry puke!"

"So be it. Until victory is America's . . . and there is no enemy . . . but peace."

16

SUMMER OF LOVE

1967, Paradise Bay

THE HIPPIES ARE CALLING IT THE SUMMER OF LOVE," HE said, tossing a stone into the surf. "More like thunder than love. Flower children singing about 'free love.' What do they know? Nothing's free. Stinking draft, the war, now this."

"Yeah."

He laughed bitterly, brushing his hand over his military-cropped hair. "Sometimes things just aren't what they seem. I think some poet said that. I used to think poets didn't know what they were talking about."

"Uh-huh."

"Doesn't seem to make much sense: you, the way I feel, and doing what I'm about to do. I can't let you go without telling you that . . ." He couldn't go on for a moment, choking on his words. "It's not fair to her. To say I don't love her . . . just a different kind, I guess," he finally concluded.

Sitting cross-legged, he tossed one more of a hundred pebbles he had thrown that day into the foamy, tumbling surf. He watched the water advance and recede, dragging with it millions of grains of sand, changing the form of the beach up and down the coast.

His thoughts turned to gravity, how it tugged, always having its way, changing the very nature of what it touched. Like the sand, almost imperceptibly, the beach moved with every wave until the entire shoreline was changed.

He felt pulled the same way, forced by a momentum he couldn't control. He was a draftee, a Marine going to a war he didn't care about. A piano man whose music was fading to the point where he couldn't hear it anymore. Getting married. Moving toward a life he was uncertain of. And the girl beside him was holding something else: a piece of his heart he had never fully understood until now.

Her presence now was spinning him out of control. She had been pulling at him emotionally from the moment he'd first looked into her eyes. He could still see the surprised eight-year-old he'd almost run over with his scooter that summer day in 1956.

Levi frowned, sighed in frustration, and stared at the far horizon.

The rehearsal for tomorrow's wedding was tonight. Soon, everyone waiting at the church would be wondering where he was.

Eyes stinging with tears, she, too, stared out to sea, where the amber colors of twilight met the smooth water.

"I can't back out," he said.

She nodded, trying to understand.

"I blew it. Why didn't you write? Why didn't you say something?"

Throaty tightness choked off any answer she might give.

"I've been in . . . well, I've always felt this way about you," he went on, measuring his words carefully. "Remember when you sat with me at the piano that day after school, right before you moved? That's when I knew for sure."

"Yes," she finally breathed.

"I was too young to reason, but I felt it here." He tapped at his chest. "God knows . . . I've prayed to Him a thousand times. He knows I wish I could think like a kid again, be that innocent, that I could undo all this."

"Uh-huh."

"She came on so strong. Then people started saying we looked good together, and I listened. How could I have known you were back in L.A.? You quit writing when you moved to Kentucky. I'm not the best at writing either, though," he apologized.

She buried her head in her hands.

"I was here, see. Helping my dad out at the cannery or down at UCSB. And there was always my music. I finally gave up school to help out, and to focus on the sounds I wanted to create. Couldn't see how college would help my music. Then I got my draft notice. I felt so bad about the way things had gotten between Carol and me . . . I had to let my dad know how things got out of control. He was trying to be understanding, but his famous 'you know what you have to do' look meant marriage. I'm sorry now."

"I understand," she said, wishing she meant it.

"I went to L.A. or San Francisco every weekend, trying to escape the guilt. Me and the boys would do a gig. I was getting real good, so I started doing solo acts in bars afterwards. I'd stay up all night long trying to compose original stuff, and I was getting really wasted. Then I'd come home, and Carol would be there."

"You really are good," she whispered. "The best piano man I've ever heard."

He tossed another stone. "Thanks. I never did record anything original, though. Got a pile of notes, sheets of what I created the past couple of years in my footlocker at the house."

Silence followed. They both wondered where this conversation would lead and how it would end.

"Do you love her?" she abruptly asked.

He swallowed hard. "I suppose so, in a way. But I . . . well, I've been letting another part of me do the thinking these last two years. The pressure, the guys hassling me, constantly asking if Carol and I . . . well, you know."

Silence again.

"Even if I didn't love her, I'd have my honor at stake. Both families expect it. Man, I had no idea what the consequences would be. I guess you know what I'm trying to say. What I mean is, I—"

"Don't say it," she interrupted. "I don't want to know what happened."

"I wish you'd never left Paradise Bay." He put a measured arm around her shoulder. "This is so hard," he muttered.

They both continued staring out to sea.

Hearts breaking.

Shouldn't be this way. Wasn't supposed to turn out this way.

He looked up the beach to the small fishing pier. No one was there. Down the beach, past the first jetty to the north, was the cove where a thousand years of crashing surf had carved out niches and caves—a place of late-night parties at low tide. No one coming from that direction either. He glanced over his shoulder to the sand dunes. All appeared quiet, sleepy.

A lot of folks walk the beach this late. So what? Maybe I'll bag this whole marriage thing. Don't care if they do see me with another woman.

"I can't stay, you know," she finally spoke up. "Kiss me one last time?"

He looked into her eyes. He slowly ran his fingers through the fine, silky strands of fiery amber cascading down her shoulders. Her hair brushed against his bare arm as he drew her in close. She leaned forward, waiting.

"I . . ." he began, then realized he was beyond words. No matter what, he would find a way to love his fiancée and leave Jenna with the kiss he desperately wanted to give her—and a parting kiss to keep for himself.

Kiss her and walk away, a voice inside his head told him.

Kiss her and back out, his heart said.

He felt her gentle embrace soothing him. His lips found her cheek, then her mouth. It was warm and genuine, but barely a kiss at all.

"I'd better be going. Don't look back, Jenna. Just know . . ." His throat tightened, unable to release the three words that were tormenting him. *I love you.*

"Hush," she said, tears running down her face as she put a finger over his mouth. "Don't say it unless you can do something about it. Just go."

He stood up, pulled her to him, and put his arms around her.

"Good-bye, Levi," she whispered. "Please make it home. Don't let anyone hurt you over there."

"Good-bye, Jenna."

She walked toward the pier and her white '65 Volkswagen Beetle, Levi toward the jetty just this side of the cove.

A girl who trusts me is waiting at the chapel. She deserves more love than I can give her. He picked up a large round stone, tossed it angrily into the surf, then turned back toward her disappearing figure.

"Jenna!"

Startled, hopeful, she turned to face him.

"I still believe!" he called out, more confused than ever as his legs propelled him in a direction he doubted so deeply.

She nodded, reached for the pearls tucked inside her blouse, and held them out for him to see. She blinked away the tears as she started toward the car again, preparing to leave Paradise Bay behind forever.

He watched and wondered; he had never imagined that love could hurt so much. Taking in a deep breath, he headed up Dockside Road to the chapel on Wharf and Main two blocks away. How could he change things and still keep his honor? By this time tomorrow, he would be married and headed off on his honeymoon, then to war.

Two hours had passed since she left the beach in Paradise Bay; her childhood fantasy of marrying Levi Harper had been dashed to pieces. Her eyes were still stinging as she drove back to her West Los Angeles apartment in the Volkswagen Beetle her parents had given her as a high-school graduation present. She had to report for the early shift tomorrow and didn't want to risk driving too late at night on Highway 101.

It wasn't all his fault. She could have been more assertive. Being in high school, living two thousand miles from Paradise Bay, other boys showing interest in her, had all made it harder to remember the childhood promises she'd made to him. *The fire is hotter the closer one gets*, she reasoned.

Until she saw him again, the flame had been just a warm

memory—certainly alive, but not hot. But an hour with him had changed everything.

She recalled how her mother had counseled her about love when she'd asked how a sophisticated city girl like herself had fallen in love with Jenna's father, a rather simple farmer type from Utah. "The heart seems to know stuff the brain doesn't," her mother had replied. Jenna was beginning to understand that now.

When a childhood friend still living in Paradise Bay told her that Levi was in the Marines, going to Vietnam, and getting married, she couldn't help but come and see for herself if that flame had been puppy love or something real, something she might regret if she didn't find out for sure.

Maybe it was puppy love, but returning to the magical seaside town brought it all back. She still felt exactly the same. Time hadn't diminished the memory that stirred in her heart.

A few words from him was all it would've taken. "Jenna, I love you, and I can't go through with marrying Carol. Marry me, Jenna." That wasn't too many words to ask for, was it? She had even prayed for those words to come. He'd wanted to say it; she'd sensed it.

She should have written to him while he was in training, arranged to meet him somewhere else. Not Paradise Bay, and not on his last day of freedom. What had she been thinking? She hadn't been. That was the problem.

She wondered about life, where to go with a broken heart. She attended UCLA now, after earning a scholarship there. She had been so anxious to be out west again, close to the ocean and her childhood memories. Her parents had wanted her to go to the University of Utah, near grandparents and relatives, but she had other plans; once Levi saw how she'd turned into a woman, he'd regret his decision to marry Carol and leave her.

So why had she waited the whole school year?

This internal dialogue raged for the entire two-hundred-mile drive back to Los Angeles. Her parents would be angry when they found out she'd risked the long drive alone, but she'd been determined to see Paradise Bay and Levi again, possibly for the last time in her life.

"It's not that I don't love you," he explained. "I'm confused, Carol. I'm wondering if this is right for us now."

"How can you do this to me? How am I going to tell my parents that you got cold feet, face my friends and family? Have you forgotten the baby? We have a child coming, Levi."

"I know, I know," he said. They were standing outside in the dark, minutes before rehearsal. "I'm just confused. What if I get killed over there? They told us in the advanced infantry training that half of us would be dead or seriously wounded within a year. It wouldn't be fair to make you suffer that."

"I'm willing to take that risk," she said. "I love you, Levi."

Guilt was sweeping through him like wildfire, and Carol had just fanned the blaze. He didn't know what to say.

"Don't you love me?" she asked.

"Not like I should," he murmured.

"Levi Harper, if you can't say you love me and that you're willing to marry me for better or worse, then fine. I'll have the baby and you'll never have to be bothered with me again." She pulled the engagement ring off her finger and slapped it into his hand.

That got his attention. He wanted to love her, to do what was right by their child, but he just couldn't say "I love you," not after seeing Jenna again. And he did love Carol, but not in the marrying way.

He turned to face her. Tears were now draining from her eyes. He sensed her mixed anger and frustration. He'd seen her unconventional wedding gown; day by day, Carol was turning into a full-blooded "flower child." And he didn't have anything in common with flower children. But he didn't want to hurt her.

"Look, Carol, we're different," he said.

She turned her back to him.

"I won't ever fit in with your friends."

She didn't respond.

"I don't totally agree with this war and I don't intend to be a 'lifer' in the Marine Corps either, but I'm also not some peace, make-love-not-war, protester type. Not like those people you've been hanging out with in Isla Vista and at UCSB."

"Oh, shut up," she allowed through sniffles.

"Look—I'll just tell everyone inside that I've decided I can't go through with it because I'm going to Vietnam, and that it wouldn't be fair to marry you when I might get killed. When I get back—if I get back—I'll do the right thing. Support you and the baby."

"I should've listened to my friends," she said flatly. "I hate you, Levi, and everything you represent." She turned away and walked into the dark.

Levi sighed as he started up the back steps of the church. A few friends and both sets of parents were there, waiting for rehearsal to begin. His father would be officiating. Levi called him over and whispered in his ear.

"Eleanor," Rex called. Levi's mother joined them.

"I'm leaving for Camp Pendleton tonight," Levi informed them. "I can't marry Carol. I thought I could go through with this, do the right thing, but I—"

"It's Jenna Bradley, isn't it?" Eleanor asked, her voice quivering. "She was here today. Things like that get around in a small town."

"Yes, she was. And yes, seeing her made me do some thinking. Doggone it, Mom, I can't help how I feel about her. And I'm going to Vietnam. Look at me, Mom." Levi put his hands on his mother's arms. "Please."

She looked up, into the eyes of her oldest child, fearful not for what the people in town might say but for what some Vietnamese bullet might do. She hadn't been willing to acknowledge that fear until now.

"I might get killed over there," he explained as gently as possible. "That's up to God, and I won't have any choice about that. But I do have a choice here, and I'm not going through with it. Carol deserves real love, more than I can give her."

Eleanor buried her face in his embrace. "I want you to live," she sobbed.

"Don't cry, Mom. You pray, and I'll come back. I'm sure of it." Levi turned to his father, his voice choked with emotion. "I'm going to the house now to get my gear. And I'll ask Jeff to drive me. Maybe Jeff can hang out the few days left before I leave for Vietnam. Okay with you, Dad?"

"Sure, son. But you call us before you ship out. We want to be there." Rex Harper blinked at the moisture forming in his eyes. He would deal with Mr. and Mrs. Santos and the situation about the marriage. But there wasn't a thing he could do to stop his oldest son from seeing hell on earth, risking his life in a god-forsaken war.

"Sure, Dad," Levi said. "I love you." His father held him in a long embrace. "Thanks, Dad," Levi offered, tears in his eyes now. He turned to his mother again, pulled her into a tight hug and kissed her on the forehead. "Good-bye, Mom. I love you, too.

And pray for me." Levi walked out of the church, then ran across the field toward home.

Jeff ran up behind him, breathless. "What are you doing, Levi?"

"Grab some clothes for overnight and get the car. We're going to L.A."

17

YOU AGAIN

Using the showers here on the beach is a lot cheaper than a motel. And the front seat wasn't so bad, was it, Jeffie?" Levi smiled as his brother walked up to the car from the showers off Santa Monica Beach. "Six A.M. and the surfers are already out there," he said, pointing to the pier. "I'm really gonna miss this."

"Too bad you can't take the surfboard," Jeff said. "Wanna go for a swim? I can always shower again."

"Nah, let's get something to eat. I have to find Jenna and then . . . I don't know, I have to make right whatever I can out of this mess. You gonna be okay driving back home by yourself?"

"No sweat. What day is this, anyway?"

"Saturday, Jeff. Remember? I was supposed to be getting married today." Levi was wearing blue jeans and a polo shirt; the only thing giving him away as military was his short hair and the dog tag around his neck. "If I find Jenna and can find a way to hang out here in L.A. for the next couple of weeks, would you mind leaving the car and letting me buy you a Greyhound ticket?" Levi knew his brother was looking forward to driving the souped-up Camaro back to Paradise Bay.

"Ah, Levi . . . you promised!"

"I know, and I'm sorry. I wasn't thinking too clearly last night. But if I hang out here before reporting back at Pendleton, I'll need wheels. You'll come to see me off, won't you?"

"Yeah, I guess," Jeff said, making no attempt to hide his disappointment.

"Well, that's twice the drive, right? I can't leave it at Pendleton for a year, can I?"

"No," Jeff conceded, "but I'll have to caravan behind Dad at fifty-five miles per hour."

"Yeah, but you'll have the car for a year. I want you to take care of it for me, okay?" Levi smiled, dangling the keys in his seventeen-year-old brother's face.

"Really? You mean it?" Jeff was beaming now.

"Sure I mean it. I love you, Jeff. I guess I've never really said it. But this war thing is getting real to me all of a sudden, and . . . well, I'd like you to remember me. You keep the car in good shape, and maybe when I get back we'll work out a deal and you can buy it. I'll get a '68 or something."

"Bitchin'!" Jeff whooped. "Yeah, man!"

"Hey, Jeff, you know what Dad says about that word," Levi scolded his brother.

"It don't mean what he thinks. It means *cool.*" Jeff grabbed the keys out of Levi's hand and ran around to the driver's side of the car. "Come on, Levi. Let me show you how good I can handle this baby."

"All right." Levi laughed. "But don't spin the tires. They need to last."

"Yeah, yeah, yeah. Come on."

They pulled out of the parking lot onto Pacific Coast Highway and up the hill to Ocean Boulevard.

"Turn here," Levi said. "She said she lives in Westwood, south of UCLA. Take Olympic Boulevard. We'll stop and grab a bite somewhere, and maybe I can get a phone number from information."

Jeff was proving himself behind the wheel, careful not to pop the clutch. He wanted to make sure his brother didn't have any reservations about letting him drive it during his senior year of high school.

"Say, Levi," he began. "I know you want to find Jenna and all. But let me ask you something," he hesitated, "and don't answer just yet. I wanna stay here with you for awhile. I can call Dad and tell him you want me to. He can find someone to fill in for me at the cannery. I got a hundred dollars in my wallet and—"

"Where'd you get that kind of bread?"

"Been saving up for a car, but I thought it might come in handy, so I grabbed it out of my dresser when we left. Anyway, I was thinkin' . . . you're staying here for a couple of weeks, so you need a place to stay, right?"

"Right . . ." Levi wondered where this was leading.

"You can't stay at Jenna's, even if you find her. That wouldn't be right."

"Go on."

"So, what if we go to an Army-Navy surplus, buy a tent, and camp out. We've got the sleeping bags in the trunk and . . ."

"And you want to hang out at the beach for a week, watch the girls, maybe go to Disneyland? Have something to talk about when school starts in September?"

"Well, yeah. And remember Gerry from Paso Robles? He's down here at his aunt's in Santa Monica. I got his telephone number right here. He'll hang out with me." Jeff looked over at Levi, a pleading look on his face, then spotted a restaurant. "Hey, there's a Bob's Big Boy. I heard they've got some ninety-nine-cent meal. You can think about it while we eat. I promise I won't be in the way, Levi. Cross my heart." He went through the motions.

"I don't have to think about it," Levi said, imitating their father's stern tone. He let it hang there for a minute, until they pulled into the parking lot and stopped. "You got a deal."

"Yeah, baby!" Jeff cried, pounding the wheel.

"It'll probably help make me more responsible. And besides"—Levi smiled—"I'm gonna miss you. Make memories while we can, huh?"

"You betcha, big brother. This is just too cool! Look out Southern California, Jeff Harper has arrived!"

They got out of the car and walked toward the restaurant, arms around each other's shoulders, patting the plastic statue of a fat and happy chef-boy as they passed by.

As Jenna drove her two-year-old Beetle the three miles to her summer job in Westwood, she felt at peace about yesterday's visit to Paradise Bay. She still yearned to be the one who was getting married today, but she realized it was the way love stories went: indecision, bad choices, and broken hearts complicating the drama of love.

Now, she wondered who would come into her future. Would some dream man come along and make her forget about Levi? She didn't see how that could be possible.

She had decided to stay and work rather than go home to Kentucky for the summer. She was sharing an apartment with her cousin and an old dorm roommate, and had gotten a job at the Hamburger Hamlet in Westwood for $1.65 an hour plus tips. By far, it was the best money she'd ever made; she averaged as much as $5 an hour on weekends. Of course, she'd rather have a job that would do more to advance her career, but this kind of money was as much as most professionals made in a week. Her goal was to hit the $200-a-week mark. With a monthly budget of $275 for rent, food, and miscellaneous, she could save more than $1,500 by the end of summer—a fortune for a nineteen-year-old girl from a small town.

Her thoughts turned back to Levi. How had the ceremony gone? she wondered. How was he feeling? How long would it take to get over him? Maybe as many years into the future as she'd known him in the past. Maybe never.

She was starting the noon shift today and working through dinner. Today would be a good payday; Saturday afternoons at Hamburger Hamlet always were. The boys trying to impress their dates always left big tips, sometimes as much as a dollar. She had made $20 Saturdays another goal.

She pulled into the parking lot and checked her makeup, fluffed her long blond hair, then got out of the car and locked the door. Once inside, she punched the time clock, put a smile on her face, and went to work at her assigned tables.

Customers were just beginning to trickle in, except for a young man who was already seated in a booth. Even with his back to her, his casual posture and military haircut reminded Jenna of someone she was desperately trying to forget. Her legs, like lead weights, carried her slowly to him; it was going to be hard to put on the toothy-smile act for this guy. *Who cares about the tip, anyway? I'll just give him the bare minimum service.*

"Excuse me, miss," the young man said before she could speak, "but I'm not sure what to order. Can you help me out?"

Jenna went speechless, tears springing to her eyes as Levi stood up and pulled her to him. She returned his feelings tentatively, afraid to let herself hope.

"I didn't get married today, Jenna. I couldn't. I had to find you. Tell me what I should ask for." He put a finger under her chin, lifting her eyes to his.

"Ask me to say 'I'm sorry' for not letting you know how I feel. I could have written . . . oh, Levi." She closed her eyes, pulled him into a tender embrace.

"I want you to forgive me, Jenna. I let you down. I want you to forgive me and tell me you'll never let me go."

They stared into each other's eyes, wordlessly saying the things only minds and hearts can utter in silence. Then Levi lifted Jenna off her feet and brought his lips to hers, sealing the promise.

Nearby, customers clapped and cheered them enthusiastically as their kiss lingered . . . much longer than the thirty seconds Levi's father allowed.

18

ADAGIO

Levi put an arm around her as they rode the Catalina-bound passenger ship out of San Pedro Harbor. He began to hum, then said, "The Four Freshmen made that song about Santa Catalina a famous one back in '59. The year you left Paradise Bay."

"I remember. I was so sad. Every time that song came on, I'd think of the sea, the fun we had while we were living there. I never wanted to leave."

"When I get back from Vietnam, you'll never have to leave again. The house you lived in is always up for rent. With the cannery all but shut down, we can get it for practically nothing."

"Really?" She sighed and laid her head on his shoulder. He held her close, and they watched the spray off the bow as the small tourist boat cleared the harbor.

"See that bridge over there?" he pointed. "That's San Pedro Island Bridge. My father said he and Mom were crossing it in her family's car when the news of Japan's attack on Pearl Harbor came on the radio. He asked her to marry him right then and there." Levi paused, then whispered into her ear, "Will you marry me, Jenna?" It was the third time this morning he had asked her.

"Yes, Levi. I'll marry you and stay with you forever," she replied happily.

"Can't ask for more than that," he said. "I made the right decision, and this has turned out to be the happiest day of my life."

"How upset was she?" Jenna asked.

"Well, she wasn't happy, to say the least. She deserved more from me, but after seeing you . . ."

"I guess I should've stayed away," Jenna said.

"But I'm so glad you didn't."

They sat on the passenger seats, just off the bow. They kissed, then leaned against the railing in front of them. The ship cut through the smooth waters, scenting the air with a cool ocean mist.

"I wish we could stay like this forever," Jenna sighed. "I'm afraid, Levi. What if . . ."

"I'll be back, you'll see," he replied before she could finish. "But I wish we could get married before I leave." He leaned over and whispered, "You know, be able to love each other legally."

"Me, too. But that wouldn't be right, would it?"

"A lot of things aren't right. Leaving Paradise Bay the way I did wasn't right. But marrying the right person is always right. Right?" He smiled.

She shook her head slowly. "We couldn't pull it off in such a short amount of time, could we?" she asked, looking at him expectantly.

"No, I guess not."

"My parents would be pretty upset if we eloped," Jenna added.

Silence followed.

"Is Carol really . . . you know," Jenna asked quietly. She had been respectfully silent on the matter that Levi had only hinted at, but had never really come out and admitted.

"Yeah." Levi groaned. He rose from the bench seat and leaned against the railing, wishing he didn't have to admit to being such a stupid failure; and acknowledging a broken covenant his heart had made to show integrity and honor by marrying Carol.

Jenna let him alone as she pondered where to go with this. It had the power to upset everything they wanted to create now. She waited a few minutes, then joined him, not touching him, just leaning against the railing toward the sea, watching the water turn and splash as they drew closer to the island.

"I thought you understood," Levi finally offered, breaking the awkward reverie.

"Not clearly," she replied gently.

"When you showed up, I thought you understood that. That it was the reason I felt pushed to the altar."

She blinked at the moisture stinging her eyes. "Sorry. I didn't want to believe it."

"Damn," he said in a hushed tone and hung his head against his arms. Jenna moved her hand across his back in soothing motions.

"I didn't mean to upset you. But I have to know. Am I a home wrecker? If I had only stayed in touch with you. If . . ."

"Nonsense," he answered, taking her hand.

"I mean, if it were me at the altar, and Carol had showed up, and you left me standing there, with a baby, and . . ."

He let go of her hand and moved away, gazing out to sea.

Jenna moved slowly toward him.

"I didn't love her. Your showing up made me realize that. She was headed for hippieland, living a fairy tale. I wasn't going to fit into her world. Yeah, I love the Santos family, and I feel like a bum, but I wasn't going to let you get away from me, Jenna." He turned to face her, and held her slender shoulders, locking his gaze with hers. "I love you, and that makes all the difference. It won't bring my honor back, but if you can forgive me, then I'll feel like the luckiest man in the world."

"If God can, I can. But you need to . . ." She paused. "I can," she finished softly, holding his stare.

"Show some honor," he finished her first statement for her. "I won't let you down. And I'll prove I can be trusted."

"I know you will," she answered, allowing herself to be tenderly wrapped in his arms.

"I accept full responsibility. You didn't wreck anything. Understand?"

She nodded.

"I wish we could stay like this. I just don't understand why I'm going. I'm not even sure what the fighting's about, if we're really saving the world from Communism. All I want is to be with you and make music."

"Let's not think about it. Look." She pointed. "Avalon Bay."

The homes and buildings of the tourist town on the hill overlooking the small bay glistened in the morning sunlight. The scene of whitewashed Spanish-style plaster and colorful tiled roofs made them feel as if they were far away from the reality of Levi leaving for war. Small sailboats and launches rocked gently in the morning swell.

"It's so romantic," she sighed.

"Let's act like there's no tomorrow while we're here," he whispered, adding a kiss upon her lips.

"There is no tomorrow, Levi," she said. "Only today."

The boat docked and they took their shoes off and walked hand-in-hand along the small sandy stretch of beach that was part of the bay.

"Almost as pretty as home," Levi offered as the cool water washed up around their ankles. Jenna looked up at him and asked him with her eyes. He leaned down and kissed her.

Lunch, strolls through the small shops, and taking a rowboat out on the bay pleasantly used up their afternoon. As twilight approached, they went out in a glass-bottomed boat to see the marine life, holding on to each other as though it could stop the day from ending. Dusk threatened, and the shadows falling upon Avalon Bay reminded Levi that they had only one hour left to catch the last boat back to San Pedro Harbor.

"Let's not go back. I don't want this to end," he said as they started up the boardwalk.

"We can't stay. You know that."

"Yeah, I guess I do. And Jenna, honey, I'll never do anything to mess this up again. I love you, and I want us to spend as much time together as possible. We'll just get separate rooms. Look," he went on, pulling a flyer from his pocket. "There's a dance with Buddy MacKay and his orchestra at the Casino Ballroom tonight. All fifties music. We'll go dancing, then get our rooms."

"What about Jeff? Isn't he camping at the state beach?"

"He's with a school buddy who came down from Paso Robles. A kid named Gerry. They're going to be too busy having fun to worry about me. Besides, I told him not to wait up. I kind of prepared him for it," he admitted, a little sheepishly.

"Do you have any particular place in mind?" she asked uncertainly, wondering if there was a way they could do this without giving up what they both needed to keep sacred. Their new beginning had already gotten off to a bad start.

"I'm a Marine, right?" Levi winked. "Trained to improvise and make do with what's at hand. Marines always find a way." He stood up, took Jenna's hand, and pulled her to her feet. "Come on. Let's look up that room for you and go dancing."

She abandoned common sense, laughing happily as they ran into the center of town to the Catalina Beach Hotel. She wondered if this was what a honeymoon felt like, being this carefree, this much in love, all the rules of caution thrown out the window.

He dangled the hotel keys in front of her, then put them in his pocket. "Miss Bradley, may I have the honor of this dance?" He held out his arm and pointed to the famous Casino Ballroom, the circular, multi-story 1930s building that stood at the tip of the harbor, where the walkway along the beach came to an end. The name wasn't exactly fitting—gambling had never been allowed there—but just being here made Levi feel like part of a slower time, a more romantic era.

"It's so beautiful tonight," he sighed. "I want it to never end." The moon hung over the small island. A lantern for lovers, its light shimmered on a calm bay. "How can I be in such a mess on a night like this?"

"Am I the mess?" Jenna asked in a hurt tone. "Is what we're doing a mess?"

"No, never," Levi said, turning to her with a smile. "It's just me. The war . . . Santos family."

"Try not to worry about it, Levi. Put it behind you for now."

He nodded toward the ballroom building. "Isn't it something, all lit up like that? The flyer said Jimmy Dorsey and his band opened it in '34. People have been dancing there ever since."

"Fifty cents each, please," the doorman said as they walked up to him.

Levi reached into his pocket and pulled out a dollar. "Keep the change." He smiled.

"My, what a big tipper," Jenna giggled, slipping her arm through his.

"He should be letting us in for nothing. I'm one of the guys who's gonna be saving this island from the Commie hordes," Levi said with a grin.

He led her inside, then onto the dance floor. They slow-danced for hours to the Big Band orchestra playing movie tunes from the '50s. By the time the final dance piece was playing, they were barely moving at all, as if they could make the song—the night—last longer.

The singer crooned "Harbor Lights," popular in the early '50s, to the ukelele and metal and bass guitars of the orchestra. Levi whispered the song into Jenna's ear, imitating Sammy Kaye.

The lights came up, the emcee thanked the crowd for coming, and the ballroom began to empty to the melody "A Stranger in Paradise." The tune couldn't have been more fitting. In the movie, William Holden and his lover were separated because of the Korean War.

"Ironic," Levi said.

"Yeah," Jenna agreed.

They stepped out into the night, a perfect Southern California evening. The cool breeze, starlit sky, and glistening sea made it all the harder for Levi to imagine leaving Jenna and going off to Vietnam.

He was glad he had convinced her to stay the night, and it made him feel good to know she trusted him. Their walk became a waltz as they returned to the small town. He could hear Tony Bennett singing in his mind: *Take my hand, I'm a stranger in paradise. . . . All lost in this wonderland, a stranger in paradise. . . . If I stand starry-eyed, that's a danger in paradise, for mortals who stand beside . . . an angel like you. . . .*

He hummed a few lines, then softly sang to her, " 'Won't you answer this fervent prayer of a stranger in paradise, don't lead me in dark despair, from all that I hunger for. . . . But open your angel arms, to a stranger in paradise, and tell him that he need be . . . a stranger no more. . . .' "

They kissed, lingering outside until the boardwalk lights went out. The Catalina Beach Hotel waited.

19

ALLEGRO

THE MIDDLE-AGED HOTEL MANAGER SHOOK HIM AWAKE. "Sir?" he said. "Come on now, Mr. Harper. I can't let you sleep here. It's morning. People are starting to wonder. You'll either have to go to your room or catch breakfast."

"What time is it?" Levi asked, rubbing his eyes.

"0630 hours," the innkeeper replied, then added, "U.S. Navy, World War Two," explaining his use of military time. "And I'm sorry, but either you're crazy, her brother, or the two of you are fighting. Why did you let that pretty dame sleep all alone?"

"Word of honor," he replied sleepily, pulling himself into a sitting position on the sofa. "You have soap, shaving cream, and a razor? I need toothpaste and a toothbrush, too."

The man went to the counter and brought out a bag of toiletries. "Here, take these." Levi dug in his pocket for money, but the innkeeper stopped him with a wave of the hand. "Forget it. Let's just say it's toward the war effort." He smiled. "My son's a Marine, too. Just left for Vietnam."

Levi decided to look for a beach shower and men's room, and headed for the front door, his wrinkled clothes desperately in need of washing and pressing.

"Come on back here," the man called out. "Use my place. The bathroom's down the back stairs. Go ahead," he urged. "There's a laundry in back for your clothes. Toss them in while you're showering." The man pointed to a door behind the front desk that led to his living quarters.

The innkeeper reminded Levi of happy-go-lucky Mr. Santos, who must have hated him by now. It had been just a few days ago, but it seemed as though ages had passed. He still cared about Mr. and Mrs. Santos, and he hoped the letter he was planning to write them from Vietnam would ease their anger and pain at his abandoning their daughter.

He sang as he showered. *This is one of those happy days that come along once in a blue moon,* he thought. He ought to convince her that they should get married now, here on the island. Forget the rest of the world. He'd already blown it anyway, disappointed his family and friends. Marrying Jenna couldn't make matters worse.

In fact, it might even make them better, might make everyone realize why he cut out on Carol. He was willing to do everything he could to be honorable about the child; perhaps this would show that he was a good man, and a repentant one.

His body was clean and refreshed now, but he still felt dirty, ashamed, as he thought about his promises. He'd been a hormone-driven fool. Betrayed his parents, the Santos family, all the stuff his minister dad had tried to instill in him growing up. And even though his strongest opinion of religion was that it interfered with boating and surfing on Sundays, there had been moments when he knew that God was for real, that he'd just delayed the inevitable by turning his heart over.

His parents had taught him well. He couldn't blame anyone but himself—and Carol, to some extent. The mistake they made took two, but he could have practiced more control.

He made up his mind that he *would* ask Jenna. They could get a marriage license, he reasoned, and begin their life together before he left for the uncertainty of Vietnam.

"Hey, thanks, sir," he said as he came back out to the lobby. "I'm sorry, but I don't even know your name."

"Ron Ringo, Senior. If you see my boy over there, let him know his dad's thinking of him and praying for him every day."

"What unit?"

"First Battalion, Fifth Marines," Ringo said, chest swelling with pride. "He's Ron Junior."

"I'll watch out for him and pass the message on if I see him. Any relation to Ringo the gunfighter?" Levi teased, referring to the song performed by Lorne Greene of the *Bonanza* television series.

"No, and no relation to that long-haired hippie drum player from England, either." The man laughed. "Guess you and the lady friend are taking off today?"

"Yeah, unfortunately." Levi sighed. "I'd love to stay, but duty calls. I plan to marry her. Sure wish we could do it here," he added, looking around at the romantic 1920s-style lobby and the portico overlooking the bay. "This would be a perfect place for a wedding."

"On the house. You come back from the war, and you can have the whole lobby for the ceremony, and the honeymoon suite, too. All on the house."

"Hey, that's awful nice. I'd have to earn it, though," Levi said.

"Find my son and tell him that I love him and I'm praying for him. That's all the payment I need." The man turned away so Levi couldn't see the emotion he had surrendered to.

"I'll be on the lookout. You can count on it," Levi said quietly. He remembered the hint of tears he'd seen in his father's eyes when they had said good-bye just a few days before. He hoped he'd get a chance to come home, let his father know how much he loved him, how grateful he was.

"Keep your head down, boy," the man offered in parting.

"Yes, sir. And thanks again for everything." Levi turned to see Jenna coming down the hall.

"Sleep good?" he asked as she walked up and pecked him on the cheek.

"Like a baby. The sound of the surf lulled me right to never-never land."

"Let's go eat." He grabbed her hand. "The hotel owner said I was nuts for sleeping out here alone."

"You won't have to someday, but you're the best man in the world for doing it now. Maybe a little nuts," she added with a laugh. "Hey—you look so . . . so fresh, clean. How'd you do that sleeping in the lobby?"

He shrugged, not letting her on to his secret, or to Mr. Ringo's help.

They ate in a café at the pier. "We'll need to leave midday if we're going to have one last night out on the town. Jeff's expecting me back, and I have to report for duty on Friday."

Jenna said nothing, but she was fingering the pearl necklace around her neck, as if to cement their childhood promise.

"I've got something else to add to that." Levi reached for her left hand and slipped a gold ring with a small diamond centered inside a tiny flower onto her fourth finger. "This should've been yours," he went on, searching her eyes.

"Yes," she whispered. "Forever."

20

FORTUNE COOKIE

It seemed weeks ago, not days. Levi looked out the solitary window of the C-130 military transport aircraft as they circled Da Nang Harbor. The blue water, the clean white sand, and the incredibly lush green of Vietnam's coast belied any appearance of conflict.

Other Marines started to gather around the single porthole window where Levi sat. The large cargo plane, with just enough bench seats for a platoon, also carried supplies, making Levi's window seat the only view out for the group of young replacements. He allowed the men to stand over him but remained seated.

He closed his eyes and considered his feelings about the choices he had made: his happiness with Jenna, his remorse about Carol and her unborn child. But his soul felt strangely free, even though he was about to descend into the valleys and mountains where so much danger and death awaited this group of men, many still in their teens.

"Hard to imagine we're really here," the young man seated beside him said, excited.

"Yeah, only thirteen months minus one day to go," Levi complained. "Ever wonder why Marines do a thirteen-month tour and the Army only does twelve?"

"Hey, I'm glad. I've been wanting to go to war my whole life. I signed up."

"You're kidding, right?"

"No, I'm not kidding. My dad was a Marine, and so was my uncle. Decorated war heroes. I'm M-60 trained, and I'm volunteering myself as door gunner to the first chopper I see."

Levi put a hand over his mouth. "I hope you're not contagious."

"What's that mean?" the young Marine asked, confused.

"Nothing. Forget it. Here, take my seat. You won't miss the action from here."

"Hey, thanks. You're all right."

Levi moved away from the growing crowd. They were all replacements. He knew only two others from training days on this planeload of fresh-faced Marines.

"Man, you can really smell that rice now," a burly private first class said. "My second tour, dudes. You guys are gonna be smelling a lot of *nuoc-mam*—fish-head soup—the gooks slop it on everything. When you're on ambush, you can smell the dinks for a mile. So you wait until that smell's about five feet away, then open up your M-16 on full auto." He laughed.

"Hey, if this is your second tour, how come you're only a PFC, not a lance corporal or somethin'?" a Southern boy drawled.

"I was." The veteran grinned, revealing a gap where a front

tooth was missing. "Decked a gunnery sergeant back at Pendleton. Good man. He didn't press charges, just took the stripes."

Levi closed his eyes and leaned back. He wasn't ready for this. His mind was back home, with Jenna. Making music. Nothing else. He thought about the Chinese restaurant in Westwood they had eaten at just nights before.

"Open yours first," she said.

"Okay." He broke the cookie in half and pulled out the fortune. "Mine says, 'You will find and marry the most beautiful girl in the world.' Your turn." He laughed.

" 'Prosperity and love will be given to you.' "

"Here, let me see that." Levi took the small white slip of paper from her hand and read it. She was telling the truth.

"Okay, then let me read yours." She laughed, snatching his out of his hand.

Jenna's smile faded as she read. " 'Beware of the dragon.' What kind of fortune is that?" she cried.

Levi put his hand over hers. "It's nothing. A fluke. Look, here's another one. This one's my fortune." He cracked the wafer open and handed Jenna the slip of paper.

She read in silence, then her eyes brightened. "This is more like it," she said. " 'You will live a long life and have many children.' "

He cracked open another one.

She read. " 'Your heart is pure, your mind clear, and your soul devout.' " She reached for his hand. "This is you. This is a true fortune."

They kept opening cookies, laughing and joking, trying to quell the anxiety of knowing that this was their last meal together. He read the last fortune, then quickly stuffed it into his pocket before she could see it.

"I'm going to keep these." Jenna put a handful of fortunes in her purse. "Except this one." She ripped the piece of paper in shreds and left it on the table.

Levi couldn't take his eyes off her. *God made a special mold for her,* he thought.

"What?" she asked, noticing his stare.

"Oh, nothing. I was just thinking," he said, then stood up and went over to pay the bill. They walked out into the night.

"What were you thinking about in there?" Jenna pressed as she handed Levi the keys to her car.

"All the things we crammed into two weeks. How beautiful you are. How lucky I am."

"We did Disneyland twice, Knotts Berry Farm, Catalina Island, the L.A. Zoo, Griffith Park Observatory, Olvera Street, Pacific Ocean Park, the carousel at Santa Monica Pier, Malibu Pier for dinner—I think we did about everything a couple on a honeymoon might do here," she said.

"Except one thing." Levi winked.

"I know, but I want it to be right." She sighed. "This stupid, lousy war."

Jeff had met them outside the restaurant, and he was following behind them now, with the Rally Sport's windows down, singing along happily to the eight-track tape of Beach Boy tunes.

Levi pulled up in front of Jenna's apartment. "Well, we're here." He glanced in the rearview mirror and saw Jeff parking behind him. "And so is Jeff. Hope he'll give us a minute alone to say good-bye."

"I told my roommates not to be here when I got back. Come on." Jenna opened her door and stepped out of the car.

"Hey, Jeff!" Levi shouted to his brother, competing with the blasting music. "Shut off the engine. I'll be back in a few minutes."

Jeff nodded, patting the car door to the beat, happily contemplating his summer vacation at Santa Monica beach.

Jenna fumbled with the keys to her apartment. Levi took them from her trembling hands and opened the door.

Once inside, he pulled her close and kissed her, unwilling to let this moment end.

"I'm afraid," she cried.

"Don't be, Jenna. Just write to me every week. Please. I'll be living for your letters," he whispered. "I'll be counting the days until I see you again. With you and my folks praying for me, I know I'll be fine." He hoped he sounded convincing.

"I can't live without you, Levi. If anything happens to you, I'll—" She couldn't finish.

He stared at the ceiling as though it might hold the answer. "I'm coming back, Jenna. I need you like a drowning man needs air. Nobody can keep me from coming back to you. Do you believe me?"

She put her hands behind her neck and removed the pearl necklace, then put it in his hand. "Bring this back to me. Every time you touch it, I'll be there. Promise you'll bring it back."

"I promise. Kiss me one last time, then I'll go."

Like a concerto played out in infinite variations, they kissed, futilely searching for a fitting note to end on.

He had to go. "This will be the last time I leave you," he promised.

"Go," Jenna sobbed, breaking away from his arms. She went to the door and opened it.

Levi looked into the azure eyes, an ocean of hope, glistening red now, but speaking to him the way only eyes can—straight to the heart. He was trying to memorize every feature of her beautiful face. He nodded, afraid to speak, and walked out the door, wincing as it closed behind him.

Those bittersweet moments had taken place just days before, but it seemed like weeks. Leaving Jenna behind that night had been the hardest thing he'd ever had to do.

He thought of the fortune cookie he'd slipped into his pocket. He'd read it over and over again, praying it didn't mean anything. *Superstition*, he told himself.

The captain's voice came over the intercom. "Marines, prepare for landing and disembarkation."

Levi buckled his seatbelt, duffel bag between his feet, as the pilot eased the large transport onto the Da Nang airstrip.

"Be prepared for rocket and mortar attack from the hills surrounding us, gentlemen. This is the real thing," the pilot went on, giving his final instructions. "We're now entering the land of the blue dragon."

So this is it. Levi couldn't get the fortune cookies out of his mind. *Beware of the dragon*, one of them had read. And then there was the last one, the one that was bothering him most.

The one he'd kept hidden from Jenna.

Innocence and time, once lost, can never be regained.

21

THE ENEMY

From the air, there couldn't be a more pleasing sight to the eye than what lay ahead. The big Marine sitting next to him pointed to the hills in the distance, the plumes of smoke rising up from them.

"Volcanoes?" he laughed nervously.

"I don't think so," Levi said, as mesmerized as the Marine private beside him. They stared at the landmass they were rapidly approaching, and the puffs of smoke, which they learned all too soon was artillery responding to the frequent rocket attacks the Viet Cong were making on the Da Nang airfields.

Their landing at Da Nang East Airfield had been smooth. Levi was the third man out, and he'd immediately felt the hit from the extraordinarily humid and sultry air.

"Man, the heat!" one Marine complained as they grabbed

their gear and waited off the runway for the trucks.

"Mmmm . . . smell that, boys? *Nuoc-mam*—rotting fish heads, garlic, spices no one's ever heard of, and all the trimmings." The PFC veteran with the missing front tooth grinned.

"Hear that exploding goin' on?" the eager young Marine said. "That's our stuff. Artillery—hot diggity damn!"

Levi shook his head.

Each Marine was not only carrying his personal gear, but an M-16 with one twenty-round clip issued out of Okinawa. The general atmosphere among the young and green fighters was bravado. Fear of never getting out of this alive, masked by the bravado, was more common than many would admit.

They had all heard the horror stories from the Marines at Pendleton who'd made it back from their thirteen-month tour of duty: best friends being killed in midnight attacks by Viet Cong sappers, body bags being shipped back to the States in stainless steel government-issue caskets, endless patrols through dense canopied forests, venomous pit vipers, scorpions, leeches, choppers loaded with troops being hit and exploding in hot LZs, booby traps of poisoned bamboo stakes, exploding land mines, snipers, rocket attacks, and the general fear that every Vietnamese was a potential Cong.

Without warning, the C-130 took off as nearby chopper pilots scrambled to their birds, but there was no sign of any staff sergeant to tell the new arrivals what was up. Staff NCOs ran the Marine Corps. Levi found it odd that one would be absent now, at a time when it seemed they needed one most.

War began crashing around the inexperienced Marines. Enemy rockets slammed into a nearby field, then the airfield, sending the group of thirty scrambling for the closest sandbagged bunker they could find.

Within seconds, Marine artillery from nearby batteries responded and sent salvos into the region's mountains west of Da Nang. Through the havoc, the unmistakable sound of an approaching Willy's jeep and troop transports could be heard.

"What do you think?" the eager Marine asked Levi as the sound drew nearer.

"Just stay put until someone gives an order."

The jeep pulled up to the bunker, and the NCO hopped out and began calling out names. "Get the hell out of there and into these trucks now! We got a war to get to. Move! Move!"

Some of the Marines came out of cover, but others hesitated.

"You cherries ain't seen war yet! This is nothin'. Now come on. Let's roll!" the replacement company gunnery sergeant yelled. He stood strangely resolute and calm through the thundering of cannon fire nearby. Levi was impressed and raced to the trucks with the rest of the new Marines.

"On the double!" the gunny called, followed by a string of expletives for emphasis.

The noise of jet engines filled any void in the bark of the outgoing artillery rounds.

Levi threw his gear in and climbed aboard the waiting truck with the others, watching in amazement as the "gunny" walked from the cab of each of the three troop carriers to the others, giving instructions to the drivers, who seemed equally unruffled.

Another rocket slammed into the nearby enclosure just off the west side of the runway. Levi wondered if he'd ever be able to tell the difference between incoming artillery and outgoing.

"They can't hit you if it ain't your time!" the gunny yelled back to the new arrivals. "And it ain't your time if you do as I say, because it ain't my time! I'll see you brave leathernecks at the drop-off. Now let's go!" He jogged to his jeep. The man commanded respect. If he had to be in this war zone, Levi was glad to witness leadership like this. If his first sergeant had the kind of character this man demonstrated, he'd be in good shape, he silently reasoned.

Levi gazed around him. They were all silent. Every man now, no doubt, was contemplating the reality of his situation.

Levi noticed a Marine arrive in another jeep from the helicopter pad. He drove over to the gunnery sergeant, exchanged words, and laughed. They slapped each other on the back, then shook hands.

When the sergeant pointed him toward the truck Levi was sitting in, the man walked over, threw his duffel bag in without any consideration for where it landed, then climbed in. Something about his stride seemed familiar. His uniform and gear looked worn, unlike the crisp green jungle fatigues the replacements were wearing.

"So you guys all new meat?" The man laughed as he sat down on the end of the bench seat and motioned the driver to put it in gear.

Levi recognized him now. He hadn't seen him since shortly after their schoolyard fight over Jenna. He had moved from Paradise Bay that year and Levi had lost total track of him since then.

"How many of you guys seen action?" the Marine went on, pulling a cigarette out of his pocket. "Any of you killed a Cong yet?"

With a jolt, Levi remembered the smart-aleck bragging about growing up and becoming a Marine someday so he could kill Reds like his father had in Korea.

"How long you been here?" Levi ventured. He sat in the rear and hoped his features couldn't be discerned in the dark interior.

"Second tour. Couldn't handle the 'world.' Damn commie-lovin' hippies. But this, boys, is what bein' a Marine's all about. Once you kill a few gooks, you'll see what I mean. If you live long enough."

Maybe he'll just go away, Levi thought. The truck rolled to a stop.

"Here we are. You boys stick close, and the gunny and I'll give you the real dope on what's up. Listen to everything the gunny feeds you. He is one mean mother of a killing machine. He knows his stuff. This is his first assignment off the line since he got here two years ago."

"Hey, what's your name, Sergeant?" a nervous PFC asked.

"Mayfield," he growled. "You new guys better get ready. The real . . ." A jet screamed overhead, drowning him out for a second. ". . . is about to hit the fan."

Levi made up his mind to stay as far away from Mayfield as possible.

After a week plus three days of hurry-up orientation in Da Nang, Levi and the other new replacements were assigned to the 3rd Marine Division and shipped out to various infantry assignments in the I-Corps area, which comprised the northern sector of the South Vietnam combat zone. Even though he was still a reluctant warrior, he had gained some measure of pride in being a Marine.

Arriving in the heart of "Indian Country," as the Marines liked to say, they came face-to-face with hardened North Vietnamese Army regulars, the NVA, who constantly infiltrated the Demilitarized Zone, the dividing line between North and South. The standing joke in Vietnam was that it was absolutely the most militarized area of all.

Levi was stunned to find out that his assignment put him into enemy territory of another kind, under the wings of the most hotheaded, foul-mouthed, mean-spirited, yet defiantly motivated platoon sergeant in the 9th Marines. They were stationed outside a hotly contested strip of land, a base camp on a hillside of red clay called Con Thien.

His first day in the field, Levi was given the dubious honor of explaining what the squad radio might need to become operable. He shot off his mouth and quickly learned to keep it shut.

"Oh, no," Levi said, laying the PRC-25 backpack radio aside and backing away. "I carried those things in Advanced Infantry back at Pendleton, and I'm not adding that weight to my gear."

"You da man, Harper!" the squad leader, Mayfield, chanted and clapped.

A cacophony of Marine voices joined in. "New guy, Harper, he's da man, if Harper can't do it, nobody can!" One guy pulled out a harmonica, and the ever-present boredom of waiting for incoming NVA rockets was lessened by the simplest form of entertainment known to Marines—a good volley of initiation rites for the greenest man in the platoon.

"You've got no choice, buddy boy." Mayfield jabbed a finger into Levi's chest. "New guys always carry the radio if the last RTO ain't no more. And since you like singing so much"—he laughed—"you're gonna be our very own Private First Class Levi Harper, radioman, so fix it and start learning how to use it."

Levi swallowed hard. "What happened to its previous owner?"

"He was our last new guy. Fritz was his name. He did pretty good, too. Fritz was on the job, oh . . . say, maybe ten days before he got it."

Levi swallowed, not wanting to give his anxiety a face.

"See there, Harper, how much we love you new guys?" May-field motioned him over as the crowd's attention turned to the noise of artillery rounds. "Look, I don't want you here, and I don't know why God in heaven put you here with me. I don't want to know anybody new. We never really liked each other in Paradise Bay, but forget all that. I just don't want to know you here. That way, if you get killed, it's easier for me if I didn't know you. Understand?"

"Understood, Mayfield. The feeling's mutual." Levi smiled stiffly.

"Still the squeaky-clean smart-mouth. Well, tough guy Harper, maybe so. See, I like the Marines. Unlike a lot of these dopes, I was born for this. I like killing gooks. I like winning, see?"

"Yeah, I see," Levi replied as artillery fire passed over and the tension eased on the faces of the men around them.

"You handled that initiation pretty well, Harper. First artillery barrage and all. And remember, I like winning as much as I did when we were kids. I didn't have the advantages you did. My dad was a drunk who never came home, except to beat me. I've had to scrape for everything I've ever had. The Marines is all I got. So don't slow me down, or make me look bad, or think I'm your friend, 'cause I'm not. You're just another cherry, a new guy, until you prove yourself, got it?"

"Loud and clear, Mayfield. I'm here to put in my time, that's all."

"Man, how in the hell did a piano-playing sissy get into the Marines in the first place?" Mayfield scowled.

"Drafted," Levi shot back, unflustered.

"Figures. Learn the radio. It's the difference between life and death for us out there. Now, get to it!"

Maybe it's for the best, he thought. Levi had a better under-standing of Mayfield now, but he still had no love for the guy. He'd be taking orders from him in the field, learning how to kill. Irony or justice, he wasn't sure.

"One day to test it out, Harper," Mayfield went on, attaching the scope to his black sniper rifle. "Goin' huntin' for Indians. You stay here, fix that radio, get used to it." He turned away, calling to one of the dozing Marines. "Let's go bag us an NVA artillery observer, Rocket Man!" The sleepy man jumped up, gathered his gear, and followed Mayfield out.

"Everybody has a nickname around here," Levi commented uneasily to the nearest Marine. "Why is his Rocket Man?"

"M-79 grenades—the blooper gun. That's his specialty. And your nickname's Cherry," the man added, turning his back on Levi. "And don't you forget it. Mayfield don't wanna know you, and I don't wanna know you. You prove yourself and maybe I'll change my mind."

"Sure wish I'd listened to you, Dad," Levi muttered as he played with the radio dials, remembering his father's advice to stay with a college deferment. Levi recalled the debate with Rex Harper now as Marine artillery opened up on enemy positions in the hills beyond.

"Damn it all, son, take the music scholarship and keep the draft deferment. This war can't last forever."

"You went to war, Dad."

"That war was different. And if we'd kept going and taken those Commies out while we had all the weapons over there in Europe and Asia, this whole mess wouldn't be happening."

"Dad, it's just something I've got to do. Besides, they won't make me an infantryman. I've practically got straight As. If I get drafted they could put me in the Air Force as well as any other service."

"Who the hell says that 'straight As' makes any difference? I was an eighteen-year-old corpsman with a twenty-five-year-old Ph.D. college professor for a squad leader—Benjamin Kelly, a doctor in philosophy. And he was a lance corporal, an infantry-man, son!"

"I should take the scholarship, huh?"

"Son, listen to me. I don't trust this government's decisions on this war. It smells."

"This doesn't sound like my patriotic dad."

Rex Harper paced the floor, trying to find the words to convince his stubborn son that it would be a mistake to throw college out the window, throw his music scholarship down the drain.

"Look, I fought for this country because everyone did. I love this country, risked my life for it. We would've been invaded, too, if we'd stood by and done nothing. Japan actually attacked America.

"Hitler was killing our men in the Atlantic. They were determined to strangle us, control us. You can't tell me that going to Vietnam to kill other young men in Communist uniforms is going to save the day. We've got missiles, defense weapons we never had before. There's no way on earth that North Vietnam's going to threaten us with invasion. Those Vietnamese in the south over there need to round up their boys and show us they're going to take a stand. Every last one of those boys on motorbikes in Saigon should be out in the bushes with our boys, at the very least."

"Dad, you're sounding political. You've never talked like this before."

"That's because I don't like talking about war. I still have nightmares, still want to dive for cover when I hear a loud noise. War isn't like the John Wayne movies you watch, son. It's dirty. People die, get blown to pieces. There's no vision of hell that even comes close to describing the fear of a man who's seen it."

"You ever have to kill anyone?" His father had never answered this question directly.

"Yeah." Rex's eyes welled with tears, and he couldn't speak for a moment. "Lots of times," he finally said, holding out his hands. "With these. I've asked God so many times to forgive me. Everyone said it was my duty, that I had to do it for the country, but the faces still haunt me sometimes. I was trained as a corps-man medic, and I never thought I'd have to kill anyone. You have to do awful things when you're defending your country-men."

A long moment of silence followed. Levi thought that maybe his father was right. He shouldn't risk the draft for a chance to get his songs recorded in L.A.

School was boring, except for the nights he played jam sessions in a small café in Isla Vista. And being with Carol made him forget he'd ever had a childhood crush. He'd always liked Mr. and Mrs. Santos. Perhaps it was meant to be this way.

His father started pacing, his words coming out in a rush. "I keep telling myself it was him or me. Him or my friends. Him or my squad. And it would've been me if I hadn't done what I did. At least that much is true. His helmet flew off, and mine did, too. He was scared; I could see it in his eyes. He was about my age—nineteen—and smaller, like most of the Japanese. I had my hands around his throat, and he was clawing at me like a rabid animal. He began to bite me, going for my jugular. I let go and grabbed my bayonet out of my boot. I thought I was going to pass out. I thrust once into his abdomen, and he let go.

"I'd never been that close to anyone I'd killed before. His eyes were frightened now, and I realized for the first time that I was looking down at a fellow human being, a young man who had dreams, hopes, people who loved him, a life to go home to. The medic in me came out. I held him in my arms and kept saying I was sorry. But he just stared up at me, gasping for air, then reached into his shirt pocket and pulled out a folded flag with Japanese writing on it. A crumpled letter and a photo fell out. The picture showed a proud young man, without the grime of war, standing with his parents and girlfriend, holding the flag he'd brought into this battle.

"He was begging for something in Japanese, for me to mail the letter. I nodded, and then he died. And I was the one who'd killed him—his dreams, his hopes. Do you understand what I'm saying, Levi?"

Levi went to his father and embraced him. No words were necessary.

But Levi had neglected to fill out the deferment papers and enroll for the next semester. The enemy had come to his door. His draft notice arrived the following day.

22

BEWARE OF THE DRAGON

Harper, get up here!" Mayfield hollered. "Get alpha
1 on the horn!"

Levi was low to the ground, behind a berm on the edge of
the forest. On the other side was a rice paddy, a small village,
and the hill that was Squad 2's objective. He was RTO—radio
operator for First Platoon, also called Alpha, second squad. And
though Mayfield was platoon sergeant, with command of all five
squads under Lieutenant Patterson, he was running with Levi's
squad, turning it into his personal reconnaissance team.

"Alpha 1, this is Alpha 2-1. Over," Levi said, almost whispering. They were two hundred meters from the village.

"This is Alpha 1 Actual. Over," came the lieutenant's voice.

Levi passed the handset to Mayfield.

"We got a situation here, Alpha 1," Mayfield said. "Quiet. Too quiet. They know we're here. I smell it. Do we have permission to prep the area with a few Willie Peters, see if we can stir them up? Over."

"That's a negative, 2-1. Hold your position. We have intel coming in now on the enemy positions at Hill 681. Over."

"I ought to do some intel on the village, 1. Over." Mayfield was frustrated. He wanted some action, and he didn't want to be the focus of enemy mortar rounds coming from the village or just beyond. If they knew the squad's position, it could begin any minute. He wanted to take the village and force Marine artillery before he and his men were scattered, or worse.

"Negative, 2-1. Hold your position! Over."

"You're breaking up, Alpha 1. No copy. Over," Mayfield lied.

"Do not move from your position, Alpha 2-1! Do you copy? Over."

"You're not clear, 1. We're taking fire now," he lied. "Requesting Willie Peter rounds to mark two hundred meters my November Echo. Over," Mayfield replied, seeking a way into the action.

"Negative, Alpha 2-1! Gunslingers on the way. Hold tight. Over!" the lieutenant ordered, promising Cobra gunships with assorted machine guns, rockets, and cannon fire instead of artillery.

"We've lost you, Alpha 1. Holding our position. Request two Willie Peters at . . ." Mayfield gave the map grid coordinates, then said, "Out."

"Willie Peter rounds" was code talk for white phosphorus artillery rounds, which were fired to mark enemy positions and the target area to make sure the artillery dropped where the infantry wanted it.

When on target, the infantry would order a "fire for effect." Suppressing artillery fire would then be dropped in patterns on the target area. The infantry had the option to advance under it while the enemy had their heads down, or wait until the firing ceased.

Mayfield wanted to let the NVA know he knew they were waiting. If the North Vietnamese opened up on them with mortars before artillery or the Cobra gunships arrived, their only options were to retreat or charge through the rice paddy under the mortar and use small arms fire to secure the village at the base of the hill.

Mayfield didn't like retreat, and he never could understand why they took so many villages and hills, then gave them back. He also didn't believe in charging over open terrain with the enemy in control of the field. Levi respected his courage and judgment, but they were made of different fabric.

"We hold . . . for now," Mayfield said to the men spread out along the dike. "Harper, see if you can raise one of those gunships."

Levi repeated their call sign, but long minutes passed before a Cobra pilot finally acknowledged him.

Mayfield grabbed the handset out of his hand. "We got a situation here," he said. "Just making sure you know our map coordinates."

"Roger that." The pilot repeated the position to Mayfield. "Coming in low. Keep your heads down. Out."

The low-flying gunship suddenly appeared out of the trees, and enemy fire with tracers opened on it at once. Precisely what Mayfield wanted. Now he knew where they were and how to flank them, how to get to the village at the base of Hill 681 without risking too many casualties as thousands of rounds of fire swept across the open space.

The Cobra gunship opened up on the far side of the rice

paddy, into the trees bordering the village and at the base of Hill 681. Rockets exploded, followed by machine-gun fire.

Mayfield waited. Levi kept his head down and watched. Mayfield wanted to attack, but with plenty of suppressing fire to keep the enemy from firing on his platoon.

The hill in front of them commanded a view of the area that was a suspected North Vietnamese infiltration route, and the Marines intended to take it and hold it while they built Con Thien up as a strategic base to halt enemy entrance into South Vietnam through the DMZ.

Undoubtedly, whoever was entrenched on the other side had been given orders to do the same thing: hold the high ground overlooking the valley.

23

GREAT BALLS OF FIRE

Levi handed Mayfield the radio handset.

"2-1. Over." He knew what was coming, and he was angry. The air strikes had obliterated the enemy positions, the ideal time for an assault. The enemy was scared, disoriented, perhaps even leaderless.

Alpha Platoon had been on the outskirts of the enemy village for twelve hours, and sunset was approaching by the time Mayfield's orders came. The battalion was to make a two-company full-scale attack at dawn. Bravo and Charlie Platoons had just arrived.

"Well, fine and dandy," Mayfield muttered. "We bomb the hell out of 'em, then leave the hill silent so the gooks can come right up the back side and reinforce. I thought this war was about taking ground and winning. I ain't seen nothing so cluster-jerked in all my days."

"You got that right." Rocket Man nodded.

Levi said nothing. This deadly game would play out at first light. For now, he was alive, and he thanked God for that, then prayed as men do when violence and death are so near.

Rain began falling, gently at first, then in sheets. He covered himself with his poncho, pulled his rifle in, and closed his eyes. Mayfield had spelled him with another new guy, who was now taking his turn with radio duty. Levi was wet and cold, but somehow sleep came easily. He left the war to Mayfield and company, drifting off to a better place.

Funny how life can get reduced to such simple luxuries, Levi thought. When daylight came, he was strangely grateful. The quick breakfast of C-ration ham and lima beans was all too short, but he managed to slurp down a can of peaches. At least now they could get on with whatever awaited—and get it over with. If they survived, maybe they'd be airlifted back to base camp and get hot showers and a real meal.

The mayhem of first light was orchestrated by Navy A-4 Skyhawks that screamed in from the east and flew low over the hills, dropping their loads of napalm, followed by pounding artillery to take out any of the enemy who might still be alive. Now came the assault. Levi was optimistic, though. Nobody could've survived that, he told himself.

"Alpha Platoon, get ready to move out. Spread out and get across fast," the lieutenant ordered. Mayfield in turn ordered the squad leaders.

This lieutenant was green. The last two platoon leaders had been killed within months of taking command. "Ready, Lieutenant?" Mayfield asked, doing his best to keep the recent arrivals, lieutenant included, from making "cherry" mistakes.

The hand signal was given, and the men, shadowy figures at

this time of day, began moving quickly across the open space. Levi stumbled along with the others through the wet ground, each step suctioned by deep mud. Mayfield signaled for Levi to join him on the top of the dike, out of the muck.

The support aircraft were gone, and the artillery grew silent as the men of Alpha Platoon neared the burned-out village. Mayfield ordered everyone to open up as they moved in and to spread out in a long line with the other two platoons.

The deafening noise of automatic gunfire and the thumping sound of the Marine 60mm mortar rounds leaving their tubes and landing ahead of them comforted Levi. There simply couldn't be any possible enemy survival after this hammering and barrage.

Fifty meters from the village, a hundred from the base of the hill, the mortars stopped firing. Now they were on the edge. As they moved through the village and into the burning brush to begin their ascent up Hill 681, the crossfire started.

Men began to fall around him. Mayfield was screaming something. The lieutenant was down. The NVA had come up from underground bunkers, poured machine-gun fire, and tossed Chicom grenades down the hill as they advanced. The cry "Corpsman!" increased across the base of the hill.

With nowhere to hide and no time to dig in, individual initiative would make heroes of a few Marines today. Levi hugged the ground a few paces behind Mayfield, who glanced back and ordered him to get on the radio, call for phosphorus rounds to mark the target of the enemy bunkers ahead.

"Add fifty! Fire for effect. Out!" Levi yelled into the handset over the cacophony of screams, gunfire, and explosions.

"It's you and me, Harper. Where's Rocket Man?" Mayfield shouted. "We need that blooper gun!"

Fallen men lay all around them. Mayfield and Levi braced themselves against the only tree stump within yards.

"Okay," Mayfield said. "Rocket Man must be down. Time to play ball like we did back home. I want you to take that machine gun out at your one o'clock, I'll take mine at eleven. First friendly arty-round that comes in, and we get up and play ball. Your pitching arm ready?"

Levi nodded. He dropped his pack and grabbed the first grenade. The artillery Levi had just called for began to strike its target ahead of them.

"Go!" Mayfield cried, and they headed toward the temporarily silenced guns, hitting the deck on their knees, throwing fast balls at the enemy gun emplacements, then falling back to the tree while incoming artillery offered a wall of steel in front of them.

In typical Marine style, Mayfield stood up and summoned the courage of the remaining platoon. They got to their feet and advanced up the hill behind the friendly artillery fire.

Levi's line of vision was narrowed to his own fear as he charged headlong into the smoke, the firing of thousands of bullets from each side, the screams of wounded men, and the barking of enemy orders in Vietnamese.

The man who played music was lost inside him as he shot, reloaded, fired, reloaded, and grabbed the submachine gun of a dead enemy soldier, turning it on the retreating North Vietnamese until it was out of ammunition. Stopping to reload, grabbing magazines from fallen comrades, he followed up the hill with his M-16 sweeping the area in front of him on full auto. As long as Mayfield was moving, Levi kept moving.

Violent insane minutes seemed like hours now as helicopters raked the hilltop to ease the pressure off the Marines on the ground. The fighting was within feet of the enemy now, and the gunships backed off. Bravo Company had been dropped on the far side of the hill and now spoiled the enemy's plan of escape. Burnt flesh, cordite, and scorched earth mixed into the familiar scent infantrymen had come to know, as a wind whipped from helicopter rotor blades above them.

Charlie Platoon arrived from reserve, dropped from the choppers, relieving what was left of Alpha. Exhausted, Levi sat down on the ground near the ridge line, then put a hand to his left eye. Moisture trickled down his face. He was bleeding, but he wasn't seriously wounded. Still, he felt faint. He reached into his rucksack for one of his two canteens, only to find it empty, a bullet hole through its center.

He felt for the other, but it was missing. A dead man was lying facedown a few feet away, both canteens in place.

"Thanks," Levi said through parched lips. He lifted the first one, drinking in gulps, then looked at the dead man again and wondered who he was, if it might be someone he'd come to know during the few weeks he'd been in country. "Thanks," he repeated respectfully, draining the last of the water.

"Come on. Let's get that head wound treated," a corpsman said, kneeling next to him. "What's your name?"

"Harper. Where's Mayfield?"

"Everyone who's still alive is down the hill. You're the last."

"Oh," he said, unaware of what that meant.

He struggled to his feet, wondering why his legs felt like Jell-O, and made his way down the hill to an open area near the ruined village.

The smoke of burning foliage, the gassy smell of spent napalm, and the stench of incinerated flesh wafted across the battlefield, choking the oxygen out of him. He dropped to his knees and vomited, gasping for air as a helicopter began lifting the seriously wounded from the field.

He'd survived.

"Take me to Mayfield," he said to the corpsman, as the man applied a bandage to his head.

The corpsman gave him a blank stare. "The sergeant's over there," he said, pointing to a row of tarp-covered bodies.

Time blurred as Levi climbed aboard the "dust-off," a Huey helicopter that was ferrying out the wounded. He lay on the deck, spent, eyes fixed in the thousand-yard stare he'd heard so much about before coming into this war. He knew why they called it that now; after an all-night battle of nerves and a day of death that took many of the men you'd begun with to their graves, you could see everything and nothing at the same time. Fourteen killed in action, nineteen wounded in action, one hundred percent casualties.

The day had surrendered to twilight. Jerry Lee Lewis's 1950's hit inexplicably came to mind as he watched an explosion lighting up against a darkening sky. What remained of the field of glory below was illuminated by the "great balls of fire" still exploding near Hill 681.

24

BY GOD AND SWORD

LEVI STOOD STIFFLY AT ATTENTION. "PRIVATE FIRST CLASS Levi Harper reporting as ordered, sir."

"At ease," the major said, still shuffling files on his desk. "Wondering why you're here?"

"Yes, sir."

"Take a chair, Private Harper," Major Donovan ordered. "You've come to my attention through one Sergeant Mark Mayfield. He thought highly of you."

"Sir?"

"He recommended a transfer to Force Recon for you two days before the assault on Hill 681. We'd put the word out that recon, both on the Battalion and Fleet level, was in need of recruits. We're looking for special skills: scuba, ability to work in small teams, focus, physical aggression. Mayfield thought you'd be a good fit. And after Hill 681, so do I."

"Yes, sir. If you don't mind me asking, what is Force Recon's mission?"

"The same as every Marine mission—kill the enemy. They're just quieter about it. But their primary mission is to gather intelligence prior to and after large-scale action. Grab prisoners, direct communications through relay teams in the heart of Indian country, after-mission artillery fire reports, set up ambushes to gather documents, monitor traffic on suspected high-speed trails, that sort of thing."

"Sounds . . ." Levi was searching for the right word.

"Exciting?" the major finished. "It is. If you like having high-priority access to artillery, fixed-wing, and gunship fire support, like working quietly and the camaraderie of men willing to die for each other, then this is your kind of job. Hell, son, Force Recon is a privileged bunch. They have so much clout, they can even call in an Arc-Light mission on word alone. Highest kill ratio of all our outfits. No one gets support like Force Recon. They're our eyes and ears."

"Sir, Arc-Light missions?"

"B-52 bombing runs. The most destructive power known to man, next to an actual tactical A-bomb blast. The bombers fly so high over the targets, the enemy never hears them until it's too late. Their loads are dropped over suspected high-density encampments and enemy shipping routes. Ho Chi Minh Trail mostly."

"Sir, forgive me for asking, but why me?"

"Why not you? Besides, your platoon sergeant—God rest his soul—recommended you. Alpha Platoon suffered one hundred percent casualties. Every man who wasn't killed was wounded. With just over half surviving Hill 681, yourself included, many of those wounded were so serious that they had to be shipped home."

Lucky devils, Levi thought as the major rattled on about valor, duty, and killing Communists.

"Alpha Platoon is being rebuilt from the ground up," the major continued. "If you decide to stay, we'll make you a squad leader, but now's the time to make a move if you're going to."

"Very well, sir."

"Glad to hear it. Mayfield was a fine Marine, one of the best I've ever met. He'll be posthumously awarded the Silver Star for gallantry in action. His family will at least be able to bury him with distinction and pride."

Are medals what I'll be measured by if I die? Levi wondered, listening respectfully as the major completed his monologue.

"He watched out for his men, and his loss is felt deeply here at Battalion Command. I hope you'll take the lessons you learned from him to Recon."

"I will, sir. Will that be all, sir?"

"No, it is not, Lance Corporal Harper."

"Sir?"

"You are being promoted in rank. You've been recommended for an award as well. Your bravery under fire was well documented by several of your comrades, Lieutenant Patterson included. The paperwork is being processed. Along with that Purple Heart of yours, you're on the way to a fine trophy collection if you make it back home from this war. Congratulations, Lance Corporal." Donovan stood, summoned the 1st Sergeant from the adjoining room, and ceremoniously took the PFC chevron from Levi's collars and pinned on the Lance Corporal chevrons.

Levi stood tall, and with the brief ceremony completed, the major continued.

"You should see that pay raise in about a month, along with a bonus for recon duty. Here are your orders. Take these to the battalion clerk and get packed. There'll be a slick waiting to take you and a couple of other Marines south to Cam Ranh Bay, then up to Recondo School at Nha Trang on the coast. Army Special Forces Staff will meet you on arrival."

"Yes, sir. Thank you, sir. Will that be all, sir?"

"Carry on, Lance Corporal Harper."

Recondo School was a mix of Army Rangers known by the acronym LRRPs—Long-Range Reconnaissance Patrols—and Marine Recon volunteers with instructors from the 5th Special Forces Group, Navy SEALs, and the Marines.

It didn't take Levi more than an hour to realize he was out–John Wayned by the volunteers in the room, highly motivated men averaging twenty years old. He wasn't surprised to see the eager young Marine who'd flown in with him on the C-130 transport a few months back, a look-who's-here smirk on his face when he spotted Levi.

"Never officially got acquainted," the young man said, extending his hand. Mike Hannibal is the name, but they call me Cannibal. Los Angeles is home."

"Harper. Paradise Bay, central coast."

The group stood in unison as the commanding general for the area of operations entered the room.

"Take your seats, gentlemen," he ordered, then gave them a pep talk about being the finest soldiers in Vietnam, the eyes and ears of MACV—Military Assistance Command, Vietnam. "Gentlemen," he concluded, "with your help in intelligence gathering, we can win this war, and God willing, sooner than later."

The men stood at attention once more until the general had exited the room.

More perfunctory introductions were made, expectations discussed by senior officers, then their first instructor—a master sergeant—greeted them late in the afternoon.

"Which one of you *is* Lance Corporal Levi Harper?" he shouted.

"Sir," Levi called out, jumping to his feet.

"I'm not some Marine Corp D.I. I'm not a *sir*. You Marines ought to know the difference, but then . . ." He didn't finish, to the guffaws of Army Rangers. "My name is Master Sergeant Paul Pitts. Sergeant Pitts, to you. And from now on, your name is Button-Fly." The laughter escalated. "Want to know why?"

"For the jeans, Sergeant Pitts?"

"Good. You're a smart Marine. You had me worried for a minute. Now be seated. We'll end the first day of Recondo School working on code. Code isn't anything new to you, but it's everything in long-range reconnaissance. The difference between life and death. We use hand codes," he said, holding up a fist as he went down on one knee. "What does this mean?" He pointed to an Army Ranger in the front row.

"Freeze. Enemy in sight," the eager Army E-5 responded.

"We don't talk in the bush. We aren't some cursed helmet-wearing platoon or gear-rattling company letting the enemy know miles in advance that we're trying to sneak up and kill them. We *do* sneak up and kill them."

He picked up a box and handed it to one of the men sitting in the front row. "Bandanas. My compliments. You'll all take one as the box comes around. This is our head gear, along with your cammie bush hats, which you'll also find in the box. Compliments of our Aussie allies." He waved a hand toward another man sitting up front. "MacGregor here is Australian Regular Army. Stand up, MacGregor. Three cheers for the Aussies!"

"Hip, hip, hooray! Hip, hip, hooray! Hip, hip, hooray!" the entire group hollered.

"For you Marines, 'cammie' means 'camouflage.' "

More subdued snickering.

"We don't stomp, tromp, or make noise in the bush. So your name doesn't really matter, but code does. And uniform code matters here, too. Army Air Cavalry pilots often interact with Marine recon units—extracting them, rescuing them, and generally making themselves available to our fellow jungle snoops—"

A loud cough went up from the back table three chairs down from Levi.

"Who interrupted me?" Sergeant Pitts bellowed.

"Sergeant Pitts, I take exception," a young Marine said, standing up confidently, his eyes telling all the other Marines what they should do. Every one of them stood up. "Marines don't require rescue, Sergeant," he went on. "Assistance from time to time, but never rescue."

Levi smiled at his boldness. The boy reminded him of his old childhood friend Albert Tenny.

"Your name, soldier?"

"Lance Corporal Ringo, Fifth Marines, sir."

Levi's grin widened.

"Well, Corporal Ringo. You now have a nickname. Who's that damn hippie drummer for the Bugs, or whatever the name of that fairy, long-haired, English rock-and-roll group is?" he asked, turning to an Army man in the front row.

Uncontrolled laughter now. Sergeant Pitts allowed it to go on.

"That would be Ringo Starr, the drummer for the Beatles, Sergeant Pitts," the man replied, trying to keep a straight face.

"Can't see how any of you men listen to that crap. Country's the only music real men listen to," he added, stifling a grin. "Now listen here, *Ringo*. You're now taking that sissy drummer's name. You're code name is now Starr. Got it?"

"Yes, Sergeant," the young man said, then he and the other Marines sat down.

"I like what I just saw. Comrades in arms. Six men per team with codes, proper comradeship, and weapons can do more than an entire company of Army or Marines on the hunt. I'm not kidding, gentlemen. And when I give a compliment, I expect something in return." He looked at Levi. "How do recon men return a compliment, Button-Fly?"

Levi stood up and shouted, "Hoo-rah!"

"Starr?"

"Hoo-rah!"

"You guys learn fast. Must've been listening to Class 2 on their run this morning. Now, 'Hoo-rah' will be repeated after each compliment I give to express brotherhood. Furthermore, I will not speak down to you intentionally. This isn't boot camp. You're trained professionals by now, and I respect you for who you are and what you're about to do. Some of you are decorated combat heroes, the very best our country has to offer," he concluded.

The remainder of the twelve-hour day was spent reading codes, repeating them, working in teams, and memorizing. The three-week course consisted of map reading, field techniques, insertion and extraction by helicopter, patrol, signaling, and Maguire rig practice—being extracted and hauled through jungle canopy by cable—then flying under the extraction chopper at high speed.

The final part of the course was Weapons Qualification, including the use of captured enemy weapons, setting friendly booby traps, recognizing enemy traps, scuba class, and nighttime practice missions in the nearby countryside with full camouflage and "war paint."

"Small world." Ringo laughed as Levi finished telling the story of meeting his father for the fourth time. They were sitting on the white, sandy beach, looking east over the South China Sea toward home. They had been given a three-day R&R to China Beach near Danang. They would receive their assignments for recon duty by the time they ended this short vacation in the rear from the real war in the jungle.

"He really wants me to take over that place someday." The stocky, fair-haired Marine from Redondo Beach smiled. "I used to love hanging out there during the summer. I'd watch the chicks on the beach and volunteer to take them snorkeling down in the bay. Man, Catalina Island." He sighed. "Stayed with my mom during the school year in the South Bay, but I've always loved Catalina. I sure miss my dad."

"Yeah, I know the feeling. My old man was a corpsman in the Pacific during the big war, and he didn't want me in this." Levi turned to his new friend. "Really. You ought to take over the place. I'll bring my piano and play songs to the guests, maybe do a Saturday-night gig down at the Casino Ballroom. Man, this is wild. I mean your dad treats me like royalty because you're a fellow Marine and all, then he asks me to give you a message. And here we are." Levi grew silent, his thoughts turning to that last day with Jenna.

"Tell me what he said again?" Ringo asked.

"He said, 'Tell him I love him and that I'll be praying for him.' "

Ringo released a heavy sigh. "I sure have mixed feelings about this war. I've never talked to anyone about it before, but I'm thinking of leaving the Corps when this is over. Funny, I always thought I'd be a lifer."

For the next hour, they talked about tactics, the politicians running the war, the lack of interest from the people back home, and the citizens of South Vietnam—who was and who wasn't enemy.

"I've been thinking about God," Ringo said. "You know, I wouldn't feel right telling many other guys this, but I've been praying lately. I think it would make Mom happy to know that. My dad is a tough old bird, but he used to pray with us, before the divorce. You don't think I'll lose my edge, do you?"

"I don't know. You can't hesitate out there, that's for sure," Levi replied. "I was brought up as a believer, you know. My dad's a preacher in our town, but he's a real man if there ever was one. It sure never hurts a man to pray."

"No, I suppose not. You know, I've thought about that myself," Ringo went on.

"What?"

"Becoming a preacher. Maybe stay in if I thought I could do some good, be a chaplain or a chaplain's assistant. I mean, I don't believe in these Communists taking over. They impose their godless will all over the planet. The Good Book says live by the sword, die by the sword. God can't blame us for standing against them with our own swords drawn, can He?"

"No, suppose he can't."

Along with the sun, silence fell between them as they wished their way to the shores of California ten thousand miles east.

"Funny," Levi finally said. "I met a former bully from school here, and fought with him. Now you. Small world, huh?"

"Sure is," a familiar voice behind them agreed.

Levi looked up, startled, then jumped to his feet. "Hey!" He laughed, giving his friend a bear hug. "How long you been standing there?" He stepped back as they surveyed each other.

"Long enough to kill you! Recon man, eh?" The two men hugged.

"Ringo, this is Albert Tenny, my best friend from Paradise Bay," Levi said enthusiastically. The two embraced again, slapping backs harder than before.

"Hoo-rah!" Albert smiled.

"Hoo-rah," Levi returned with a grin. "Now don't start on me, Al. I can't handle the emotion." He chuckled.

"Music, eh? Not gonna join with me, eh?" Albert ribbed.

Ringo smiled and shook Albert's hand.

"Last I heard, you were stateside," Levi went on, shaking his head in disbelief. "What are you doing over here?"

"Didn't get the job done on my first tour. I'm back to form a recon team. Tag, you're it!"

"No way!"

"Yes, sir. I have five guys picked already, and you're the sixth."

"You sneaky devil." Levi laughed. "How'd you know I was here?"

"I didn't. Just looked at the roster and bingo! Half my last tour was recon. You're gonna like this job, Levi," Albert assured him with a grin.

"This calls for a celebration." Levi waved for both the men to follow him.

"I'm buying," Albert said. "Join us, Corporal Ringo?"

"I'm in."

"So you wouldn't join up with me, huh?" Albert teased Levi relentlessly. They headed down the resort beach, created expressly for battle-weary GIs, to the nearest enlisted men's club. Laughing at the irony that they had ended up together here, Levi fended off Albert's noise about how God had his hand in it.

"Coincidence. That's all it is, Al. Pure and simple."

Tenny didn't let up. Ringo enjoyed the friendly jabs.

Levi filled him in on his adventures in the DMZ, his experience under Mayfield's tutoring, and Mayfield's last charge into the fire. "A heck of a fighter," he finished.

"Last I saw him was in a fistfight with you," Albert said. "I admire him for his courage. Too bad about the guy," he added with genuine regret.

Levi went on to talk about Jenna, his called-off marriage to Carol, his regret over disappointing his parents and the Santos family. How much he missed the music, how he wasn't sure now that he could ever play the same music again.

"Well, Corporal Ringo, what do you think of this friend of mine?" Albert chuckled. "Didn't want to join, didn't want to be a Marine, gets drafted and finds himself in the toughest, meanest Marine outfit in Vietnam. Recon! Hoo-rah!"

"I just wanted to make music," Levi explained, his tone cynical. "Wanted to be a peace-lovin', long-haired, maggot-infested hippie." He laughed, imitating the deep voice of his favorite drill instructor from boot camp.

"Well . . ." Ringo began hesitantly, "if you can't make music with the band, you might as well make it with the sword."

25

EVE OF DESTRUCTION

Cautious, Levi crept forward through the thin brush. He was first, point man, and his entire team was depending on his eyes and ears. Except for a crying baby, the mountain village ahead was eerily quiet.

Albert was tail gunner, or "drag," the last position on the patrol. He loved his work, covering tracks, putting brush and path back in an undisturbed condition to keep the enemy from tracking them, making sure the first five pairs of eyes hadn't missed anything. As team leader, he had his choice of patrol assignments, and this was the one he usually chose.

The RTO was Chavez and, except for the rest of the long-range recon patrol, he and his radio were at Harper's heels.

"Burned-out yards," Levi whispered. They called the Montagnard mountain people "yards" to distinguish them from regular

Vietnamese of Asian descent. These people were often brutal-
ized by the Vietnamese of both sides. "Village totally burnt out
except one or two hooches."

"Who done it? Air attack? Napalm?" Chavez whispered back,
noting the burning Montagnard hooches, which all stood on
poles. The closest were nearly intact, the walls still standing.

"No. Our intel knows this was a friendly vil. This is NVA
work. A couple of hours, no more. Except for that baby crying,
it's awfully quiet. Too quiet."

"Trap?" Chavez whispered.

Levi shrugged and signaled the squad with hand gestures, in-
dicating that they should take up defensive positions and spread
out into a wheel while he made his way to the first hooch, the
source of the crying.

"Signal Tenny," he mouthed to Chavez. "I'm going in. Be
ready to call for extraction and gunships if I get nailed. And get
that blooper gun ready." Chavez was trigger man for the team's
M-79 grenade launcher.

If you're going to die today, this is where it's gonna be, Levi told
himself as he left the sanctuary of the bush to cross the twenty
open meters.

He took a deep breath, ran to the cover of a tree, then a few
more long paces to the back of the hooch, where he rolled under
the structure and came up on his knees, his eyes and ears tuned
to any sign of an enemy trap. The crying was almost directly
above him. He felt something dripping onto his arms and glanced
up at the plank flooring above him. Blood.

He unpinned a smoke grenade and held it ready in his left
hand, with his .45 handgun in his right. Levi now crept silently,
inches at a time, toward a hatch-type door in the wooden floor
above him. He'd use the smoke grenade to cover his retreat if

anyone fired on him. Then, firing back, he'd *didi mau* out of there.

Carefully, he eased the door up.

He took a deep breath and moved inside the hooch, handgun ready, his heart beating loud enough to alert the enemy. *Oh hell, if I'm gonna die, might as well get it over with.*

Crouching low, he moved quickly into the open room. He paused, listened for movement, then rolled to the doorway leading to a smaller room, a bedroom no doubt, toward the crying sound.

A wounded NVA soldier was holding the baby, rocking it. His eyes met Levi's, but he made no move toward his AK-47, which was lying at his side. He was near death, gut-shot, and bleeding profusely.

Levi kicked the AK-47 away and stooped down to examine the dying man.

"GI, take baby," the man whispered, pushing it toward Levi. "I die."

"You're going with me, pal," Levi said. This wasn't a killer mission, it was an intel-gathering mission. Their orders were to make a "snatch and grab," take a prisoner back to Battalion Intelligence for interrogation. The North Vietnamese had moved into this "secured" and friendly area of Montagnards, the village of mountain people who, once the Army Special Forces had supplied and trained them, were supposed to have been able to deter Communist infiltrators.

Levi tossed the smoke grenade out to cover their retreat. Shouldering the AK-47 and holstering his .45, Levi checked the man for other weapons, tucked the baby under one arm, then lifted the wounded soldier and dragged him out through the floor hatch and into the open.

He had no choice but to risk the exposure of being out in the open as he made his way back to the bush where his team was waiting. The smoke would offer some concealment, but it couldn't stop bullets.

"What's this?" Tenny asked when Levi returned. "Stuff a rag in that kid's mouth!" He reached for the baby, but Levi pushed him away and pulled the child closer as he laid the wounded man down.

"*I'll* check the baby out," he said. "This *is* our snatch and grab," he added irritably. He looked the baby girl over. "Oh, man . . . she's been hit. Her neck is grazed. No wonder she's been crying." He applied pressure to stop the superficial bleeding.

"This guy's as good as dead." Albert was crouched down beside the dying soldier.

"Me Tran," the soldier managed. "You talk Viet?"

Albert nodded. The wounded soldier struggled but spoke to him in Vietnamese.

"Okay, maybe this guy's worth saving," Tenny said, sounding humbled. "Seems he fell out of favor with his Communist bosses. He wouldn't shoot the baby, so his commanding officer shot them both and left them to die. Made an example of him. He says he's a private, a draftee from some fishing village in the north. Near thirty years old. Can you believe it? Had a wife and kid who died from fevers, when he was younger. Damn! A draftee. I thought all these guys—"

Levi cut him off. "Call an extraction for him and the baby."

"Yeah, okay. But only one of us goes. We still need intel. We're supposed to locate a site for a communications relay team up here. The POW snatch and grab was secondary to this mission. We gotta know what we're getting Battalion into."

"I'll take 'em in," Levi replied. Chavez was already calling for a medivac chopper on his PRC-25 radio.

Albert gave Chavez instructions. "Tell the LT we got bad guys up here. Let's give him the landing zone coordinates one klick, our September, from the ridge line where we were dropped off. Have them send a diversion chopper to the original LZ. Let 'em know we need a good amount of gunship fire support on the tree lines surrounding the new LZ at . . ." He gave the map location. "Tell them we have one Papa Oscar Whiskey—just one—and that he's severely wounded but talking. Tell them to keep him alive, and that this NVA wants to cop intel. I want plenty of fire on that spot, and call for two birds. I want the bad guys to think the whole team's being extracted. Copy?"

Chavez nodded and tuned the radio for transmission.

"Look, Levi," Tenny went on. "You get that NVA back, and tell Doc at the dispensary in Dong Ha to take good care of him. He saved this kid. Maybe we can turn him into a Kit Carson Scout if he makes it."

"Man, is everything war to you, Tenny?"

"Yeah. Everything between here and the freedom bird back to the world." Tenny slapped Levi on the back. "Now, get out of here."

Corpsman "Doc" Hall from Nevada, who occasionally ran patrols with them, came up out of the bushes and gave the man a shot of morphine, then dressed his wound. He put a compress on the man's stomach wound and wrapped it, showing the NVA how to put pressure over the area.

"Okay, here we go," Levi said. He lifted the soldier to his feet and tucked the baby under his arm. *If Dad could only see me now*, he thought, smiling to himself.

The soldier was holding the bandages over his wounds, chanting low, like a Buddhist monk in prayer.

Henderson, the newest member of the six-man team, stepped forward. "Here. Put the kid in this." He had fashioned a sling out of mosquito netting so that Levi could carry the baby papoose-style against his chest, leaving his arms free to support the wounded soldier and keep his rifle at the ready.

"Thanks, Gomer," he smiled. Henderson was from the hills of South Carolina, and it hadn't taken him long to be nicknamed for the comic Marine of television fame, Gomer Pyle.

"You got a smoke grenade?" Albert asked as Levi started away from them.

"Just one."

"Here, take an extra." Tenny attached it to Levi's rucksack straps, then put a hand on his arm. "For your second recon mission, you done real good, Levi. I'm proud of you. See all the fun you've been missing out on?"

Levi knew Albert was referring to his invitation from two years ago to join the Marine Corps with him. "Sorry, buddy. Paradise Bay is for me." Levi smiled, then moved out. His reason for joining recon in the first place was to get as far away from the hill-assaulting, rice-paddy-stomping, noise-making grunts as possible. Being on assignment with six other men was far better than fighting with a whole platoon of would-be heroes killing people and blowing up things. At least, that's how he'd felt after the hill assault with Mayfield.

The war was changing him. He could look at a dead Marine now and feel regret and sorrow, but not grief. He learned to shut down emotion. *Better him than me*, the voice inside him said. His world was shrinking to gunfights, and whatever happened between them. A world of counting days until he went home to Jenna and his music.

He pulled the man and baby along in the direction of the ridge line, trusting that Chavez had made the call and given the coordinates to Control and Command at Dong Ha.

Barry McGuire's 1967 hit put beat and rhythm into his steps as he made his way forward:

> *The eastern world, it is explodin',*
> *Violence flaring, bullets loadin'.*
> *You're old enough to kill but not for votin',*
> *You don't believe in war, what's that gun you're totin'?*
> *And even the Jordan River has bodies floatin'.*
> *But you tell me over and over and over again, my*
>   *friend,*
> *You don't believe we're on the eve of destruction.*

26

RAG TEAM BAND

On average, they were down no more than four months "in country" when the recon team was put together. Albert and Levi were the twenty-year-olds. Henderson was the eighteen-year-old comedian from the hills of South Carolina. Cannibal was nineteen, a surfer from Southern California who could never get enough to eat. Ricky "Ricardo" Chavez, twenty-one, had escaped Cuba as a boy in the late '50s. His father and uncle had been killed in the Bay of Pigs fiasco, and this was his way of fighting Castro. At twenty-three, Mike Paulos was the oldest, the son of first-generation Greek immigrants who had fought the Communists in their home country right after World War II.

They all hated Communists, but Tenny, Chavez, and Paulos were the most vocal on the subject. Most Marines were simply there to do their duty, some for the adventure, others, like Levi, because they'd been drafted. These three, though, were on a mission to rid the planet of as many Karl Marx and "Uncle" Ho Chi Minh–loving Communists as possible.

"I guess you know what this code means?" the radio operator at Battalion Command chuckled. He slipped the piece of pocket-size notepaper into Levi's hand. A single line from a radio transmission was scribbled and addressed to "button-fly."

Levi grinned as he looked at the note. "Ollie-ollie-oxen-free!" he read.

"Al ." Levi laughed. "They made it out," he whispered to himself, satisfied. He crossed the field to the enlisted men's club for a quick drink before continuing on with what he needed to do.

"Hey, piano man! Play us a song!" a happy but weary Marine called out as he entered the small but well-decorated hooch.

"Just one." He smiled as he sat down at the beat-up and slightly out of tune piano. "That's it, guys," he said as he finished a Beatles tune.

"One, two, three, four . . . piano man, do some more!" the battle-weary enlisted men from Force Recon cried in unison.

"Sorry, guys." Levi laughed. "I'd love to, but I gotta find out what happened to my team, check on that NVA and the baby. Just one question, though. Who brought this piano up here, anyway?"

"Dice Man!" one of the Marines shouted, clapping the guy beside him on the back. "He won it in a card game down in Chu Li, and our pilot buddies on helo-insert owed us one. A CH-46 might be slow, but we got the piano. No bullet holes or nothin'. But no one knew how to play it."

"Oh, all right. Here's one." He started to play, then spoke over the tune. "Kind of slow, but next time you're out there in the bush late at night, snuggled close to your buddies, and you look up at that moon shining down over the killing zone, I want you to think of this Andy Williams song. And I want you to visualize some guy from the neighborhood back home making a move on your girl—singing it to her—and you, out here fighting for his freedom."

Men were in hysterics at Levi's ability to pause, putting the right accent on a word or idea, just at the proper moment, and then back it up with some piano chords that dramatized it all.

"Moon River," he sang.

One hour, then two passed as Levi lost himself in the music. He didn't notice that his team had arrived until Cannibal called out.

"Hey, piano man! Give us that Box Tops song!"

The team was back safe and had pulled up chairs and busied themselves with cold drinks. Levi smiled. "Chavez, front and center." Ricky Chavez grabbed a set of bongos from a shelf behind the bar. Some Marine had willed them to the club along with a considerably spent guitar. "Gomer," he called, waving his hand for the Southern boy to join in with his harmonica. "Paulos, grab that beat-up excuse for a guitar behind the bar." Levi pointed, then shouted some chords to him. "Cannibal, bring your lousy voice up here." The big man grinned, a stale Hostess Twinkie, sent weeks before from home, stuffed into his mouth. "Where's Tenny?" Levi continued as he played a medley of '50s and early '60s pop songs to warm up.

Albert had just walked in. He waved Levi off and took a seat at their table in the back.

Levi nodded toward the four men up front with him. "We're

known as the Rag Team Band." He laughed. "Straight from the West Coast and other places. One, two, three . . ."

Albert smiled at the irony, then held up a handful of mail. Levi grinned and mouthed,

My baby just wrote me a letter.

27

WOOLLY BULLY

Months Later

W HY DID YOU HAVE TO GO AND GET THESE GUYS MUSI-
cally inspired? I need them to focus before missions," Tenny
growled as they sat in the chopper waiting for the signal to take
off.

"Hey, it's just a ritual. Good for morale. Ease up, Sarge." Levi
grinned.

Levi hadn't been able to pull Tenny out of the dark funk he'd
been in since killing the woman and boy near the Hai Van Pass
a month before.

"He was tossing you a live grenade, Al. And she was giving
him instructions."

"War wasn't supposed to be like this," Tenny moaned.

"We found a gun on her," Levi insisted. "Now, get over it.
That's an order."

Albert shook his head. "Hmm . . . a pacifist telling me to get over it. Makes me hate Commies even more."

"*Uno, dos, tres, cuatro*. 'Hey! Woolly Bully. Watch it now, watch it now. Here it comes, here it comes! Watch . . . it'll get ya!" Ricky Chavez sang out, beating his drumsticks against the chopper floor as they readied for takeoff.

The team had just been assigned to Phu Bai, south of Hue, to work several special ops missions under the direction of Fleet Force Recon.

"Why does he have to carry those drumsticks on our missions?" Tenny complained.

"Luck," Chavez said, taking a break from his song. He took up where he'd left off. "Watch it now, watch it! Hey! Woolly Bully. Here it comes, here it comes, watch it now!" Chavez pointed a stick at Cannibal.

" 'Tenny told Harper, let's don't take no chance,' " Cannibal sang off-key, " 'let Cong learn a lesson, learn M-60 dance . . . Woolly Bully, Woolly Bully, watch it now, watch it, Woolly Bully . . .' "

Levi laughed, then turned to the Kit Carson Scout, the man he'd rescued with the baby months earlier. "You like, Tran?"

"Numba one!" Tran replied, always eager to please.

Tran An, the wounded North Vietnamese prisoner of war, had been given an opportunity by the South Vietnamese and American surrender programs to convert to the ideas of democracy and freedom. But to prove himself worthy, he had to pick up the rifle and work as a scout for American patrols in the heart of enemy territory.

The risk was great, but the offer of freedom, benefits, and the promise of life in the South induced many North Vietnamese to defect. Tran An had always secretly admired GIs, and his English, though improving, consisted mainly of "GI, numba one," meaning best, or "GI, numba ten," meaning worst. If he had a bad feeling about going down a particular trail, he'd simply let Levi and Albert know by saying, "Numba ten." He understood instructions and had taken a crash course in basic military English and commands. He knew what questions to ask prisoners and how to make them feel at ease in giving up information.

All in all, it was the rescue of Tran An that had turned the team's attitude about the Vietnamese 180 degrees. Tran was grateful and showed it. He had a zest for life, and he also had a girlfriend in Hue, a woman who'd fled to the South because of religious persecution. The baby he'd brought out of the village that day was now in her care. They intended to marry next month and raise the girl as their own. This now was his tenth mission, and everyone aboard had reminded him that it was going to be a "numba ten."

The insertion chopper still on the ground, Tran was apprehensive now, alternately peering out the open door to the jungle beyond and showing his approval of the singing with a smile.

"What's a woolly bully, anyway?" Albert yelled into Levi's ear, over the "whop, whop, whop" sounds of the chopper rotors spinning.

Levi pointed to Paulos.

"My grandpa's a sheepherder back home in Greece. Wool comes from sheep, right?" Paulos said.

"Yeah." Tenny nodded.

"So, you want to sneak up on sheep, you dress like a lamb, right? Big bad wolf puts on camouflage. Like us, in cammies and war paint, right?"

"Go on," Tenny replied, straight-faced.

"But the wolves are bad guys. So a 'woolly bully' is a bad guy in sheep's clothing. Or like us, the good guys on the hunt in camouflage. A 'woolly Cong' is a bad guy, a bad guy trying to be tougher than us . . . a bully. Get it?"

"Not funny," Albert shot back. "Doesn't make sense anyway."

"Makes perfect sense to me," Paulos countered.

"Clear as mud." Tenny frowned.

Levi elbowed Tenny. "Hey, lighten up, man."

Luckily, Paulos let it go, slipping back into song with the rest of the squad.

They sang like kids at a beach party as the Huey lifted off the ground. Chavez beat his sticks even more furiously against the deck.

Tenny shook his head and pulled out his map. "I know we've all been over this at least three times today. But once more," he said above the noise. "You take point, I'll take rear." He moved his finger on the map toward the river and the bend where they would set up their ambush. "Here's our bait—the point of the river. Here's where we lay out the claymores as we draw the suckers in. Here's the escape route. We lay more claymores here and here. White phosphorus trip line. They jump over here, then boom! Anyone who's left jumps to the opposite side, and we rake 'em on full auto." He folded the map up and tucked it back in his shirt.

"I thought this was intel," Levi said, surprised. "What's the purpose?"

"We'll be in the Ashau Valley for this morning's little adventure," Albert explained. "I know I should've told the truth back in our briefing, that this was more than intel, but the guys were acting goofy. We got to stop this music nonsense."

"Okay, okay," Levi answered, irritated now. "What's the real scoop," he asked, shouting to be heard above the noise of the helicopter.

"Definite Indian country, loaded with gooks. The LRRPs from the Airborne and Ranger outfits have been getting some pretty impressive kills, even when they weren't on killer missions up there. Up until now, we've avoided fights. Force Recon wants a body count this time."

Levi shook his head, exasperated. Every base in 'Nam gave out extra beer rations for body counts. Young soldiers eager to please shot at anything in the kill zone. Some captain or major could report his count and add some citations to his record. "This stinks," he said.

"War is hell," Albert offered, for lack of a better response. "Okay, boys. We got the crack of dawn and nobody's awake. Hit the deck, spread out, and make for the tree line."

The men's sense of fun vanished as they stood and made their way to the door, faces painted with camouflage, headbands around their foreheads to hold back the sweat. They wore no helmets, nothing that might rattle. They were no longer fun-loving, music-making boys, but professional recon men with an awesome array of killing power available to them.

The chopper set down just long enough for them to hit the ground. They cleared the Huey in seconds, then ran through the six-foot elephant grass to the tree line on the northern edge of the landing zone. The most dangerous moments on a recon mission come during and just following insertion. If they were spotted before they could take cover, they would lose the element of surprise and fall under gunfire.

They began making their way to the river, their planned kill zone. Along the way they established their avenue of escape, planting claymore antipersonnel mines as they moved.

Each member of the team carefully noted the locations along a "high-speed trail," one reported to be used frequently by the enemy. The team would then stay clear of the main trail to avoid falling into their own traps should they need to make a quick escape.

Levi held up his fist and dropped to one knee, alerting the others to possible danger ahead. He motioned with his right hand that two men should flank right, off the trail, two to the left. He withdrew farther from the path, staying parallel to it with just enough view of his teammates to maintain communication through hand signals and gestures. The jungle was so thick, he could see only yards ahead, make out only shadows.

Albert passed the signal up front that he was in position. Levi looked to his left, and Henderson nodded. Levi quickly placed the claymore mines on the opposite side of the trail from where his patrol was positioned. They would let the enemy pass, then take down as many as they could with a single blast.

They repeated this until they reached the river, then waited for the optimum time to spring their ambush. When it came, they would initiate contact with small-arms fire, then withdraw toward the landing zone, lure the enemy into the open. Cobra gunships would fly over and let go with rockets and machine-gun fire. Once it was over, a rapid-reaction platoon would land, mop up and count the bodies, gather weapons and evidence, and report the body count.

Easy. It was done all the time.

Levi sensed danger, and he could smell the enemy close by. The odor was unmistakable—the food they ate, the clothes they wore. He was beginning to understand the adrenaline rush that Tenny, Cannibal, and the others saw in this. In spite of himself, he was becoming a very good Marine, and a very good killer.

It was kill or be killed, either in a regular combat unit or here. And out here, there was no stinking officer seeking a medal at his expense, no one breathing down his neck. All he had to do was look out for these men, loyal comrades who also looked out for him. He was nearly half finished with his tour now. He'd do whatever it took to get back home to Jenna.

Albert was another story. He *wanted* to be here. He actually believed that killing Communists would make the world a better place. Crazy, patriotic Albert. Cannibal was seeking adventure. Henderson wanted to find out if he was a man. Chavez and Paulos hated Castro and all the other Commies in the world. Levi would simply kill to go home.

So, if there was going to be any chance of getting his wish granted, the North Vietnamese or Viet Cong guerillas on this trail would have to lose their lives today.

KIA—killed in action—would be an honorable death for them, after all. They might own the jungle but the recon Marines were better trained, better killers. And killing the Woolly Bully was really all that mattered anyway, Levi reasoned. Levi glanced over to their loyal Kit Carson Scout. He showed no emotion, simply nodded that he was ready.

Another Marine might have killed Tran An that day four months ago. It would have been justified. After all, he had an AK-47 sitting next to him.

Now, whatever a Woolly Bully meant to the Marines, Tran An was one of them and along for the ride.

28

A THOUSAND EYES

Thanks, guys." Levi grinned, admiring the gift, a teakwood-encased brass captain's clock. "Six days and a wake-up, and I'm outta here." He read the inscriptions of each team member's name, then added, "No Tran?"

"He's got a little surprise of his own," Tenny said, just as Tran walked into the barracks with a package in his hand.

"For numba one Jenna." Tran smiled, handing the package to Levi. "Numba one moon-honey."

The entire team busted up at Tran's innocence.

Levi untied the string, fully enjoying the comic relief. Tran stood by beaming, proud of the gift as Levi folded back the brown tissue and found a long colorful *ao dai* inside, a dress with a slit up the side designed to wear over pants. Levi was moved by the gift, already imagining its silky pattern of flowers accentuating Jenna's blond hair and slender curves.

"She ain't gonna wear no pants under that fine dress, is she?" Gomer drawled, reaching over to feel the fabric.

"A fine woman wears no more than what enhances her natural beauty," Cannibal offered with a grin.

Levi was preparing to leave for Hawaii, and his destined rendezvous with Jenna. They would be married by the end of the week, then spend the next full week of his R&R forgetting about everything but each other.

"Don't mean to be a spoilsport," Tenny said, "but you'd better stow that in your locker. Captain radioed. Wants us to report for the mission briefing with Major Thompson."

"You ought to sit this one out," Chavez said to Levi as they walked from the barracks to the company command post.

"Wouldn't be right. I can't leave you guys out there on your own," Levi replied.

"Nothing's going to happen to lover boy here. I'm right behind him," Paulos interjected.

"Tran, too," the little Vietnamese added.

Levi put his arm around Tran. "You're number one. I'm going to sneak you into Paradise Bay and buy you a boat someday."

Tran laughed. "And take me to Hollywood. See John Wayne, too?"

"John Wayne's right there." Levi pointed ahead to Tenny as they walked into the command building.

"Why don't you boys scoot over to the mess hall. Grab some hot chow. Piano man, here, and I will fill you in," Albert offered to Rocker Team, the code name they had adopted.

"Hot chow." Cannibal nodded. "Yeah, you fill us in." Chavez, Paulos, Henderson, and Tran followed the big man. The Marines laughed at some offhand silent communication Tran made with pointing gestures to Cannibal's backside.

"Numba five," he mouthed.

The briefing began with congratulatory remarks, followed by comments about why they had been selected—the team's outstanding record together, the water skills many of them possessed.

"We're going to provide two motorized junks to give you the best possible opportunity to penetrate what we believe is a highly concentrated NVA buildup five to ten klicks east of Hue in this mountain range skirting the Perfume River, here," the major said, jabbing a finger into the map. "Our downed pilots reported what appeared to be unusual and heavy movement along known high-speed trails in the mountains east of us here." He pointed again on the wall map. "You will have your Kit Carson Scout, Tran, dressed as a river boat operator for boat number one, and one South Vietnamese Marine in civilian clothes running the second boat."

Levi gazed over to Albert. Their eyes met. Albert would want Levi to get out of town, make it to his R&R in Hawaii, but Levi had to know if it was right to abandon his team. This was family, too, and they were being given an assignment that left Levi feeling uneasy. He couldn't ever forgive himself if one of them were lost while he was enjoying life safe in Hawaii.

The major continued. "Our two pilots were last seen here," he said, marking the spot on a map laid out before them on the table where they had gathered. "They went down yesterday, and we want them back. So your mission is twofold. Verify intel on an enemy buildup east of Hue near the village of Song Ba, and seek out our pilots."

Albert raised his hand.

"Yes, Sergeant?"

"Do we coordinate with the Navy river patrol boats? I'd hate to be mistaken for an enemy junk and blown out of the water."

"You'll be escorted within two kilometers of your area of operation by a Navy Whiskey boat. From there you will be on your own. Your Vietnamese operators should be able to handle it and get you in at dusk from there. Anything else?"

Tenny shook his head.

"Then good luck, gentlemen. You have your briefing materials. I'm proud of you men and I know this is a dangerous mission. Just so you know, this mission comes from the top. This enemy buildup has Fleet Command concerned. We need that intel and want those pilots out of there. That'll be all."

Tenny and Levi returned to their hooch to lay the mission out to the rest of the team. Normally their platoon leader would have briefed them, been in charge of the details, not Major Thompson, but the other three teams and the lieutenant were all out on missions themselves. Their company commander, Captain Roberts, had recommended them to the major even though he was down at Recondo School in Nha Trang. So the team was receiving its orders as directly from the top as it ever got.

"I'm going," Levi said.

"You don't have to," Al responded.

"Never break routine. It's bad. I'll do this last mission. Someone's got to look out for you."

"Look, Levi. Just sit it out here at the base, then catch that freedom-bird to Hawaii. You've earned it!"

Levi shook his head. "Got to watch out for you, buddy-boy." He smiled, slapping his friend on the back.

"I'm a big boy. You won't be blamed if something happens. It's war. That's all it is. You think too much," Al observed.

"I'm going," Levi replied.

This mission was supposed to be an overnighter, so they would be taking minimal gear. The most important equipment was their weapons, extra ammunition, radio, extra batteries, grenades, and a one-day supply of water and rations. They might end up swimming, if anything happened to the junks while on the river, so they had to travel light.

"Never done an insertion from water. This should be different," Tenny said to Levi as they entered their hooch.

"I don't mind going for POWs. I'd rather go on rescue operations any day of the week. Wish we had better intel. This is going practically blind," Levi observed.

"Yeah, well . . . I guess that's what they're paying us for."

"I'd love for us to get those pilots out," Levi went on. "I think we ought to focus on them and get intel on the enemy buildup as we go. I feel sorry for those poor suckers."

Albert winked at him. "I hear one of the pilots is Huish."

"No way! We owe Huish. Yeah, we need to go for those guys. You think we can get some native intel?"

"Can't tell who's VC and who's not up there in the hills."

"Tran?" Levi questioned.

"I was thinking the same thing," Tenny answered.

Tran could pose as a VC scout, claim he was separated and question villagers ahead of the team's movements. They didn't know the Vietnamese Marine, but Tran had proven himself. Besides, he was married, had adopted the baby Levi had rescued that day months ago. His wife and child lived in Hue. He wouldn't turn traitor on them now.

"You can get out of here, you know. No one will blame you or think bad about you for it," Albert offered one final time. He knew Levi belonged with Jenna and that the wedding was more important than one more mission.

"Don't suppose it would be right to leave you guys out there without my eagle eyes. Besides, it's just an overnighter. Right?" Levi answered.

"Right," Tenny answered. "But . . ."

Levi cut him off. "Like I said, no messing with routine. Bad stuff can happen when you mess with routine. Let's get some chow and fill in the boys."

Levi began to whistle, and Albert tried to carry a tune. It was Bobby Vee's hit "The Night Has a Thousand Eyes."

29

LUNAR NEW YEAR

January 30, 1968

Remember, we cut the motor at two hundred yards and use these." Albert held up the small oars.

Levi nodded and started the engine in his assigned "junk," a long fishing boat used by natives along the river and the coast. Albert followed with his engine and then hid himself. The team was split between the two junks, also called "sampans," and were sitting low inside the boats, covered by tarps, with Tran and the other Vietnamese Marine guiding the two craft.

A Navy Whiskey boat escorted them within the two-kilometer cutoff point and then turned back downriver toward Hue, leaving them to finish their upriver journey alone.

It was dark by the time they reached the point above the village where they hoped to gain information on the pilots and the enemy buildup reported before the Marine helicopter crew went down. They waded the final fifty yards in waist-deep water, quickly concealed their boats in the underbrush, then moved inland.

Tenny motioned Tran to take point. He was good at smelling trouble. Both Levi and Albert took comfort in that.

It was close to midnight, January 30, the eve of Tet—the Vietnamese celebration of the Lunar New Year. Levi sensed a different kind of danger in this mission, a foreboding he'd never experienced before. He brushed it off as the jitters. He was so close to seeing Jenna now.

The village they were heading for was up a steep trail, one they had to stay off to avoid detection. It made the going slower, but stealth was key to survival, if the enemy buildup reported by the two downed pilots was accurate.

From this vantage point the lights of the city of Hue, east of their position, were dim but visible. No doubt, Tran was thinking of his new bride, wishing he could be there to celebrate the new year with her and the adopted child he had saved from an NVA officer's bullet.

The Vietnamese Marine who had accompanied the team in the second junk was left with the boats on the beach. Levi felt unsure and uncomfortable with the new man. They'd never worked with him. He wondered, if it came to a fight, how the Vietnamese Marine would do. *He must be good*, he consoled himself. Command had assigned him. They wouldn't assign a questionable man to this mission.

Tran, on the other hand, left Levi with no fears, no doubts. On more than one occasion in the past two months, Levi had enjoyed dinner at Tran's humble home, which he and his new bride shared with her relatives in the center of the South Hue shopping district. Levi had cuddled the baby girl in his arms and, for one shining moment, felt glad that he had come to Vietnam, that his presence had made a difference.

They had named her Lin An. They were raising her as their own, believing God had placed her in Tran's path that day for a reason. And because of the child and the soldier Levi Harper, the entire chain of events that began when Tran An was brought to the door of his beloved Mai Ky was now complete. Now, Tran knew there was a God, that his humble prayers as a frightened soldier in the North Vietnamese Army had indeed been answered.

Tran held up his fist and went down on one knee. Levi followed, and each of the team members passed the same signal to the man behind him: *Freeze. Enemy.* Tran gave the next signal by pointing to his eyes: *The enemy is in sight.* He held up two fingers: *Two enemy soldiers.* Then three fingers: *Three enemy now.*

Shouts in Vietnamese were heard as a patrol of pajama-clad Viet Cong came toward them along the trail, dragging the two beaten Marine chopper pilots with ropes around their necks.

Couldn't be easier. Levi smiled. The pilots were being brought to them. Sometimes things worked perfectly. Grease the gooks with silencers and grab Huish and the other pilot.

A feeling of relief came over him. This mission could be accomplished with the intel the pilots would offer. They'd be back to the boats in a fast jog downhill and into the safety of Hue in hours.

Levi signaled the team to set up an L-shaped ambush. Albert was at the tail end; he'd be final man in this trap. If they were going to free the POWs, they had no time to lose.

Tran was at the top of the trail, positioned to stop any escaping Viet Cong who might try to make their way back up the hill and "wake up Dodge," as Tenny liked to put it.

Tenny signaled for silencers: Cannibal, Henderson, and him-self. Three shots at close range. The American POWs would be grabbed by Harper and Chavez, who would then head back to the boats, with the rest of the team covering the escape.

The mission seemed easy and painless, and the major wouldn't be able to fault them for returning without intel. In-stead, they would have two happy Marine pilots, with all the "poop" on the enemy they could want.

As the three-man Viet Cong patrol approached, Levi recog-nized one of the Americans. It was indeed Lieutenant Tom Huish from Colorado, nicknamed "Huey" for both his surname and the UH-1E Huey slick he flew. Beaten up and struggling to support a more seriously wounded copilot, he was being shoved and nudged by a Viet Cong behind him. Levi's team had hitched rides into and out of missions with Huey on several occasions.

And since Huey had saved their tails more than once, rescuing him would be doubly satisfying. *Payback time*, Levi thought.

"On the count of three," Tenny mouthed to the men waiting with silencers, then gave the hand signal: *One, two, three.*

Zip, zip, zip! The Viet Cong who now lay dead never heard the muffled gunshots. The American pilots stood frozen, surprise registering on their faces.

Camouflaged men greeted them from either side of the trail. "How ya feelin', Huey?" Levi asked.

Tears sprung to his eyes. "Oh, man, am I glad to see you guys!"

Tenny and company pulled the dead Cong into the brush, then Tenny held his finger to his lips to let the pilots know they had to be quiet. When he gave the signal for *evade and escape*, the team began making its way back to the boats. The second pilot, who was wounded, started to collapse as Chavez reached out to support him.

The race to safety was on. More enemy soldiers certainly followed. They could only hope the night and silence would bolster their odds of getting away without casualties.

When they reached the beach, Huish tapped Tenny on the shoulder, and they crouched down in a huddle with Levi. Huey told them what he knew in whispers, as Tran An and Paulos went to find the Vietnamese Marine assigned to stay with the motorized junks.

"Something big's going down," Huey said. "Over a hundred VC and a battalion-size NVA force dressed to dance. From what I could tell, a regiment was moving in from the hills behind them. Fully loaded with ammo, rockets, C-4. These guys are sappers, and they've been training for something major here. They're headed for the big city. Hue is going to get nailed big time. We have to warn command at Phu Bai."

"He's gone. He's gone with one of the sampans. The lousy . . ." Expletives rolled off Paulos's tongue as he related that the Vietnamese Marine who had escorted them in was nowhere to be found, and had no doubt taken one of the junks downstream with him.

"Damn," Tenny exclaimed. "Well, doesn't that just figure. Chavez, raise Major Thompson. Give him our position, the intel Huish just shared. Tell him our Vietnamese Marine is a traitor— just in case he shows up with some other story. Make sure they arrest the guy." Tenny turned to Levi.

"Take these guys with you. Everybody goes but me and Tran. We'll cover the escape. Call for a chopper. Let them know I'll 'pop a smoke' to give them our position."

"I'm not leaving you. There's not enough room in the junk anyway."

"You are leaving." Tenny demonstrated with a hand gesture.

"You can hang on to the sampan. Float alongside, I don't care. But you are leaving."

Levi knew better than to argue. Time was working against them. "Let's go," he said to the rest of the team. Tran was already manning the trail. Levi grabbed a rucksack full of claymore mines from the small narrow craft and handed them to Tenny. "See you back at Phu Bai. Putting the call in now. The extraction chopper will be on its way."

"Yeah, I'll be waiting for you. Now go! *Didi mau!*" Tenny ordered in Vietnamese, telling them to hurry.

Levi embraced his friend. "Don't be a hero, Al. Don't do anything stupid." A dark feeling had been dogging him for more than a day now, and he didn't feel right about leaving Tenny behind.

Their exchange was brief but meaningful, the depth of their friendship expressed in less than five seconds through the strength of their grasp and a long look into each other's eyes.

"Give my love to Jenna," Tenny said as they pulled away. Al took off toward the brush and the trail to set up an ambush, and hold off any Viet Cong coming toward them.

Levi shoved off, then looked back one last time.

Tenny was a Marine's Marine. A different flavor than Mayfield but the same "can do" gung-ho spirit. Tenny wouldn't give up his life without a fight. He'd improvise. Somehow, he'd find a way to escape without waiting for an extraction chopper or letting the team risk their necks trying to rescue him.

The boat was a hundred yards out on the river when the beach suddenly exploded in gunfire. Levi hit the motor full throttle. He looked back in horror, and it took everything in him to keep from going back to save his friends.

Ahead of them lay Hue. A sudden explosion sent a wave

through the air, rippling toward them from the direction of the city.

"That isn't fireworks," Chavez noted.

"Fuel, ammo," Huish agreed. "That's a big hit."

"Man, it's all over the place. Look in the direction of Phu Bai." Henderson pointed and the men turned, mesmerized by the noise and flames five miles away. They were at the base of the mountains; the river ran swift here. They would be back in the city in no time, but what lay ahead was uncertain.

The firing and explosions of claymore mines behind them told him Tenny and Tran had at least accomplished the element of surprise. "Chavez," he whispered. "Is that chopper on its way?"

"I haven't been able to reach command yet," he returned.

"Keep trying," Levi ordered, as the river turned and the site they had just launched from disappeared with the river bend. As violent as the battle behind them was, he knew Albert was exactly where he wanted to be.

What lay ahead appeared equal to everything the team had in them. Explosions in and around Hue were clearly visible now, lighting up the night sky in some sort of Lunar New Year welcome the enemy had carefully orchestrated. The reports of enemy buildup were no joke. They might very well be fighting all the way back.

"Happy New Year," he whispered.

30

BY THE PERFUME

Hue—February 1, 1968

Gentlemen, I want to congratulate you on yester-day's rescue of our two pilots. After receiving your radio call we put a priority flight together to rendezvous with you outside Hue. I want you to know, with all hell breaking loose all over South Vietnam, it was a task raising an available chopper. You are important to us. I just want you to know that."

"I can speak for all of us. Thank you, sir, for getting us the hell out of there," Levi spoke up.

Major Thompson nodded. "I'm sorry to hear that Sergeant Tenny and the Vietnamese scout Tran An were left behind, but we're doing everything possible to get them out of there. And Sergeant Tenny, as you are all aware, is a resourceful man."

Major Thompson had called the five remaining recon team members in to brief them on another mission by water.

"I'm not going to con you," he went on. "This may be the deadliest and toughest mission I've ever asked you to go on."

"Sir," Levi dared, "we owe it to Sergeant Tenny and Tran to get back upriver as soon as possible. His radio is out and he could be wounded."

"You will follow orders, son. And we're not leaving Sergeant Tenny behind. We have a team of Navy SEALs mounting up as we speak. So, at ease, gentlemen. Back to the map. You will be inserted under cover of darkness. Here, up the Perfume River. Until we can get First Battalion through these city streets in South Hue"—he showed them on the map—"you'll be behind enemy lines."

"What's new," Paulos muttered to Chavez.

Major Thompson heard the exchange but chose to ignore it. "This bridge is your objective. It's to be held until dawn. A river assault will take place here, here, and here. The bad guys are holding the high ground—the fortress walls of the Citadel. We have access to the east entrance to the Citadel at the Hau Gate. Our allies, the first ARVN Division compound, controls it. It is the only position inside the walled city that we do control.

"We're not yet authorized to pulverize the place with arty and air-support ordinance. As you know, the Imperial City, as the Citadel is also known, is sacred to the Vietnamese, so we're trying to respect that."

"I wonder if those boys on the NVA side are going to show some 'respect,' " Cannibal grumbled to Henderson.

The major shook his head but still said nothing. He knew it was quite possible that he was sending these men on an impossible mission, perhaps to their deaths. And he was willing to cut them all the slack they needed.

"You'll receive all the fire support you need," he continued.

"We'd like to keep this bridge intact, but if it aids the enemy in any way, then we blow it. It is possible they are infiltrating from the hills in the east and entering the Citadel across it."

"Begging your pardon, sir," Levi interjected. "But we've never done street or city fighting, let alone recon in a city. We're trained for the bush. Wouldn't it be better to bring in someone trained for this; I mean, we are recon, sir," Levi emphasized.

"I am very well aware of that, Lance Corporal Harper. Now, as I was saying, we don't have enough information on their strength. All we know is that they took most of Hue while the city was celebrating Tet. They're killing civilians, and they've captured the Citadel, the most important symbol of Vietnamese nationalism for both North and South. It's imperative that we get the upper hand in this. And we fully expect this to be the largest street battle to date in this war. Any questions?"

"No, sir," Levi replied, speaking for everyone.

"You'll need to load up with C-4, plenty of extra ammunition, and two radios, gentlemen. It's imperative that we know what's going on out there minute by minute. And I want you to know that I appreciate what you men are about to do. You're the finest in the Corps, and I know you'll make us proud. Men"—Major Thompson sighed—"there is no safe place in Vietnam tonight." He walked down the line, shaking each man's hand, then turned back to face them. "Sergeant Andrews will take you to your point of departure on the Perfume River. God be with you," he concluded.

"And with you, sir," Levi replied.

They walked out of the command center to a thunder of artillery, rocket, and mortar fire being returned on the base perimeters. The initial wave of enemy attacks had been fought back with intensity. Suicidal sappers—enemy high-explosive experts—

had attacked every military compound in the country, including the U.S. Embassy in downtown Saigon.

Marine casualties had been high, but the body count of the Viet Cong and the North Vietnamese was even higher. The Marines were already finding that the Communists had murdered entire families, their bodies left to rot in the streets or open fields.

Levi was quiet as the men jogged to their hooch to gear up for the mission. They felt lucky to have gotten back from yesterday's mission alive, but Tenny and Tran were heavy on their minds. Each knew, without a word being spoken, what the other was thinking. They should be going to find Tenny and Tran, not guarding some bridge in Hue.

Levi thought of Jenna, and his parents, what they must be thinking as they watched the news back home. He prayed a silent prayer for them.

Jenna must be anxious, too. In just three days, she was supposed to meet him in Hawaii. He knew he'd never make it there now. He turned around and went back to the command center, where he asked Major Thompson if he could speak to him on a personal matter, asking if there was any way she could be contacted and told to cancel her trip to Hawaii until the Tet battles were over and he was cleared to leave.

Thompson was more than understanding. He immediately assigned a staffer to telegram her.

Where were Tenny and Tran? Levi wondered. If they were still alive, they'd probably taken out at least half of the enemy on the strip of river beach where they remained. He'd have loved to get his hands on that lousy Vietnamese Marine who had abandoned them with the other boat.

Now he could only hope. And for now, he needed to keep a clear mind, use what Mayfield and Tenny had taught him to keep the rest of them alive.

Besides himself, there were only four remaining team members. Chavez and Paulos would both be on radio for this mission. Cannibal and Henderson would be carrying M-60 machine guns. An extra machine gun was an addition to their normal lay-down fire power, which made Levi feel a little better. Having two radios was crucial. If one went down, the backup was essential for passing along intel, and getting rescue if needed.

"Should've listened to Dad," Levi muttered to himself.

"I've got to go." Rex Harper switched the television off, kissed Eleanor, and went out the screen door. Trying desperately to sound cheerful, he called back over his shoulder. "Going to get the Ford down at the church." He had left his Ford Fairlane in the alley behind the chapel earlier, rather than inch it home in the soupy fog.

Jeff noticed his mother's eyes filling with tears. "He'll be okay, Mom," he said, trying to comfort her. Karen Sue went to her room, unwilling to watch the violence in Vietnam unfolding on the evening news with Walter Cronkite.

Levi had written them about the city of Hue and his visits to the home of Tran An, his team's scout. Told them how beautiful the country was, that it would make a first-class tourist destination if not for the war. He described wide sandy beaches north and south, a certain dignity to the people of Hue that he hadn't seen in other parts of Vietnam.

Rex Harper walked slowly across the field, hounded by a sense of foreboding, then stepped inside the dark chapel to be alone with God and his thoughts. He knelt down beside the piano, which somehow made him feel closer to his boy.

"Father," he prayed, "I've never asked for much, but I'd like to ask You a favor. I came home from war to raise a family, and I've done my best. If my son is destined for death today, I ask

You to take my life for his, let him live to know the joy of having a family, as I have. He's a good boy, Lord. I ask this in the name of Jesus. Amen."

He got up from his knees and reached for the hymnal Levi kept on the piano. As he picked it up, it opened to an Oliver Wendell Holmes hymn, one of his favorites, and a letter in Levi's handwriting fell out.

Dear Dad,

I know you'll open this hymnal at some point before I return. I hope you'll forgive me for anything I've done that brought shame or embarrassment to you. I think you're the greatest man on earth, and I promise to make you proud. I love you and Mom with all my heart. I've put myself in God's hands, so I'm sure I'll come back from this war. It doesn't get much better than that, does it?

Your son,
Levi

"No, Son, it doesn't," Rex whispered, then read the final verse of the hymn through his tears.

We thank thee Father; let thy grace,
Our loving circle still embrace.
Thy mercies shed its heav'nly store,
Thy peace be with us ever more.

31

DANGER CLOSE

Death was everywhere tonight, in the flares overhead and the firefights echoing in the air. Levi and his team were players in a surreal drama, a nightmare of carnage playing out in every town, city, and village in South Vietnam.

They were up the Perfume River now, a hundred meters from their designated insertion at the bridge. Just as Levi had hoped, there was no need to cut the engine and use oars; the explosions of artillery, mortar rounds, and automatic gunfire were rocking the entire city.

He signaled to Paulos, who was sitting at the controls of the second craft. Having two inflatable rafts and two radios evened the odds of some of them making it out alive if the worst happened. The mission was highly dangerous; their orders were to gather information, secure the bridge with silencers, knives, even bare hands if necessary, then blow it up to deny the enemy re-inforcement or retreat.

The best they could hope for was to get the job done while the Fifth Marines and the South Vietnamese Army did theirs—retake Hue with minimal loss of life.

Paulos returned Levi's hand signals, acknowledging that he was to head for shore fifty yards ahead of Levi's craft. All of the men were wearing black paint on their faces, arms, and necks, with black bandanas over their heads and regular cammies—jungle attire. There was no need for camouflage in street fighting, but to a man they were certain that changing their routine in any way would bring bad luck.

Lying low, Paulos headed toward the north shore, close to the bridge. Just as Levi started to follow, flares ignited over the water, and an explosion capsized Paulos's raft. Levi and his team were thrown overboard, another mortar slamming into the water ahead of them.

"Get rid of the packs," he ordered his men, spitting up water. "Weapons and radios only. Head to the south shore." He spotted Paulos swimming the wrong way. "No!" he shouted. "Swim south!" The NVA had zeroed in on them, and mortar rounds were falling all around them.

Disoriented, Paulos continued swimming to the north shore as Levi and the other three team members crawled up the south bank.

Gasping for breath, Levi crouched down with Chavez, Henderson, and Cannibal, and pulled out the small pair of binoculars he carried in his cammies. Flashes of gunfire erupted as Paulos brought down half a dozen of the enemy before disappearing in a blast.

"Okay," he said to his men. "Paulos got some of them, but

he's down. Can't get to him now. Let's find cover. Move!"

They scrambled up the bank toward a nearby factory building which had been considerably damaged by artillery fire, then took positions on opposite sides of the open door.

Levi gave hand signals: *Two through the door. One up, one down. Two cover at the door. Go!*

Levi motioned for light-footed Chavez to take point, followed by Henderson. Henderson and Chavez, weapons ready, went in. Levi, outside with Cannibal, pointed up the stairs. If the enemy was inside, they'd most likely find him on the top floor—a good observation post. Cannibal closed and bolted the sliding door behind them. He and Levi would follow once Henderson and Chavez reached the top floor. They had failed to secure the bridge, but they still had a radio, could serve the Marines battling their way in this direction by guiding them through. Perhaps a Marine company could then secure the bridge.

They made it upstairs, where they found a long corridor running the length of the building. Levi signaled again. *Go, one! Go, two!* They crept forward and checked each room. To their surprise, the building was empty. Levi motioned Chavez to bring over their radio and try to raise someone.

When Chavez finally contacted a commanding officer for the Fifth Marines, Levi took the handset.

"Harper, Force Recon," he said, then used code to describe their position and situation. "Team Rocker at . . ." he said, offering the street and coordinates. "Recommending fire mission for . . ." He gave their position plus fifty meters as a target. Chavez had just pointed out the window to a platoon-size enemy grouping being staged outside the building to their immediate south.

"That's affirmative. Danger close. Confirmed target. Fire for effect."

Marine artillery immediately opened up on the NVA platoon outside.

"Heads down, boys," Levi mouthed. They all lay flat, hands over heads as shells screamed toward them. The first round hit the east corner of the building away from them. Four remaining explosions shredded the street below and blew remaining glass out of the windows.

Levi exhaled audibly. "Too close," he said.

He scanned the scene from his perch on the top floor. The five rounds had torn the thirty NVA troops into pieces. The effect of ordering fire on their own position offered a deterrence to any other NVA thinking about gathering near the team's hideout, and took care of the immediate problem—the thirty enemy who might have chosen to take up residence with them in the building.

The CO for the 1st Battalion, 5th Marines took over as temporary commanding officer for Team Rocker. The team now became the new forward observation post. Alpha, Bravo, and Charlie Companies continued their desperate street fight against the North Vietnamese this side of the Perfume River.

"Danger close." Levi sighed. "Okay, spread out. Keep alert. I don't want us to go through that again."

32

PIANO MAN

Two Days Later

L EVI WAS DRIVEN TO HIS DECISION BY THE MEN'S HUNGER, lack of water, the distance behind enemy lines, and their lack of usefulness to 1st Battalion.

"We go tonight with the tide. Grab hold of some debris and float down the river. The enemy movement around here is going to completely compromise us. They're falling back, and it's only a matter of time before we have to fight for this building."

"I'm going to kill someone if I don't get something to eat pretty soon," Cannibal complained.

"Good motivation," Levi replied, "but we need water more. We haven't got a drop between us. And Charlie Company out there knows more than we do. The batteries are nearly dead. Got to conserve the juice. Can't do much good if we can't give radio communication."

Levi wasn't about to lose another man, but he didn't mention Paulos. He was frustrated. First Al and Tran, then Paulos. Miracles did happen in war, and it was possible that he was still alive, but it was more likely that he wasn't. And talking about team members getting zapped brought bad luck to a mission.

They took turns for the next five hours, alternating watch through the top-floor windows.

Henderson nudged Levi. "Bad guys," he whispered.

Levi looked out and spotted the NVA patrol below. "Okay, time to go. Bad guys on the ground floor," he said, shaking Chavez awake.

At that instant, the sound of M-60 machine-gun rounds rattled the building.

"Cannibal!" Levi shouted.

They ran down the corridor toward the stairs, Henderson leading the way with his M-60 in "rock and roll" hip-firing position. By the time they reached the stairs and started down, the firing stopped.

"All clear!" Cannibal shouted. "That'll teach 'em to make me miss dinner," he added, motioning the others to follow him down.

"Geez," Chavez breathed, seeing the four dead NVA sprawled out before him.

"Don't look so surprised, Ricky," Cannibal said. "I'm good at what I do. Sure hope these guys got some food on 'em." He opened the dead men's packs. "Look at this! These guys got some of our C-rats! Lima beans, peanut butter, and crackers. I can't believe it!"

"Okay, grab 'em," Levi said. "But we got to get down to the river. I wanted to wait until dark, but someone's gonna be checking on these guys when they don't hear from them." He turned to Henderson. "Let's hide these guys behind that wall. Come on."

They completed the task, then cautiously stepped outside and inched their way along the back wall of the building. A lower wall surrounded the factory, concealing them from anyone who might have been watching from the other side of the river.

Reaching the corner, Levi had to make a decision. "We got fifty yards to the water, minimum, and twenty yards to those houses over there. You guys see anyone around them when we came down?"

All three shook their heads.

"Okay. Let's make it to that house on the corner. We hide out for a couple of hours, then get down under that beat-up wharf and slide out of here on the river. Go!"

Levi watched as each man covered the open space, waited for Chavez to signal him the all-clear, then sprinted across and dove through the door. "You know, we're some lucky—"

"SOBs," Cannibal finished, smiling through a mouthful of lima beans mixed with peanut butter. "Mmmm . . . Peanut Butter–Lima Bean Surprise." Cannibal beamed.

"I'd rather die than eat that garbage," Chavez said.

Levi motioned to them. "Henderson, Cannibal, each of you take a window. Chavez, you get upstairs. Call me if you see anyone coming our way."

Posting himself at the front door, Levi stared at the sun through the smoky haze of the battle-caused fires. "Come on," he said, urging it to set, then spotted enemy movement across the river. "They're using the damn bridge," he swore, knowing his team should've been there to blow it by now. "They're reinforcing the Citadel. Call it in, Ricky."

When the sun finally surrendered the day, Levi motioned the others to the door. "Let's go," he whispered.

Each man took his turn running back across the open space to the first single-story building on the river. Levi watched, considering their position.

Down from the factory, a cluster of small shops and houses lining the street here. NVA doesn't know we're here. More dumb luck. Or is it?

God, if You can hear me, help me now, he prayed silently.

He ran to his men, crouched down, laid the coordinates map on his lap and studied it for a moment, then peered through a hole in the wall.

"What are you thinking?" Henderson asked, joining him. The enemy was digging in roughly two hundred meters away, on the opposite riverbank.

"That I should've listened to my dad," Levi replied. He pulled the binoculars from the pouch around his neck and took a closer look.

The Citadel was a thousand yards distant, a jewel of architecture that was about to be hammered by Marine gunners. A battalion of Marines would soon be charging into the fire against the well-entrenched and recalcitrant enemy making a suicidal attempt to hold on to the prestigious real estate.

They couldn't be allowed their victory. Now, Levi knew what he could do before they made their way to the river. He could order artillery fire on the opposite bank, and also behind them. "Kill two birds with one stone," he muttered.

"What?" Chavez asked.

"A ring of steel," Levi explained. "We hightail it for the river by calling in arty on the NVA's position across the river behind us, and also make it into these buildings in front of us. It should give us time to get to the water and discourage the bad guys from sticking their necks out to fire at us."

"What did he say?" Henderson asked.

"What did *who* say?"

"Your dad."

"Stay in school," Levi replied, then motioned them to gather around him. "On my count of three," he said. "Suppressing fire, Cannibal," he ordered. The big man nodded. "Lay it on heavy toward the rooftops over there." He pointed. "We pop smoke for cover when the artillery rounds start hitting, then hightail it to the buildings on the dock and into the water. How many smoke grenades we got?"

"Two," Chavez replied.

"I'm going over third man, Cannibal, then I'll pop the smoke and we'll all lay fire down so you can come across."

Everyone nodded once. They understood.

"Give me that radio." Levi took his coordinates from the map, then called in a Willie Peter round before ordering a fire for effect.

"Affirmative. Out," Levi responded after reaching fire command. "Sixty millimeter," he muttered.

"What did they say?" Chavez asked.

"No arty. Just mortars. Six-zero mortars. The best they could do."

Cannibal shook his head.

Chavez groaned. "Not too accurate sometimes. I've seen those guys miss on the marker rounds when I was in a combat platoon. They get nervous, or don't get the grid right. Lands right in your lap and you ain't there to tell 'em to adjust."

Levi folded up his map and slid it into his shirt. They looked at each other. They knew it was time. The four men stuck their closed fists out and gave each other good luck raps against their knuckles.

"I'll tell you what . . . when we get back, if those guys haven't found Tenny and Tran, I'm going MIA—stealing a boat and taking a trip back up the river. I'd rather fight in the jungle than this mess." His show of bravado was as much for himself as the others. His hands were shaking, palms slick with sweat.

This is it, a voice inside him said. *You will never hold Jenna in your arms again, feel her body against yours.* Levi tried to push the thoughts away as he prepared to move forward, into the open killing zone. Someone else was controlling all this, and he had no choice but to play it out.

"Here it comes," he whispered to the others, hearing what he thought was the hollow thud of the smoke round blasting out of the mortar tube. "Go!"

Cannibal opened fire with his M-60 as Levi, Henderson, and Chavez began their race across the deadly space, explosions, dirt, and hot metal piercing the air around them.

Levi fought off panic by focusing on the house in front of him, then dove through the door of the cinder-block structure like a rabbit ducking into its hole.

As he lay on the dirt floor, gasping for breath, his first thoughts were of Jenna. *Does she know what's happening? Did she get the telegram Major Thompson promised to send?* Right about now, he should've been getting off an airplane in Hawaii.

A blast just outside the door snapped him back to reality. When the dust settled, he crawled toward the opening, his mind racing with the probabilities. Where was Chavez? Was he wounded? Was Henderson hiding in the rubble somewhere?

Levi wiped the grit from his eyes and saw that the Prick-25 radio backpack lay just ahead in the street. Chavez must have dropped it. His eyes moved to the wall, looking for Cannibal, who should have been waiting there to come across. Nothing.

"God help me," Levi whispered. He was bleeding from a gash

above his left eye, and his ears were still ringing from the crushing explosion moments before.

He reached into his pack for a roll of gauze and quickly wrapped his head to keep the blood out of his eyes. Everything depended upon his knowing where he was, where the objective was, and getting his team back together.

Where are they?

He had to get that radio pack in the street.

Helmet's missing, he thought, then remembered he hadn't been wearing a helmet. That was before, with Mayfield. *I'm recon now,* he reminded himself. Ground pounders wear helmets. *I'm recon. . . .*

The radio was only a few yards away. If he went for it, he'd be hit by a sniper, or another mortar explosion, and be dead. He sat there staring at it, convinced now that Chavez was dead. Along with the others. *They'd all be in here by now if they made it across.*

His mind grew numb to the noise of the thundering around him. Everything went back to Jenna. Where it all began, with her and the music.

"Come in, Rocker One!" Their call signal. *I am Rocker One.* "Come in, Rocker One. This is . . ." Squelch sounds. Static came from the radio in the middle of the rubble-strewn street.

"Got to call. Get to the radio," he supplied to anyone who might hear his weakened voice. "Can't be this way. Not now," he assured himself. He crawled toward the open door once more.

He imagined he was a boy again, a boy at play in the sunny summers of the hilly central coast town he'd grown up in. The memories came easily, passing before him one by one like the frames of a movie. Mayfield, Tenny, and he were playing war on the beach. The good guys were winning.

"Come in, Rocker One!" the voice repeated again, more ur-

212 James Michael Pratt

gently this time. "Rocker One, this is Charlie Actual, over!"

His head was pounding, as if a vise had gripped it and was tightening slowly, squeezing his brain to darkness. He tried to focus on the PRC-25, reaching out dizzily, then fell back again, faint, aware, fighting loss of consciousness.

"Come in, Rocker One. Charlie Actual. Over!"

"I want to go home now," he whispered to the squawking box in the street, oblivious to his surroundings. He was sitting at his piano, and everyone was clapping.

"Piano man!" someone in his father's congregation shouted.

Levi stood up and bowed.

Pretty Jenna Bradley came up and took his hand. She kissed his cheek.

He blushed.

Then the room emptied. Jenna disappeared. Everything turned dark except for the soft voice that whispered, "Piano man."

33

STACCATO

Tran an ventured closer. he had seen the american Marines from a distance and, even in the shadowy darkness, recognized each one of them by their height, weight, the color of their hair. They were wearing headbands, camouflage to hide the stark whiteness of their skin in the jungle.

But this was no jungle, it was a way of fighting they hadn't practiced or prepared for. House to house, a lot of open deadman zones. Staccato bursts from submachine-gun fire, M-16 bursts on full automatic. Fifty-caliber rounds, enough to cut a man in half, raking walls, crumbling buildings. Grenades, violent clashes—dozens of small squad-size wars raged in those buildings as the North Vietnamese fought the approaching Marines of the 1st Battalion to the death of their last man.

He had made it to shore just hours before, by paddling down

the Perfume River in the enemy sampan he had discovered during that night's firefight upriver. He came with the body of Albert Tenny, who'd been shot in the back as they floated the sampan out to the middle of the water during their escape two nights before.

Tran had left Tenny's body in the small boat on the south shore. He had come back to Hue to search for his wife, his baby, and his relatives, only to find the streets had become a battlefield.

He hurried through the darkness, dressed in a dead NVA soldier's uniform. If the Communists caught him, he planned to act confused, explain that he'd gotten separated from his unit. But only if they caught him before he reached friendly lines. Once he was back with the marines, his recon team, he'd strip the NVA uniform off, right down to his shorts, and his former countrymen from the north would be the enemy again.

He slung the M-16 over his shoulder and dashed between houses, then along the low wall where he'd last seen them running for cover.

"It Tran," he called up from the window, keeping his voice barely above a whisper. When he heard a man groaning, he cautiously entered the house and found Levi. "It Tran's turn now," he comforted his friend. "I take you, Harper. No sweat." He lifted Levi up, dragged him out the door, and down to the riverbank. Levi was twice Tran's size, and the effort was considerable.

Staying close to the bank, in water up to his neck, Tran floated Levi down the river on his back. Each step in the muck of the river bottom was a struggle as he moved his human cargo closer to the sampan on the shoreline one kilometer away.

The night sky was still blazing. There was no letup in the deadly game. Tran's thoughts turned to his wife and child. Were they alive? Where had they gone? What direction? As soon as he delivered Levi to the Marine medics, he would go looking. But where would he begin?

He finally reached the sampan, where Albert's body lay, the smell of death strong and lingering over it. Levi's breathing was shallow, his pulse faint. Tran had no time to waste. He lifted his friend into the small, narrow craft beside Tenny. Levi's limp right arm swung freely across Albert's body in a surreal unconscious embrace of friendship. Tran pushed off into the water.

His only mission now was to save Levi Harper, the man who had saved him.

34

SYNCOPATED TIME

Present Day

Jack Santos rubbed his eyes, his vision blurry from reading journals around the clock. The life-and-death drama portrayed in them made him agonize not only for his father but for the loss of his father's friends.

Tenny, Chavez, Cannibal, Henderson, and Paulos. Their names were now somewhere on the wall at the Vietnam Memorial in Washington, D.C., names that would've meant nothing to him just days before. But now he realized the real impact of war. Those names represented people just like him—people with faces, loves, cares, and dreams. Those men not only lost their lives, but the chance to bring new lives into the world as fathers. With their deaths, an incalculable "what might have been" was lost to the world forever.

Jack brushed back his thick black hair, yawning as he leaned back in his chair. He turned his weary eyes to the window, gazing out at the lush grounds.

The first sand dune separating the property from the long shoreline was a stone's throw from the porch. The home had been built on the point just outside the cove that extended down to the shore on one side of the property and rose up on the opposite end, offering an elevated view of the bay and the magnificent sunsets. A man could easily lose himself here.

"Time to eat," he mumbled, realizing that his stomach complained. He was accustomed to staying up all night, composing or jamming with other musicians, so lost in his music that he often forgot to fuel his body. When he did get around to it, though, he made a point of eating health foods. His mother, the eternal hippie, had raised him on earthy, organic fare.

He wondered where he could get a good salad, maybe a wheat-grass sandwich with avocado and mayo. Probably nowhere. But a town like this would have plenty of seafood, maybe some salmon. He pulled himself out of the chair and glanced at his watch. A full night and day had passed while he'd absorbed himself in Levi Harper's story.

Slipping around the house to the front gate, Jack walked up the street to the first intersection, where a rusty sign hung over an old barnlike building. He could just make out the faded block letters. "Gus's Feed," it read. Jack smiled.

Over there, a voice inside his head whispered. *Over there is the boat tie-up, the main dock just beyond the wharf café. See it? That's where we kept the skiff. And going out through the wakeless zone, you just head her up north around the point and there's the bay and cove, the beach where we all played.*

"I see it," Jack replied to ghosts from the journals. As he made his way into the small commercial section of town, he felt as though he were seeing Paradise Bay for the first time, through Levi Harper's eyes.

A grocery store stood on the corner of Main Street, and he realized it must have been Grandfather Santos's store at one time. He looked through the window and saw a spotless deli case, an ancient soda chest, and wooden shelves for boxed and canned goods. *Some things never change*, he thought, seeing an old Wonder Bread sign that had to be twenty-five years older than he was. "Building strong bodies in twelve different ways," the sign read.

He chuckled as he noticed the stack of Twinkies dominating the pastries section of the cookies and candy aisle. *Probably left over from Grandpa's days.* He smiled.

He recalled from college chemistry how his fun-loving professor had asked the class to determine what the white, fluffy, pasty substance with a 500,000-year half-life in the petri dish was. Best guess won 100 percent on that week's quiz. Jack had joked that it probably came from a Hostess Twinkie. The professor pushed a desk alarm, and awarded him the "prize" for coming up with the correct answer. "Twinkies will be here long after man destroys himself." He'd laughed out loud, allowing the words to tumble from his lips unconsciously.

Jack was glad that he'd come. He'd been carried back in time, into Levi Harper's world. Perhaps being here was the only way to really understand the journals.

An old hippie in a 1967 Volkswagen van passed by. Jack recognized the year because he'd spent hours traveling with his mother in one, had practically grown up in it. Jack smiled and nodded at the long-haired man inside, then started walking again, deciding he'd get something to eat at the café down on the wharf.

He forgot about his hunger when he reached the corner of Wharf and Main and found himself walking up the steps to the door of an eighty-year-old church instead. He tried the doorknob. It opened. He realized that this was the kind of town that didn't need to keep locks on its holy places.

The main chapel was dark, lit only by the rays of the setting sun coming through the stained-glass windows, but he could see that it was being completely remodeled. The walls were being repainted, the flooring replaced, the pews sanded and revarnished. Curiosity satisfied, Jack stepped outside again and closed the door behind him. Grandfather Rex Harper's congregation met here, his mental voice announced, *I would have loved to have met him.*

The café was only a block away now. A middle-aged and diminutive Asian-looking man on the wharf was untying a small fishing boat and casting off. The man looked up and stared. Jack ventured a wave, the man returned the gesture and shoved away from the pier. Jack thought of Levi's friend Tran An, wondering what kind of contact the two men had while Levi was in the VA Hospital. He knew that Tran An had been there when his father, Levi, awakened from the coma. And he'd read that Tran had been invited to live here, had purchased a boat with his life's savings. No doubt, if Tran An were still alive, he'd be happy to be here in Paradise Bay, light years from his troubled past.

Beginning to feel the effects of two days without sleep, Jack slowed his pace as he reached the wharf and walked past the old cannery building on the right. The small commercial fishing boat, moored just moments before to the tie-downs, had already disappeared into the darkening sea. Odd, he thought, but he was tired, and a poor judge of distance at any rate.

Tran had disappeared at sea. It was a dark night when his fishing boat went down, Jack had learned from the journals.

"Imagination, the potent force behind my music," he recalled reading in one of Levi's journals. He must certainly be seeing things.

The open sea greeted him around the end of the building and pier. Jack leaned against the rails and stared at the horizon. The glorious amber fireball, beginning to turn iron red, would soon dip below the sea for the night. The vista was incredibly romantic, made for lovers.

He was grateful for this experience, wherever it might lead him. Somehow, it helped assuage his sense of failure with Claire, the only woman he'd ever really loved. Levi's own expressions of hopelessly losing his heart to Jenna made all the sense in the world now.

For the first time, Jack understood that a man couldn't think love away. It just was. And the pain of losing love, or losing at love, could only be eased with time.

He turned his back to the setting sun, walked the opposite length of the pier past the other side of the warehouse, and looked in through an open window. Building materials were stored neatly on pallets.

The last two days and nights had been so full of odd and unexpected answers to questions about his father, about this place, that he couldn't stop wondering about the fishing vessel and its caretaker he thought he'd seen just moments ago. He decided he'd ask the next local he ran into about it.

He reached the café, opened the door, and stepped inside. "Hello?" he called.

"Take a seat," a voice replied from the back. "We're just about ready to close, but I've still got coffee and apple pie."

"That'll be fine." Jack took a seat at the counter as the waitress walked into the room. "What happened to the fisherman who owns the old boat that docks just up from your café?" he asked.

She placed a slice of apple pie in front of him. "You tired, honey? You're seeing things," she said, setting a cup of coffee in front of him. "There's no boat down there. Hasn't been since . . ." She didn't finish the sentence, just shook her head.

"Guess I am tired," Jack muttered. She was probably right, though. He'd been in a whirlwind for the past week. She simply hadn't seen the boat dock, or his mind was so exhausted and filled with war stories and boat rescues, he was simply seeing things.

"What's a good-looking young man like you doing wandering around this ghost town?" she went on. "Are you in real estate? A lot of them been poking their noses around here lately. And it's about time, too. Why no one's seen the potential of Paradise Bay before now is beyond me."

"I'm here on family business," Jack replied, then took a sip of his coffee and went on. "How do you manage to keep this place running? Seems pretty dead around here."

"I own it. It used to belong to my folks, so there's no mortgage. I think that's what my boyfriend Bob likes best about me." She laughed, checking her hair in the pie-case glass.

"I haven't eaten all day, and this is probably the best pie I've ever had." Jack smiled, downing the last bite.

"Thanks. I call it Paradise Apple. And if I do say so myself, it's the best on this coast. Vacationers, truckers, and folks from nearby towns come here just for a slice. And the view, I guess." She nodded toward the sunset. "I wouldn't live anywhere else. Been here all my life. Played in the cove, right over there," she pointed. "One of the first to get a two-piece bathing suit. Boy, did I catch it from my parents. . . ."

"Did you know Levi Harper?" Jack asked, excited to know she'd grown up here.

Her smile vanished. "I'm not selling Mr. Harper out," she said angrily. "He's the best thing that happened to this place in years. He was going to rebuild it—" She stopped herself abruptly.

Jack was taken aback by her mood change. "No harm meant," he apologized. "I've just been reading some stuff about life here in the sixties. About Mr. Harper, Jenna Bradley, and a guy named Albert Tenny."

She said nothing, still glaring at him.

He tried another approach. "I'm a musician, and I'm here to get some peace and quiet so I can compose. I've always been curious about people and places, and this place is right out of the fifties and sixties. I'm just curious about what it was like back then, what the people were like."

Her mood transformed and she came alive again, as if he'd hit on her favorite subject. She poured herself a cup of coffee, pulled up a stool, and sat down beside him. Her tone was buoyant as she described the days of innocence and pleasure the people of Paradise Bay had found while the rest of the world marched headlong into the torment of war, sex, drugs, and rock and roll.

"The big companies came in and took over the fishing business," she explained. "When the cannery dried up, the town just died away. There were no jobs here anymore, so people were forced to look elsewhere. A few hung on, but just a few. Things are changing again, though. Before long, we'll be as important as Pismo Beach and Morro Bay. You wait and see." She glanced at her watch, then stood up and switched off the lights. "Now, scoot," she said. "WWF night on TV. But you be sure and come back."

"You can count on it. And by the way, my name's Jack Santos." He extended his hand as he stood up.

"Santos? As in Carol Santos?" She stepped outside with him,

studying his face, then slapped him on the back. "I know who you are now!"

"Good," Jack laughed. "Because I've been wondering all my life."

"You're her kid. I can see it all over your face. And him, too." She paused, then added uneasily, "But I guess you don't want to talk about that."

"About what?"

"Well . . ." she began, whispering as if afraid of being over-heard. "What happened between Carol and . . . you know, one of those names you mentioned earlier."

"Oh, that!" Jack smiled, relieved. "I know all about that."

She relaxed, as if suddenly freed from some invisible restraint. "I promised not to talk about it, way back. Carol was a good friend of mine, and when she left town for the last time, she swore me to secrecy. But here you are, so I guess it's no secret anymore, is it? You're their kid, right?"

"Tell you what. I'll make you a deal, okay?" Jack leaned forward as if to share a secret.

"Sure. Anything for Carol's boy."

"What's your name?" Jack asked.

"Fran. Fran Swartz."

"Okay, here's the deal, Fran. You don't tell a soul about me, not even old Bob. And if you keep up your end of the deal, I'll see that your pies are packaged and sold all over the country. We'll call them 'Fran's Paradise Apple Pies.' How's that sound?"

"You could do that? I'd be famous if you did that!"

"I know lots of people in Los Angeles, including a man who owns several restaurants. I'll bet he'd take them as fast as you can make them."

"You've got a deal!" She laughed, pumping his hand. "So how long do we keep this little secret between us?"

"Until I get moved into the old homestead, the one up on—"

She put up a hand, giggling like a schoolgirl. "Don't say another word. I know the house. It's the one that belonged to you know who."

Jack smiled, shaking his head. "You're good, Fran. You'd make a great detective. Well, I'd better get back up to the house, catch up on some sleep."

"Need a ride?" Fran pointed to a white '70 Chevy Impala with gray primer patches.

"Thanks, but I think I'll walk. Take in the breeze."

"Suit yourself. Good night, Jack."

"Good night, Fran."

He turned the corner in front of the wharf, then froze at the sight of the empty pier. Fran had told him he must've been seeing things when he asked her about the old boat. Could he really have been that tired?

He shook it off and let his thoughts drift back to the things he'd read in the journals. If only he had Claire to talk to . . .

Jack forced himself back to reality, looking around him as he started walking again. The place seemed a beat off rhythm from the rest of the world. *Reality*, he laughed inwardly.

A Simon and Garfunkel song was playing on some lover's radio up the beach, near the sand dunes.

He thought for a moment of Claire. How much he had loved her, how he had sung this song to her. She loved Emily Dickinson, just as the song proclaimed.

These had been Levi's borders. Carol, his mother, had lived here, too, but Levi had left this place, spent nearly one year in Vietnam, and returned here as a middle-aged man. Within this small place on the California map were indeed the borders that had defined how Levi saw life, what he loved and lost.

" . . . in syncopated time . . ." The song finished.

Syncopated time, a half-beat held just a little longer.

He had seen a lot of things tonight. Unexplainable things. A man, or the ghost of a man. A boat, or a hallucination of his mind.

If I ever own this town, I'm going to rename it, he told himself. *And the sign will read, "Caution: You are now entering Paradox Bay."*

The perfect place for those who knew the secret, as Levi Harper did, of playing life's experiences in syncopated time.

35

LOST TIME

Jack Santos awakened to the squawking of sea gulls and the crashing of the surf on the stone jetties down near the wharf.

It was his third day in Paradise Bay, but last night had been his first night of sleep. He tried to remember what day of the week it was as he pulled the lace curtain aside and caught the first rays of the sun glinting on the ocean.

He had decided to use the guest bedroom on the second floor, uncomfortable with the idea of disturbing the master bedroom. Levi and Jenna's clothes and personal belongings were still there, as if awaiting their return.

Upstairs were five bedrooms. The one he'd chosen was as large as the master, with a balcony that boasted a view of the coast, all the way from the bay up to the sandy beach at Paradise Point.

A small lighthouse stood perched upon the rocky outcropping of the point, the highest elevation along this part of the coast. The lighthouse had served as sentry for years, but now that the fishing wharfs were abandoned, it was no longer needed as a guide for the maritime craft in dark and forbidding weather.

Jack stretched, scratched his head, and glanced at the alarm clock. He'd set it for 6:30 A.M., half an hour from now. He let his head hit the pillows again. *Who had slept in this room as a child,* he wondered. *Levi, Jeff, or Karen Sue? What did siblings do together?* Jack couldn't imagine.

He was sure he would have liked it, though. Had he been granted a more perfect life, these rooms would be very familiar to him by now.

A sense of happiness seemed to hover here, a tangible warmth in the cleanliness, the furnishings, and the pastel color of the walls. He could almost hear its former inhabitants, their conversation, laughter, and tears. The simple things family life was filled with.

Enough ghostly voices filled Jack's head to make him believe that this turn-of-the-century Victorian actually had a soul.

"Talk to me, Levi Harper," he asked out loud. "What do you want of me?"

Live here, the voice in his weary mind replied. *Your audience will come to you. Music is magic, remember?*

The place was an artist's dream, but it was also a lonely environment. *Great music is magic,* Jack replied to himself. *Not the stuff I do.*

Great music comes at a price. Sacrifice and convenience don't coexist. When has convenience ever created anything extraordinary?

"This is absurd," Jack voiced. He switched off the alarm before it had a chance to ring and headed into the bathroom for a shower.

He pulled the glass door shut and turned the water pressure to high. He stood underneath it, letting it beat against his head, hoping it would bring him back to reality. He'd talked out loud to himself before, but now he was actually hearing voices. Worse, he was enjoying it.

He vowed to stop listening to the voices and be clinical about reading the journals. But just as easily as he made the promise, a question popped into his mind. *What am I going to do with this place? Sell it, or live in it for awhile?* After all, it would be legally his as soon as the attorney for the estate processed the paperwork.

Jack pushed the question aside as he stepped out of the shower. He threw on a pair of jeans and a T-shirt, then slipped into his Nikes. Time to watch the sun come up, he told himself. Maybe catch Fran down at the café and get a hot breakfast. He could use some real food right now.

He hurried down to the wharf, only to find the café dark and locked up. Disappointed, he decided to walk out to the end of the pier before heading back to the house. Maybe he'd walk back on the beach, through the water in his bare feet. The tide was low, the sea calm, and he'd always enjoyed being near the surf as it gently lapped upon the shore.

Standing beside the wood railing, he watched the fog burn off as the sun came over the coastal mountains, warming his back. The gulls swooped into the water, catching their breakfast. A small fishing vessel floated in the distance. He could make out the outline of a man standing on the upper deck. He looked away for a moment. The boat disappeared as quickly as it had appeared. Jack smiled, remembering the boat from the night before. *Imagination, seeds of song,* he mused, reciting a line from Levi's journal.

Time to get back to my history studies, he thought. He started walking back the length of the pier, then turned around again at the sound of a ship's horn. The same boat he'd seen a moment ago was now heading in the opposite direction, moving slowly up the coast.

Jack made a dash for the street, then raced across the pavement to the beach, searching the fog two hundred yards out. The boat had vanished again. He slowed to a walk, shaking his head in disbelief. His instincts were telling him that the boat was the same one he'd seen down at the pier the night before. But according to Fran, that wasn't possible.

Right now, though, he was hungry. He'd go back to the house and whip up some scrambled eggs and toast. He could surely cook well enough to do that. Once he'd eaten, he'd bury himself in the journals again, take a well-deserved nap later in the afternoon, then come back to the café this evening for a good meal.

He smiled at the cliché that came to mind as he considered everything he'd read, seen, and heard the past two and a half days. "Something fishy in Paradise . . ." If this was a normal place, a normal time, he might be convinced he was losing his mind. But this was Paradise Bay.

He opened the parlor door to the sunlit room, wondering what it might have been like if he'd had the chance to grow up here. Something about this place made him feel that, with just the right measure of belief, he could walk through one of these doors and find the whole Harper family gathered in front of the television, enjoying an evening together.

He went to the kitchen to make his breakfast and found himself thinking about Lin An. He was intrigued by her natural intellect and warmed by the tenderness with which she cared for Levi. He considered calling her, using the excuse that he had questions about her father and the boat he'd seen. After all, she fit so perfectly into this place, into this story.

"Lin An." He paused. "A lovely name." His mind had wandered to the stories, to Tran, and back to Levi. After he'd read more of the journals, then he'd give Lin a call, see how Levi was doing, ask if they could meet, have dinner—and discover who Lin An really was.

36

CONCERTO FOR THE DEAD

Veterans' Hospital, Los Angeles

I WANT YOU TO TAKE A LOOK AT SOMETHING," DR. JENKINS said. He pushed a folder across his desk to Lin An. "It's a case study that was recently published in *JAMA*, conducted by a well-known physician at Jaffa University Medical Hospital in Israel. It contains data from a two-year period in which three separate groups of twenty people each, all either in fetal or walking catatonic-like conditions, were compared. Group one was played Mozart twenty-four hours a day, seven days a week, over that period of time. Group two was played a combination of contemporary, baroque, and classical. No music was played for group three at all."

Lin An pored over the information. "This is remarkable," she said after a few moments. "Five of the twenty patients in group one actually emerged from a state of complete catatonia!"

Jenkins smiled. "I also have something else I think you'll find very interesting." He slid a manila envelope toward her. "This is from your father's personnel folder. Apparently, he'd asked the nurses to save his notes. It's in Vietnamese, and it was written over a three-year period."

"Notes? My father was just a custodian here." She held her breath as she opened the folder and began thumbing through the small stack of handwritten papers inside.

"He was a friend of Levi Harper's, wasn't he?"

"A very close friend. My father wanted to work here at the hospital from the time he left the refugee camp in the Philippines and came to the States, back in 1979. He offered to work for free, said he owed a debt to Mr. Harper. I wouldn't be here today if Mr. Harper hadn't risked his life to save him."

Jenkins pointed to the papers. "Can you translate them? I have to admit I'm more than a little curious."

Lin picked one written on Marine Corps stationery, with their globe-and-anchor logo and the motto *Semper Fidelis*—Always Faithful—at the top. She began to read. Her eyes moistened as she read the Vietnamese handwriting of her gentle father. She stopped several times to regain composure.

Each note contained a record of visits to Levi's bedside, from the day her father started his graveyard shift in 1995 until Levi came out of his coma in 1998—exactly three years to the month after her father had begun his surreptitious effort described in the note.

"A covert operation, wouldn't you agree?" Jenkins laughed.

Lin An started to cry as she read the last one. "It says, 'Levi awake. He called me by name. My prayers answered. My mission is complete.' "

Dr. Jenkins allowed Lin An to take it all in before interrupting her mental wanderings. Her eyes were closed and she clutched the notes tightly; he knew she was alone with her father.

"Thank you," she said. "I'm sorry. I shouldn't be so emotional." Her lips quivered in an attempt to form a smile.

"You should be proud. He really was one of a kind, wasn't he?"

"Uh-huh." She sniffled. "I miss him. May I keep these?"

"Of course."

"What does this mean? Does it have something to do with the Israeli music case study?"

"Well, you must admit, it is pretty impressive. We have a verified case study conducted by a hospital attendant who could barely speak English. He played Mozart and other classical melodies to Mr. Harper two years before the study in Israel began. What do you think we should do with this information?"

"I know what I'd like to do," Lin An replied, wiping her eyes. "I'd like to clinically verify it—reproduce the experiment. But I'd also like it to be a secret between us until it's complete."

"Absolutely. But are you also going to include the prayers?"

"Sure. I think I remember a few of them." Lin An laughed nervously, then grew pensive. "I loved Father so much . . . whatever made you look in his file?"

"Actually, it's a little strange. Personnel files are kept for several years after an employee leaves. What's uncommon in this case is that one of the nurses called me from her station yesterday to tell me that a young man, a Marine, had dropped this file off. I immediately called the clerk in personnel to find out if she'd given the file to any unauthorized person, and she didn't have a clue what I was talking about. When she went to check, your father's file was missing."

"Maybe he was an old coworker of my father's. Maybe he

knew about Mr. Harper and had kept the file for safekeeping. I mean, there was quite a bit of publicity about the case. But why would a coworker have my father's personnel file?"

"We don't know. But this *is* your father's file. It even includes his personal identification information, including his photo." Jenkins stood up, smiling at Lin. "Anyway, you should be very proud."

"I am." She beamed.

"Then let's get to work." He escorted her to the door. "Oh, one more question. Did you know of any friends who . . ." He paused. "Never mind. It isn't important."

"What?"

"Stranger things have happened than old files showing up in odd places at appropriate times. Some of the veterans who knew Levi when he was bedridden before mentioned that, in a similar way to the nurse's experience, a young man in a Marine Corps uniform had passed through the recreation hall the day this file showed up. I know this is way out in left field, but do you have a family member or close friend of your father's who might have been in possession of some of his personal information? Perhaps sent a son or someone else they trusted, a Marine, to deliver the file?"

Lin An thought for a moment, then shook her head.

"Well, that's that. We must have a dozen employees with military sons or relatives. I'll leave that part of it alone now. Go ahead and buy any amount of Mozart you think you'll need, and we'll reimburse you. In the meantime, I'll make a call to Israel and find out if any particular pieces were played more frequently. And we'll get started on our secret experiment." He smiled and held out his hand.

"Thank you, Dr. Jenkins."

Lin An returned to her office. She needed time alone to digest what this meant. And not only for what she'd just learned about her father's role in Levi Harper's miraculous awakening.

One man, a Marine, had saved her father and a young child long ago. And now this same man, Levi, lay waiting for the child—herself—to follow her father's example and save him once again. She was being pulled into the center of Levi Harper's debate with the gods of fate over his life.

She also felt a strange new light filling her, and it was somehow connected to a man named Jack Santos.

37

CRESCENDO

Jack finished the breakfast dishes, cleared the table, and sat down in front of the journals.

He hungrily consumed page after page of an era lived in black and white. The '50s had been a mixed bag of new gadgets and old ways, full of surprises as the country emerged from the shadow of World War II and an economic depression of global proportions.

He was surprised at the history he was learning from a personal journal. Like a good novelist weaving his way through periods of time that history classes never fully explored, Levi Harper had unwittingly offered a glimpse into a world lived decades before.

After a full day of reading, he planned to visit with Fran at the café and try to get one of the bizarre experiences he was having in Paradise Bay figured out—the disappearing boat. But discovering his father's identity and learning that he was still alive, then inheriting his estate, had probably been enough of a strain to induce hallucinations. And there were voices Fran could never help him with—voices from the journals that he'd have to work out for himself.

Jack also realized that he was gaining a wealth of knowledge from the journals, subtle truths that Levi Harper seemed incapable of *not* declaring. The pages of his diaries were sprinkled with philosophies, the kind of things sons usually heard from their fathers as they grew up. A piece of life he would never have understood was comprehensible after all. He had a father, and he had his father's thoughts, his soul.

He picked up where he had left off, thinking about the statement Levi had made about the dreams that kept him company for three decades. During a sleep of Rip van Winkle proportions, his father had been mercifully entertained with the visions of the night. No ticking clocks had stirred him, alerted him to loss, beckoned him to duty. Only sleep, dreams, and a boy frozen in an aging, but to Levi, a twenty-year-old Marine's body.

38

A TEMPO

Spring 2002

TIME WAS SO ELUSIVE TO ME IN THAT DREAMING STATE. I couldn't measure it, nor did I care to. Time was simply now. I was aware of the music constantly played for me. And I thought I was with my Marine buddies because they visited me.

I may have lost time as we know it in the waking world, but I gained something else in the place of dreams. I now have knowledge of things being a certain way without evidence of the facts. My senses are keen and highly intuitive. They flourished even when deep slumber forbade me from mingling with others in the living world.

Perhaps being dead to this world for so long made me alive to the things that the spirit creates. Everything has two creations, after all. Perhaps because creative sensitivity is aroused and cultivated in the absence of distractions, my inner musical and native knowledge about life peaked during those years of sleep.

Awakening had its unique challenges and lessons, as well. I soon found myself a young man in an old soldier's body.

February 10, 1998

The Vietnamese hospital aide was taking him for a walk, his customary evening stroll down the corridor to the recreation hall, just far enough to tone his aging muscles and give his respiratory tract a workout.

He was in his thirtieth year at the West Los Angeles Veterans' Hospital. His fifty-first birthday was today, February 10th, the date of his family's yearly visit for twenty of those thirty years. He was not aware, in the sense of being alert to questions and capable of answering them, but his catatonia did not prevent Levi from mild exercise, a short walk, sitting up, standing on his own. He was literally a "sleep walker."

Levi's father had passed away after a stroke, and Levi's in-heritance—the Harper genetic propensity for stroke—had been partially responsible for this catatonia at the age of twenty, while he was recovering from the blast in a military hospital in Japan. The mortar explosions had killed his friends and nearly killed him.

Tran An had served as his aide for three years now. The strange friendship that had compelled the aging Vietnamese man to seek this employment also brought him here today, Sunday, his usual night off. But it was Levi's birthday, and Tran had decided to bring him a gift, a tape he'd made of all the piano greats from the latter part of the twentieth century.

His daughter, though born in Vietnam, was now an American in every way. She knew the popular American music backward and forward, so he'd asked her to tape the famous piano artists from the '50s to the present. She'd recorded them all, including many newer artists: Billy Joel, Elton John, Yanni, Jim Brickman, Kurt Bestor, Sam Cardon, Paul Cardall, Clyde Bawden, David Tolk, and John Schmidt, among the many.

And the contemporary composers of so many soundtracks— John Williams, Ross Williams, Randy Edleman, Kenneth Cope, Jay Richards, Rob Gardner, and others—were mixed to bring a startling array of soothing talent to Levi's bedside.

Lin An had finished her residency program at UCLA Medical School, and the veterans' hospital was her first choice of medical assignment. Like her father, she, too, felt the need to serve, somehow pay her debt for her family's freedom from the Communist terror so many years before.

Tran An was playing the tape in a small boom box as he and Levi made their way to the recreation hall. Finally reaching it, Tran helped him sit down on the piano bench to rest.

That's when it happened.

"Well, if that don't beat all!" the nurse on duty exclaimed. "Hey, everybody! He's awake! He's playing the piano!"

Some came because they thought there was an emergency, others because of the simple melodies they heard, played in perfection as his fingers fluttered over the keys of the tired-looking Steinway someone had donated to the hospital. Old and young alike, veterans stood and listened. The harmony of carefully chosen chords plucked the piano strings in orchestral timing. He finished with the words of a song no one had ever heard before:

> *Paradise girl, hair aflame and chains of pearl,*
> *She danced to music soft and sweet, wind beneath her*
> *feet.*

Paradise girl, hair aflame and chains of pearl,
Pretty Paradise girl . . .

The piano grew softer, quieter, each note savored like a light dessert after a feast. When it ended, he turned and smiled, though haggard and unaware of his appearance.

"I know you, don't I?" he asked, looking up at the aged Vietnamese fisherman.

The small man nodded, too moved to speak for a moment. "You numba one, GI," he finally said.

A puzzled look of recognition crossed Levi Harper's face.

The veterans applauded. He bowed. A nurse came forward, and Tran slipped quietly to the back as people gathered around Levi.

The nurse nervously called the nearest nursing station and then slipped beside Levi on the bench. "Hi, Mr. Harper. My name is Nurse Hollins. That was very beautiful. I've never heard that song before. What's it called?"

"Uh . . . 'Jenna's Theme.' I, uh . . . played it when she moved."

The doctor on call for the night walked in. He listened intently as Nurse Hollins explained how Levi's awakening had taken place.

"Mr. Harper, my name is Dr. Jenkins," he said, walking up to him. "Let's go back to your room, shall we? I'd like to check you over."

"Okay," Levi replied in a childlike voice, as Jenkins and the nurse helped him to his feet. They walked out of the room and started down the corridor. "I'm hungry," he complained, more alert now. "How come my legs are so wobbly?"

Nurse Hollins answered. "What would you like, Mr. Harper?"

"There's always room for Jell-O!" Levi laughed. "My friend

Albert likes Jell-O. Do you have red Jell-O? Albert calls it Commie Jell-O." His words were coming easier with each sentence.

"Sure, sweetie. Red Jell-O, and lots of it," she called out to a
staff member down the hall. Dr. Jenkins and other staff hurried
into the room to prepare Mr. Harper for the inevitable—tests,
and the revelation that his awakening was to a world that was
not what he thought.

His Jell-O arrived, a large bowl with whipped cream on top,
just as Nurse Hollins was settling him back into his bed. "Oh,
boy!" Levi pointed. "Jell-O!"

"Anything you want, Mr. Harper," she laughed. "You've been
away for some time now, you know."

"I have?"

39

ENCORE

He had fallen asleep immediately, and the members of the staff took turns recording him throughout the night, the vital signs, his alertness, watching for any sign that he was falling back into a comalike sleep. His rest was hailed as completely normal by every shift the next morning.

Dr. Jenkins felt it would be unwise to give Levi too much information so soon. Telling him too suddenly about the loss of thirty years would also alert him to other losses, like deceased family members or a girlfriend who was now married with children. In short, a world totally distinct and foreign from the one he'd last known. Giving him too much to swallow at once could endanger the fragile ecology of his awakened state. Better to give him the facts in small portions, see how he handled one thing at a time.

Specialists were brought in to begin a series of extensive neu-
rological tests. They would check complete body functions, re-
actions to certain stimuli, and memory.

Exhausted after all the poking and prodding, Levi was resting
when Albert appeared. He smiled down at Levi from the foot
of the bed. He pointed his index finger at Levi, then held it
straight up. *You're number one*, it meant.

"Oh, Albert. It's so good to see you," Levi murmured. "I'm
kind of confused. I've guess I've been recuperating for awhile,
huh?"

Albert, wearing his dress blues, smiled and nodded.

"So how are the rest of the guys?" Levi asked, his voice gaining
strength. "Chavez, Cannibal, Paulos, Henderson. Are they coming?"

"They'll be along when you're ready," Albert smiled.

"You sure are dressed spiffy. What's up?"

"Oh, just a special-duty assignment. Got a new guy coming
into our unit."

"Hoo-rah!" Levi laughed. "Man, were we ever something to
behold. All cammied out, war paint on our faces, rocking and
rolling to 'Woolly Bully' with that crazy Huey pilot . . . what's
his name? The one with the handlebar mustache?"

"Huish," Albert replied.

"Yeah, that's it. Huish. We called him 'Huey,' after the type
of chopper he flew, right?"

"Right," Albert smiled.

"Boy, he sure loved his bird. I forgot what he named it."

"Helen," Albert reminded him. "His wife's name."

"Helen," Levi repeated, smiling at the return of memory. "*Helen's Huey* he called it. Remember?"

Albert nodded.

"He sure took it personal when he found a bullet hole in it." He paused for a moment, then asked, "You ever see old Huey after that rescue on the river east of Hue?"

"Every now and then." Albert smiled again, then turned serious. "Look, Levi. You've been through a lot, and I've gotta go now. I was given leave for a few minutes to come by, drop some paperwork off, and tell you not to worry about what the doctors say. Just trust and believe in God, the way your dad taught you back in Paradise Bay—all those Sundays in church you hated so much."

"I don't understand," Levi said, his mind going fuzzy.

"You will. You'll understand one line at a time. *Semper fi*, buddy. And take each day as it comes. One line and one day at a time. Finish your music, Levi. I'll be back when you've written your last note."

Levi blinked, and Albert was gone.

Puzzled, Levi closed his eyes and relived their visit. It felt so good to be back in the States, and having Albert there when he woke up had been a pleasant surprise. He sure missed Jenna, though. *But I don't want her to see me like this*, he thought.

He remembered blacking out in that firefight in Hue, just after the explosion. He'd lost sight of Cannibal, Chavez, and Henderson somehow, but they must've made it out okay. After all, Tenny had just said they'd be coming by as soon as he was ready.

Levi put a hand to his face and realized he needed a shave. He sat up on the edge of the bed, then gingerly tested his balance and made his way to the bathroom. He looked around on the sink for his shaving mug and brush, a can of lather, and a single-edge blade, but nothing was there except a new toothbrush and tube of toothpaste.

Levi looked up, reaching for the mirrored medicine cabinet door, then cried out in shock. "Hey, somebody help me! Please!" He crouched down on the floor, arms around his knees. *The man in the mirror looks like Dad, only older. It's just my imagination. A bad dream.*

Slowly, he pulled himself up, grabbing the porcelain sink basin to steady himself. He looked in the mirror again, then ran out of the bathroom to press the call button, his heart racing.

Nurse Hollins hurried into the room. "What's wrong, Mr. Harper? Are you all right?"

"No, I'm not all right!" he shouted. "What happened to my face? I look so . . . so old!" He pulse quickened. He steadied himself by sitting on the bed. He reached up to his face and ran his fingers nervously over the stubble. His breath picked up to that of a sprinter's on a dead run. In his eyes the nurse read of his search for an answer to the illusion the mirror must have created.

Nurse Hollins sat down and put an arm around him, patting his shoulder as if she were comforting a child.

"What happened?" he asked, voice cracking and giving way to emotion now. "Why hasn't my family come?" he asked. "I want to see my mom and dad, Jeff and Karen Sue."

Before she could decide how to reply, Dr. Jenkins came in, followed by the staff psychologist and the chaplain.

"Hello, Levi," Jenkins said, as though unaware that something was wrong. "How are you today?"

"Not good."

"Well, let's see what we can do. This is Dr. Royal, chief psychologist, and Lt. Commander Ronald Ringo, a chaplain with the U.S. Navy. They've stopped by to see you."

"Hello, Levi," the chaplain spoke up. "Mind if I sit down? I'll just pull this chair up closer so we can visit."

Levi sighed. "Suit yourself."

"I think I'll sit down, too," Dr. Royal interjected. "So tell me, what has you so upset?"

"I look like an old man. What happened to me?" Levi looked at each of them, eyes pleading.

"What do you think happened?" Royal replied, crossing his arms.

"I don't know. I remember a blast, that's all. Plastic surgery, maybe?"

"You know, your focus is really improving. When you really want to say something, you speak perfectly, clearly." Royal whispered something to Jenkins, jotted down a few notes, then added, "Good for you, Levi."

"So what happened to me? Where am I?"

"You're in West Los Angeles Veterans' Hospital," Chaplain Ringo answered. "You've been recovering for quite awhile. Levi, I know this may be difficult for you to understand, but . . ." The chaplain couldn't seem to find the words. He and the doctors had tried to prepare for this moment, deciding it might be best for a man of God to break the news, but he was finding it harder than he'd expected.

"How long?" Levi looked directly at Jenkins.

Dr. Royal spoke up. "Mr. Harper," he said in a calming tone, "you've been in a coma. Sometimes shock sets in after an injury occurs, and a coma is how the body protects the brain from further trauma. You sustained shrapnel wounds to the head, then a stroke. You were in critical condition when you were finally brought in. You weren't expected to live."

"That was a number of years ago, Levi," Chaplain Ringo said. "I was there, too. I was a Marine, like you."

"You were a chaplain in Vietnam? How many years ago?"

Tears ran down Levi's face. Nurse Hollins, a large, maternal-looking woman, put her arm around him, offering reassurance as she stroked his hair.

"No, I wasn't a chaplain back then. Just a Marine lance corporal." Chaplain Ringo had answered only half of the question, still trying to find the right way to tell Levi exactly how many years had passed.

"So how long has it been?" Levi pressed. "I can handle it." He remembered Albert's advice to take it one line at a time, one day a time.

The psychologist intervened. "How old do you think you are, Mr. Harper?"

"I don't know . . . the shrapnel must have messed up my face, then I had a stroke, so I've been in a coma for maybe a couple of years? I'm probably twenty-three now?"

Chaplain Ringo looked down at the floor and shook his head. "We've been debating about how to tell you this, Levi. May I ask you to trust me?"

Levi hesitated. "Sure, I guess. Albert told me I should."

"Albert's your friend?"

"Yes. We've known each other since we were kids. He was team leader in my recon squad."

Chaplain Ringo hoped that the shock he felt on hearing the word "recon" wasn't registering on his face. His mind raced back to the time when he was a member of Marine Force Recon, recalling the face of the young musician he'd met at Recondo School during the war. China Beach. His friend Albert Tenny. The drinks they had together before going separate ways.

"Would you like to see your family, Levi?" he asked tenderly.

"Yes, please. When can they come?"

"Jeff's on his way now. We expect him tomorrow."

"Great. How about Mom and Dad, and Karen Sue? Has anyone called Jenna? I need to know. I don't want her seeing me like this, but she needs to know. She waited for me, right?"

"Please, Levi," Chaplain Ringo said. "Let's just take this one thing at a time. We'll explain more once Jeff arrives, okay?"

"Yeah, sure. Okay. But I need my family . . . and Jenna."

"I'm going to go in a minute, Levi, but I want to ask you a question first. Do you believe in God?" Chaplain Ringo had last talked of God and life with this man thirty years ago, when his own beliefs were being tested. At the time, he wasn't sure he could unleash the sword of death as a Marine much longer, and wondered if he should serve God some other way instead. *So now we've come full circle*, he thought as he waited for Levi's reply.

"Yes, of course I believe in God," Levi said, brightening. "Bet my dad would like to hear that, wouldn't he?"

The chaplain nodded. "Do you also believe in His plan for us?"

"Yes."

"Then keep that in mind when your brother gets here, okay? What's the Marine Corps motto?"

"*Semper fidelis*. You know, you were a Marine. Funny, Albert said the same thing today."

"So Albert visited you today?"

Levi nodded.

"And what does *semper fidelis* mean?"

"Always faithful."

"Then *semper fi*, Levi. Now, you get some food, some rest, and let Nurse Hollins give you that shave. I'll be back tomorrow, okay?" The chaplain stood up and went to the door, then turned around. "Oh, and one other thing, Levi. Hoo-rah."

"Hoo-rah," Levi echoed, confused. "I know you, don't I?"

Chaplain Ringo's voice tightened. He couldn't speak. He nodded, saluted, and walked out the door.

40

JEFFREY

CHAPLAIN RINGO ARRIVED BEFORE THE OTHERS. "HOW ARE you feeling tonight, Levi?" he asked as he sat down and opened his Bible to Ezekiel.

"I feel okay. Is my brother here yet?"

"Yes, he's here. But he's getting a report from the doctors right now. Can I read you something from the Bible before he comes in?"

Levi nodded.

" 'Son of man,' " Ringo began. " 'Behold, I take away from thee the desire of thine eyes with a stroke: yet neither shalt thou mourn nor weep, neither shall tears run down.' " He looked up at Levi. "That promise, made thousands of years ago by God, seems to be made for this day. I believe He had you in mind."

"Oh," Levi replied, confused.

"We're going to bring Jeffrey in now, okay?"

"Sure," Levi grinned. "I can't wait to see him. I'll bet he's all grown up. Is he in the military, too?"

"No, he's not in the military." Ringo sighed heavily, then went on. "Levi, your brother is older than you think. And so are you."

"How much older?" he asked nervously.

"For now, let's just say we're living in a different world than the one you knew in 1968, when you went into a coma. I was a boy at the time, an eighteen-year-old Marine rifleman."

Levi paled, memories fighting their way to the surface of his mind. "Hey! Wait. I knew someone with your name. I just can't remember where," he said, fighting off panic. "No! It can't be! You're old! This is just a bad dream." He panted heavily, his eyes closed. *Maybe they will all just go away and I'll wake up, and it will be okay.*

"Remember what I told you about God's plan, Levi? That everything will be all right if you keep that in mind? Jeffrey's here now. Let me bring him in."

Levi finally nodded through tears he fought off by rubbing his palms heavily against his closed eyes. Ringo got up and stepped out the door. He returned a few seconds later with Nurse Hollins, Dr. Jenkins, Dr. Royal, and a man Levi didn't recognize.

"Where's my brother?" he asked, gazing at the group of people so new to his life.

The stranger stepped forward, a stout middle-aged man in a dark blue suit, his voice choked with emotion. "Hello, Levi. It's Jeff, Levi. Your little brother."

Levi stared for a long moment, trying to understand. *How could this be possible? Jeff had been a senior in high school the last time he saw him.* "Albert was here yesterday," he finally said.

"He told me I might not understand a lot of things." Levi smiled weakly. "I guess he was right."

Jeffrey returned the smile, but tears were running freely now. "I'm sorry. I told myself I wasn't going to do this." He wiped at his eyes, shaking his head.

Levi raised himself from the bed, walked up to his brother, and gently laid a hand on his face. "It's okay," he said, sniffling, fighting back the emotion, as well. "But if you're really my brother, tell me what happened to Dandy."

Jeff threw his head back in spontaneous laughter. "Gus's dog had him. I said that even if we glued his head back on I didn't think it would stay."

Levi stepped back and took a long look at him. "Is that really you in there, Jeff?"

"Afraid so," he nodded. "I'm forty-eight now, Levi. God knows I've missed you so much!"

Levi stepped close. They looked into each other's eyes and recognized the spark. In unison they threw their arms around each other and wept.

The silence in the room deafened the others, uncomfortable with this type of emotional response from brothers lost to each other for so very long.

"You have no idea how hard I prayed after you left. I really didn't give a damn about driving that Camaro. With you gone, it wasn't the same." He wept unashamedly, the younger brother in Jeff rising to the surface. They were sitting on the edge of the bed now, arms around each other.

"One day at a time," Levi comforted him. "That's what Albert said. So, do you still have it?"

Jeff looked up, confused. "What?"

"My car."

"Yeah," Jeff laughed. "And it runs even better now." He launched into a detailed explanation of the overhaul he'd given it, the glass packs he'd installed, the chrome wheels he'd replaced. He kept it stored in the old garage in Paradise Bay.

The others present continued to remain silent, keeping a respectful distance as the two brothers reacquainted themselves with each other.

"So, how's Mom and Dad, and Karen Sue?" Levi finally asked. "Have you kept in touch with Jenna?"

Jeff didn't know how to answer immediately and he looked up to the professionals for some hint. He remained silent, in search of a response, as Levi's mind quietly did the math that living in a coma meant.

"Let's save all that for tomorrow, Levi. It's late," Jeff begged off.

Levi reclined against the cushioned mattress, his home for three decades. He stared heavily at the ceiling above as if answers were contained somewhere in the whiteness.

"You're forty-eight. I'd say it is pretty late," Levi returned, stone-faced but innocently.

"You still have a way about you," Jeff smiled, wiping at his face with the back of his hand. "Levi, I need some extra time before I go into details on how everyone is. Can you wait until then?"

"Tomorrow?"

"Yes."

"Sure," Levi agreed, without expression or emotion. "But you'll come first thing in the morning, right?" He turned to the chaplain then, as if realizing for the first time that he and Jeff weren't alone. "And you'll be here, too?"

"Yes, I'll be here," Ringo replied. "*Semper fi.*" He winked at Levi, then walked out with the others.

•   •   •

Tran slipped quietly into the room while Levi slept. He would sign in and take care of his duties: empty the wastebaskets, mop the floors, and clean the sinks. But first, he would start the music for his friend Levi Harper, as he had for over three years now.

A flutter of the eyelids was the first thing he'd noticed when he began his work here at the hospital. Then Levi's eyes would open for an instant. Tran would take him on daily walks down the corridor, and as time went by he was certain he noticed improvement, especially when they stopped in front of the old Steinway in the recreation hall. The doctors didn't think there had been any change, but Tran believed that Levi was reaching some state of consciousness as he stared at the keys.

He intended to spend the rest of his days taking care of his friend, if necessary. He loved Levi, and it was also his duty. *So now he is back*, Tran thought.

A life for a life.

41

ADAGIO

TODAY, LEVI SEEMED CONTENT WITH ALBERT'S COUNSEL. Both Chaplain Ringo and Jeffrey were grateful for whatever dream or imaginings had brought Albert Tenny to his bedside. Levi was holding on to those words as his anchor.

"So let me get this straight. Vice President Nixon became president, Bobby Kennedy and Martin Luther King were both assassinated, all in 1968?" Levi was incredulous.

The answers Jeff had given him to his questions about his parents and Jenna had already put him under considerable stress. He had gone to his bed and hadn't stirred until morning.

"Did we win in Hue? Did the Marines take the Citadel?" he asked the chaplain.

"Yes, we won, and the Marines took the Citadel. But . . ." Ringo hesitated. He had been there for the full twenty days, a brutal human tragedy that still haunted him. "Your friends," he finally went on, "didn't make it."

"That's not possible! I've seen them! Tenny was here!" He started pacing, agitated. Reality was turning out to be more of a nightmare than anything he could have experienced while he was unconscious.

"I'm sorry, Levi. Truly. Maybe their memories and the sweet dreams God gives us are what you've seen. Even if they were alive, you were comatose."

Levi sat down on the edge of the bed and buried his head in his hands.

Jeff spoke up. "Levi, get some rest now. We'll come back later, okay?"

"No. I want to know more. Is everyone I loved gone, except you and Karen Sue? Dad is dead, Mom's in a rest home dying, and Jenna is married, almost fifty years old? I need to get out of here before I lose what little is left of my life. Get me checked out."

"Levi, you know we can't do that," the chaplain said softly. "You'll need to be here a few more months." Dr. Jenkins and Dr. Royal had just entered the room. They stood quietly in the doorway, taking notes.

"Months! No way! I've already been here thirty years! And married or not, I'm going to find Jenna. I'm due for a break from this place, right?" he demanded.

Dr. Jenkins intervened. "The world outside is a different place than it was in 1968, Levi. You need some time to adjust, and we also need to observe you for awhile, make sure you're on the mend."

"That's right." Dr. Royal nodded. "We have a lot to learn from you, Mr. Harper. You've gone through something so rare that it's never been documented in the medical books."

"So I'm a guinea pig? Is that what you call it?" Levi was grow-ing more agitated by the minute. "I've already lost thirty years, and I don't want to waste any more of it here. I don't care how old the world is now. You hear me? I . . . don't . . . care!" He stood up abruptly and headed for the door. "I'm going to play the piano."

When Jenkins tried to stop him, Jeff held up a hand. "I'll take him." He took Levi by the arm and led him out the door.

"Jeff?" Levi asked once they were alone.

"Yes, Levi?"

"Can you talk them into letting me out of here? You can say you'll take care of me until I can make it on my own. Please?"

"Levi, you're not a normal coma patient. There's a lot of things you need to relearn. Please, try to be patient. You'll be out of here soon enough."

They had reached the recreation hall. Levi sat down without saying a word, but his mood seemed to brighten as his fingers touched the keys. Jeff pulled up a chair, and the people in the room gathered around.

"Remember this one, Jeff? It's the Moody Blues." The aging veterans clapped to the rapid beat of the music as Levi took them back to their youth. He played the four-minute piece with the energy of a twenty-year-old. A virtuoso without prompts or sheet music, drawing the music up from his soul.

"Ride My Seesaw" was played as if he'd performed it one hundred times since the '60s.

He finished and stood, bowing to the cheers of the men sur-rounding him with congratulatory slaps on the back.

"I'm going to find her, Jeff," Levi said when he finished. "She's out there waiting for me. I was dead, Jeff! I'm alive! I need to at least see Jenna! Call her. And if you can't help me, I'll make it on my own."

"Oh, Levi," Jeff sighed. "I . . . oh, what the . . ." He didn't want his brother here a minute longer either. "Listen, let me make a few calls. I'm a lawyer, and they can't keep you here if I'm your legal guardian. Come on." He held out his hand.

Levi jumped up, grinning from ear to ear. "Jeff, you're the best brother ever!" He grabbed him around the neck and rubbed his knuckles against the crown of his head.

"Hey, knock it off! I worked hard on that hairdo!"

"Promise you'll get me out of here," Levi said, serious again as they made their way back to his room.

"I promise. Just give me a week. Slow and easy, like adagio. Can you do that?"

"Okay. Adagio. But just one week. If you don't have me out of here by then, I'll have to do a little E&E like I did with the boys of Team Rocker in Vietnam."

"E&E?"

"Escape and evade. Once a Marine, always a Marine."

42

TRAN AN

Tᴙᴀɴ sᴛᴏᴏᴅ ɪɴ ᴛʜᴇ ᴅᴏᴏʀᴡᴀʏ. "ʏᴏᴜ ᴋɴᴏᴡ ᴍᴇ, ɢɪ?" ʜᴇ asked as Levi packed his bags.

"You do look awfully familiar," Levi said with a puzzled expression.

"You numba one. Tenny numba one. Chavez, Paulos, Gomer numba one. Cannibal, numba five, I think," Tran smiled.

Levi stood back and examined the small Asian man from head to foot. His eyes widened, his mouth fell open, and he shook his head back and forth, trying to make what he was seeing fit the last mental image his memory had stored of the agile thirty-year-old Tran An.

That was a mental snapshot of Tran An smiling to him on the Perfume River, letting him know it would be okay, as he left Tran and Albert to fight it out alone with the enemy the night they had rescued the two chopper pilots.

"Tran! It's you? I can't believe it!"

"Yes. It Tran."

Levi pointed at Tran's graying head. "So it happened to you too, huh?"

"Yes. I sit now, okay?" Tran pointed to a chair.

"Sure!" Levi pulled it closer. "Tran, I am so glad to see you! No one told me you were here. I thought you were in Vietnam, maybe even dead. I . . ." He couldn't finish. He reached for the small man and embraced him like a brother. "I am so, so very glad to see you," he offered in a hushed, almost reverential tone. "It's just you and me now."

Tran smiled, eyes moist, and nodded to confirm Levi's last statement.

"Sit. Tell me everything, Tran. What happened to you and your family? What happened that night on the river when I left you with Tenny?"

"A lot happen." Tran went on to explain the entire nightmare of his escape with Albert from the Viet Cong, describing the enemies' anger when they discovered one of their boats was missing. Albert had fought until his ammunition ran out, then they'd made a dash into the river with one of the sampans they had discovered nearby. They made it out to the middle of the river, but one enemy round—one of hundreds fired in the frenzy that followed—found Tenny's back and exited out his chest.

Singlehandedly, Tran had caught the current and powered the boat downstream until he reached South Hue and the confusion of the Tet battle. Albert had remained conscious throughout the night, and said many kind things, but died before Tran could get medical help.

Tran had used his recon training to evade the Americans, the South Vietnamese, and the North Vietnamese, all fighting for control of Hue on the south side of the Perfume River, and for control of the city fortress on the north side known as the Citadel.

He had taken Albert's body down the river in the sampan, trying to get closer to the center of the city, changing into the uniform of a dead NVA soldier when he found himself in an area totally controlled by the Communists.

He had hidden out the first day, then crawled to his wife's home that night on his hands and knees. But they were gone, and he prayed they weren't dead.

Then he found Levi. He dragged his friend back to the sampan, laid him beside Albert, and pushed off. He had progressed only one kilometer down the river when he came upon the Americans, who started to lift Levi into a body bag along with Albert.

"No way!" Tran had told them. "GI alive!" He pointed, showing them the moisture, the tears from Levi's eyes.

" 'Take body out of bag,' one big recon Marine say. He say he know you and don't give a damn what other Marines say. He take you himself to aid station," Tran explained.

Levi wondered who the big Marine might have been, but it didn't really matter. Marines never gave up on each other.

Tran went on to recount the sad story of the surrender of South Vietnam to the North Vietnamese in 1975, his ultimate escape with Lin An, the baby Levi had rescued, and the tragic loss of his wife and two small sons in their escape to sea by boat.

Jeff had told him the rest of the story. How he, Levi, was shipped out to Japan, then back to the States. How Jenna came faithfully once a week for two years, then finally accepted a marriage proposal from a radio executive. How his father had suffered a stroke and died soon after, as much from a broken heart as anything, Jeff believed.

Eleanor Harper had remained in Paradise Bay. She and Karen Sue visited Levi often and kept the old homestead up until Alzheimer's claimed her final years.

Now Tran's addition to the story had Levi spellbound and deeply moved. "And you came to work here? Just to help me?" he asked, incredulous.

"Marine don't leave Marine behind," Tran replied.

"Thank you, my friend. I don't know how I'll ever repay you, but you can stay with me from now on. Remember my promise to you in Vietnam?"

Tran hesitated.

"Would you like to live by the ocean, have a boat?"

Tran nodded, his face brightening. He seemed unsure of what to say.

Levi stood up and extended his hand. "I'll talk to Jeffrey right away. And as soon as you're ready, you can come to live with us in Paradise Bay. I insist. The last two Team Rocker Marines need to stick together!"

"You good GI, Levi. We go fishing. I show you numba one *nuoc-mam* dish!"

"Mmm!" Levi smacked his lips.

"You no fool me, Levi Harper. You think *nuoc-mam* numba ten, but I show you new way!"

43

GOING HOME

THREE DOLLARS AND FIFTY-NINE CENTS EACH! DID AMER-
ica lose all its cows?" Levi asked as the clerk handed him the
frozen yogurt. "You sure you can afford this, Jeff?"

"Yes, Levi, I can afford it. And there are as many cows as ever.
It just costs more to get milk out of them nowadays. Just like
everything else," he smiled.

They were walking through the Oaks Mall, just off Ventura
Freeway in Thousand Oaks. Jeff was enjoying Levi's reaction to
the maze of air-conditioned stores. He had forgotten that malls
didn't exist back in 1967, when Levi left for the war. He was
doing his best, as well, to help Levi forget about Jenna Bradley.

"Everything's so fancy. I can't get over it," Levi said, spooning
a mouthful of yogurt into his mouth. "Tastes like soft ice cream,"
he added with a smile. Levi stopped and thought for a minute—

strange how even ice cream reminded him of something he and Jenna had shared. "Good stuff," he finally offered, realizing he needed to just take it a day at a time.

Levi's perspective was refreshing to Jeff, who was no longer amazed by the space-age technology that ran the world and dictated people's lives. Like everyone else, he'd been too busy with his day-to-day life to stand back and appreciate how truly mind-boggling it all was.

"Levi, you could use some new slacks. Maybe jeans. What do you think?"

"Whatever you think," Levi said, still distracted by his dessert. "Man, this stuff is great. I'm gonna gain so much weight!"

Good, Jeff thought. Levi was too thin, and he had no muscle tone. Getting him back in shape would take time. "You still like the jeans that carry your name?" he asked with a smile.

"Yep. They still have 'em?"

"Sure do. Straight leg and loose fit, zipper and button-fly." Jeff led Levi into a store and walked up to a clerk. "Take this man's measurements and give him anything he wants." He turned to Levi again. "I'm going to pick out some shirts for you, okay? Try on anything she suggests while I'm gone."

Jeff returned an hour later carrying several bags.

"Thanks, Jeff," Levi said. "I'll pay you back. I guess I've got a good chunk of disability coming from the Marines."

"You've already paid me back plenty by coming home."

Levi stopped in front of a music store and tugged on Jeff's arm like a child. "Let's go in here, Jeff. Let's buy some of those little records you play in your car."

"They're called CDs. Compact discs." Jeff chuckled at the guileless boy he saw in his older brother.

"Oh." Levi nodded. "Let's get a bunch of 'em. Moody Blues,

Simon and Garfunkel, Beach Boys, Righteous Brothers, The Doors, Grass Roots, Sonny and Cher, and that new guy, too . . . something John."

"Elton John." Jeff laughed. "He's been around since 1970."

"Good piano man," Levi returned.

Jeff nodded with a grin.

They were in the store for hours. Levi found all the artists he'd mentioned, along with pop groups from the '60s and '70s, classics from the '50s, and piano music by all the best artists of the century.

Jeff didn't even blink when the clerk gave him the total, just pulled a VISA gold card out of his pocket.

"Over six hundred dollars!" Levi gasped. "That's more than I made as a lance corporal in four months!"

"It's a new day, Levi. People who made one hundred fifty dollars a week back then make fifteen hundred dollars a week now." He pointed to the exit. "Come on. Let's get out of here while it's still daylight."

They were in the car and several miles up Highway 101 before Levi finally managed to get a CD case open. "I'm in the mood for the greatest crooner of all time," he said, gingerly taking the CD out of its case. "Perry Como. Did I tell you I met him once? I was playing a hotel lounge in Hollywood, and he came up to me and told me I was good. Left twenty bucks in the jar." Levi leaned back and closed his eyes. "Man, those were the days."

"Yeah," Jeff agreed, happy to see his brother finding some comfort in this big bad new world he was facing. "I know this is hard for you, Levi," he said. "I don't want you to get hurt."

"What could happen now that could possibly hurt me more than I've already been hurt?" Levi shrugged. "Maybe send me to Vietnam? Hah!" He leaned into the cushioned passenger seat, closed his eyes, and listened to Perry Como. Occasionally Levi glanced over to the slow lane. "Hey, look! There's an old Volkswagen van like the one Carol had. Remember?"

"Yep."

"But that's an old man driving it. I thought old guys drove Fords, Chevrolets, or Cadillacs."

"They do," Jeff said, realizing his brother still didn't comprehend his own age, that the "old man" in the van probably wasn't more than a couple of years older than Levi. "Shall we listen to something else?" he asked.

"No, not right now. Let's talk. Just put Perry on low," Levi said. He was wound tight and he knew it. Jeff was making this easier, but he was still in a dream. If he hadn't felt the love from Jeff, Tran, Chaplain Ringo, and others, he would be hospitalized for sure. The fears caused by this strange world would be too much to handle. Now all he could do was go ahead.

"I made a mental list of questions, and I was hoping you could catch me up some more," Levi opened up.

"Shoot."

"Okay. First of all, what did that girl at the store mean when she asked you to swipe your card through that machine? 'Swipe' used to mean 'steal.' "

"Yeah, but it doesn't mean that anymore. It means to pass a credit card or a debit card through the machine."

Levi nodded. "What's a debit card?"

"It's like a credit card, except the money comes straight out of your checking account when you use it."

"Wow. That's pretty dumb, if you ask me."

"Yeah." Jeff smiled. "Sometimes it really is."

"Someone said Elvis was dead."

"Don't believe it." Jeff laughed, even more amused at his

brother's innocence. "He's bigger than life!" he announced, choking on the humor Levi's childlike questioning produced.

"Well, is he or isn't he?"

Jeff's subdued chuckles burst out into a full roar. "Man, Levi," he said struggling for composure. He begged Levi to hand him the drink from the cup holder. "Oh, man. That was good. Whew."

"What's the big deal?" Levi asked, stone-faced.

"See, Elvis is dead, but not really," Jeff answered, unable to maintain a straight face. "See, some say he is, but other people see him driving up to their local café in a Cadillac asking them for leftover burgers, fries, milkshakes, that sort of thing." Jeff's eyes watered as he tried to finish. "Can I finish this question later?" He laughed, unable to go on.

"Sure," Levi replied, still out of touch with the humor Jeff found in the King's possible death.

"Next question?" Jeff asked. He still grinned widely at the thought of explaining the Elvis phenomenon to Levi.

"Tell me the order of the presidents after Lyndon Johnson one more time."

"There was Nixon for one full term, then he got re-elected but resigned. And then his vice president served, a fellow named Gerald Ford. Ford lost to a Democrat named Jimmy Carter from Georgia."

Levi nodded, trying to take it all in.

"Then Carter lost to Governor Ronald Reagan. You remember the actor who was our governor when you left?"

"Yeah. I remember. Strange."

"Then his vice president won, George Bush, and he served four years. Then he lost to our current president, a Vietnam War protester named Bill Clinton. And that's it."

"A war protestor became our president? What's happened to this country?"

"I told you things have changed, Levi." Jeff went on to explain some of the incongruousness associated with the politics of the time, truth, appearances, and social expectations.

They were silent for awhile, through the Ventura County cities all the way to the Santa Barbara County line. Levi looked out at the Pacific Ocean, the oil rigs, the Channel Islands, the surfing spots at the oil piers just above Ventura.

"People don't really believe he 'didn't inhale,' do they?" Levi asked, in reference to the Clinton legacy.

Jeff smiled and nodded as they drove on.

"I've sure missed this place." Levi took in a deep breath of ocean air. "Hey, look! Santa Claus Lane! Do they still have those date-flavored milkshakes?"

"Sure do. Let's go have one. Time to fill up anyway." Jeff pulled off the freeway into a parking stall in front of a group of buildings that had been a landmark tourist trap for years. "We stopped here in your Camaro Rally Sport on our way to L.A. just before you went overseas. Remember?"

"It seems like yesterday," Levi replied happily as they stepped out of the car.

Jeff purchased the large milkshakes, and they sat down at a picnic table to eat them.

"I miss Dad," Levi said. "And I can't bear to think of Mom the way you described her. Will she know me?"

Jeff shook his head slowly. "I miss Dad, too. And he sure missed you. They both did, but I think it was worse for Dad."

Levi was quiet for a moment. "Is Karen Sue coming up to see me?"

"Yeah, and she can't wait. You know, she's in her mid-forties now, and she's getting a little gray around the edges."

"So what's new?" Levi shrugged, as though nothing could surprise him anymore. "Catch me up some more on politics. Who's
the enemy nowadays? We still got ten thousand nukes pointed
at the Soviet Union? Is Red China still Communist?"

"Well, there is no Soviet Union anymore," Jeff replied.

"How'd that happen? Did we beat 'em in a war?" Levi asked
between spoonfuls of the date-flavored milkshake.

"No, they just gave up."

"No way!"

"It's like this. Ronald Reagan came into office, built up the
military, and told them where to go. By that time, the Soviet
Union had tried its Communist experiment for seventy years and
was burned out. See, the young people behind the Iron Curtain
had telephones, fax machines, computers, rock and roll, American movies, McDonald's hamburgers. They weren't stupid, and
they decided they weren't going to take the utopian dream, so-
cialist baloney from their commie leaders anymore.

"So they rebelled, went to the streets, just as people in the
good old U.S.A. do when they're fed up. On top of that, the
governments of the Communist block in Eastern Europe were
made up of younger people, too. They didn't have it in them to
shoot their own. Not like Stalin, Lenin, and a lot of others. So
the countries fell and opened up to capitalism.

"We outspent them on weapons—so much so they couldn't
keep up. And they couldn't make their people happy because
they had to spend so much on weapons, they couldn't afford
luxuries. When their people found out what Americans their age
had, the Communist promise of a better life became the lie."

"How many countries fell?"

"All of 'em, except Red China, North Korea, and Cuba. Oh,

and Vietnam. Funny thing, though, South Vietnam's a far cry from Communist. Saigon was renamed Ho Chi Minh City, but it's still every bit the capitalistic Saigon you knew. Those South Vietnamese love that money, and they hate the sternness of the Northerners. The North is so broke, they just look the other way. Oh, and Cambodia fell, too, just like the domino theory said it would. The Communists came in and massacred over two million of their people."

"And we didn't do anything?" Levi asked, stunned.

Jeff shook his head. "We lost fifty-eight thousand men in Vietnam. No one was willing to have the same thing happen in Cambodia."

"So, they did exactly what we predicted, and we just let it happen?"

"Yep. After they killed their educated, their professionals, and anyone else standing in the way, the country was such a mess it eventually fell by its own dead weight. It's not Communist anymore, but half of all the Cambodians alive in 1975 died. People don't like to talk about this stuff. Makes us look bad."

"Castro is really still around?"

"Last I heard."

Levi was feeling the sting of defeat that men who'd served and won their battles but lost the war had felt decades before him. When he left for Vietnam, literally half the planet was either Communist or under the influence of Communist nations. To the soldiers, Vietnam wasn't just about killing Viet Cong and Communists from the North; it was about the lurking Communist menace trying to do what Hitler and his Fascist allies had done in the '30s and '40s. It was a war made for the Albert Tennys.

They were told it was a new type of world war, *a war of ideas,* being fought in the jungles of South Vietnam. They'd been taught that invasion, nuclear war, every scenario but western capitalism would beat the Soviets and Red Chinese at their world domination game.

"Maybe we just should've waited," Levi whispered under his breath, unaware that he was speaking out loud.

"What?"

"Maybe if we had waited, my friends . . . all those GIs dead."

Jeff could see the tension in his brother's face. The bullets, the bombs, the whopping sound of rotating helicopter blades— all of it was coming back. The doctors had cautioned Jeff not to let Levi fall into a depression, that he should tread carefully when it came to news about the past.

"Hey, look!" he said, pointing, trying to divert Levi's attention. "Over there, driving up in that Cadillac!"

"What?" Levi looked around, confused.

"Elvis!"

44

BACK IN TIME

Three Months Later

Jeff quietly stepped out onto the porch. He was working long-distance now, using faxes, e-mail, and phone calls to keep up with clients. With his family still back east, he had taken up residence in the old homestead with Levi until he could bring them out to stay permanently. He had decided to make Paradise Bay home once more.

He never tired of watching his older brother taking in knowledge like a sponge. Right now Levi was sitting on the porch, reading another copy of *The Twentieth Century*, a compilation of photos, newspaper articles, and pop culture trivia.

Levi tried to hide it, but Jeff knew he was grieving over the loss of Jenna. He could see it in his face, read between the lines. More than once Levi had asked to call her, to find out where she was so he could simply say "Hello." Jeff's answer was a request for more time. He sensed Levi was growing impatient. So at least once a day he'd take Levi down to the chapel to play the piano. Levi would lose himself for awhile on new creations. His music had a new quality now, as if a genius had been born with his awakening. Music wasn't just therapy for Levi, Jeff realized, it was his salvation.

"It's time, Levi," he said, hating to pull his brother away from his reading.

"For what?" Levi asked without looking up.

"A trip to the hospital for your checkup. It's just for a couple of days."

"You aren't leaving me there, are you?" Levi asked, startled.

"Are you kidding? I'm having too much fun staying home with you. But I do have to pick up Allie and the kids at the airport, and then you and I have a couple of television interviews to do. A lady from *20/20* called. Her name is Barbara Walters, and then CNN's people called from *The Larry King Show*."

"Do I know them?"

"No." Jeff laughed. "But millions of Americans do." He handed Levi a copy of *USA Today*. "Look at this."

Back from the Dead: Vietnam War Hero Plays His Music Again, the headline read.

"Go ahead, read it," Jeff urged.

Levi read out loud. The article included a photo showing him kissing his parents good-bye, with Jeff and Karen Sue standing in the background. "You gave these photos to them?"

"Yeah. Seems the hospital got a call from someone wanting to do a lead story for their newspaper on you and then I got involved."

"They want to interview me on national television?" Levi asked nervously. "Why?"

"Because you have a unique story to tell. The whole country wants to hear it."

"What, that I can't remember the last thirty years? I don't want to be treated like some freak at a sideshow."

"They're going to ask you to play the piano." Jeff grinned.

Levi brightened. "On national television?"

"Yes, sir. And you're going to knock 'em dead."

Levi passed his checkup with flying colors. Between tests, he performed for the veterans in the recreation hall. He played his "Believe in Paradise" to perfection, "Jenna's Theme," and a medley of the '50s songs he'd last heard at the Casino in Avalon so many years ago: Tony Bennett's "Strangers in Paradise," Sammy Kaye's "Harbor Lights," "Que Sera Sera," made famous by Doris Day, and "It's Not for Me to Say," by Johnny Mathis. No message he could give would be more appropriate than those songs.

"After more than thirty years, I'm finally getting a break on national television," he told his audience. "You guys are the greatest. I'm doing this for you, and for the men who served and didn't return."

They cheered as Jeff gently tugged at his arm.

"See you guys soon!" He waved.

"You look great, Levi," Jeff smiled as they walked down the hall. "Casual but real GQ."

"What's that mean?"

"It's a magazine. Never mind. We're going straight to the CNN Studios in Hollywood, then we'll head back to the hotel to meet the famous Harper family."

"I'm so glad they made it. I just wish Mom and Dad could be there. Will Karen Sue be watching?" Levi asked. He wondered even more if Jenna would see him. He had allowed Jeff to believe his desires for her had cooled, but it wouldn't hurt his feelings if she saw him, connected, and gave him a call.

"Yeah. Karen Sue's not only watching, she'll be in the audience. We get to make a brief appearance with you," Jeff explained.

"Whew! Maybe that'll make it easier. What's this Larry King like?"

"He's nice, fair, asks good questions. He's watched worldwide. Don't worry, he won't embarrass you."

"A worldwide debut . . . almost worth the wait."

His performance on CNN made news around the country, and Jeff had to parry offers from talk shows until he could organize a sane schedule for Levi. Radio stations called for copies of his demo CD, and two recording studios made offers the morning after his interview. A record company bidding war ensued, which added to the news of Levi Harper's awakening and of his piano genius.

"Larry King sure knows a lot of people," Levi said, then yawned as Jeff showed him the list of offers the next day. After the interview the night before, he had met Allie, Jeff's lovely forty-something wife, and his niece and nephew for the first time. They had stayed up into the early morning hours, getting to know each other and talking about the interview. Even after all that, Levi couldn't sleep, reliving the interview and his piano performance.

"So tell us," Larry King had asked. "What's it like waking up to a new world?"

"Like Disneyland. Like Fantasyland, Frontierland, Tomorrowland, never-never land, all rolled into one."

Larry had laughed at that, then asked him a few questions

about the war: what it was like, what he last recalled, what he felt when he woke up. They went on to discuss Levi's reaction to the new technologies, then Larry had turned to the camera and announced a commercial break.

"Don't go away," he said. "Levi Harper—the true piano man—is going to play us a few songs from the past!"

Larry King was generous with his praise as Levi signed off with the song Jeff had asked him not to play, a medley that began and ended with "Jenna's Theme."

45

JENNA

SIX MONTHS AFTER HIS AWAKENING, LEVI HARPER FOUND himself bowing to a standing ovation at the Hollywood Bowl, where he was the opening for the main act, Reunion. Members of the Lettermen forty years ago, they were playing to a sold-out audience.

Levi chose "Believe in Paradise" as his encore, a simple tune with a pure lyrical message that played like an adult lullaby. He still didn't completely understand why it was received so enthusiastically by everyone who heard it.

"Thank you, ladies and gentlemen. I was asleep when I wrote this next song." He laughed. "It's true. It was just there when I woke up from a thirty-year coma induced by a mortar blast back in Vietnam. I wrote it in my dreams for one of the most important people in my life, a person who shared a childhood motto with me: Just believe. I've never forgotten that motto, and it's gotten me through some pretty tough times. This song is for you, Jenna, wherever you are."

He played the opening measures twice as he readied his voice for the lyrics. But before he could begin, a lovely female voice started singing—a voice he thought he recognized. He turned toward the audience.

And found her.

He stopped playing, standing up to gaze at her, transfixed.

"Finish the song, Levi," she said, her eyes glistening with tears as she stepped up on the stage to stand beside him at the piano.

Wordlessly, he obeyed. He sat down and played, closing his eyes as she sang the lyrics, her golden voice carrying him back to the place of his dreams.

> *Believe in Paradise,*
> *You and me,*
> > *where the deep blue ebbs eternally.*
> *Where mystery and nursery rhymes*
> > *are always solved in Paradise time.*
> *Believe in us, our second chance,*
> *A lovers' waltz, a sacred dance.*
> *And in the end, your child and mine*
> > *will sing all songs in Paradise time.*
> *Believe . . . in Paradise,*
> *In you and me . . . just believe . . .*

He bowed his head at its conclusion, unwilling for the moment to end. A fanciful dream, an illusion, his mind playing tricks. The song, his desire to believe he could have Jenna again, had all brought him to this point. She wasn't really there, he reasoned, seeking a measure of control.

The applause was deafening as she moved to the bench and sat down beside him. Jeff had helped orchestrate the moment without Levi's knowledge. Light as a feather, he felt her lips brush his cheek.

"I love you, Levi Harper," she whispered. "I always have."

He turned, gazed into her blue eyes, then softly kissed her lips. The twenty-year-old Marine again, he allowed the delicate moment to linger.

"I won't let you go, Jenna," he whispered. He was powerless to control the dam bursting from behind his eyes. "You're beautiful. You haven't changed. But I . . ." He stumbled and bowed his head in embarrassment.

"You were, are, and always will be the most handsome man in the world, Levi Harper," she tearfully voiced, meeting his lips once again.

The audience was on their feet, the applause growing even more deafening as he pulled her into his embrace.

"You're my breath, Jenna. It was you who gave me the will to awaken. I swear, nothing will make me ever leave you again."

Jenna put a hand to her neck and showed him the pearl necklace. "I've never stopped wearing it," she said. "You brought it home like I asked you to. Stand up. Thank your audience."

Levi stood up and bowed, but the only word he could manage as he extended one hand toward her was "Jenna."

Jeff Harper was perfectly at ease in his behind-the-scenes role. It made him feel proud, fulfilled, gave him a zest for life that he hadn't known for years.

"She isn't married anymore, Levi," he explained to his brother backstage. "She needs you, and you need her."

"But how did you make the arrangements so quickly, and without letting on?"

"It's what I do. You signed the papers I put in front of you. Took the blood test and physical I asked you to take. You didn't even question it. *Voilà*, a marriage license, signed, sealed, and delivered. I'm an attorney, remember. And I'm your manager," Jeff said. "Don't you forget it." Jeff beat a retreat to the door. He had already explained that Chaplain Ringo was waiting, that a special suite at the Catalina Beach Hotel had been reserved—compliments of the Ringo family—and that the marriage license was ready.

"Hey, wait a minute." Levi walked up to his brother and threw his arms around him. "I love you, Jeff. I don't know how to thank you. For everything."

"Go have some fun, will you? Take those tickets and get on over to Avalon. The helicopter's waiting." Jeff slapped his brother on the back.

He watched as Jenna took Levi by the hand. He was such a child. *A glorious, adult child,* Jeff mused as he saw them disappear into the limousine he had rented. He had made sure Levi's clothes and the other things he would want were all packed and ready to go. This truly topped off a satisfying six months with the awakened Levi. And there was more joy to come, he was certain. Levi had revived the child in Jeff again, the one that had been smothered by sophistry for so long. His big brother's ways had softened the cynic in him, the pragmatic attorney mind that had to have an answer to everything.

He got into his leased Grand Cherokee and pulled out of the lot. He would drive up the coast tonight to Paradise Bay and tell his wife and children that they were just about finished with their West Coast vacation, that it was time to pack their bags and get back to reality. Soon, Levi and his bride would be inheriting the old Victorian homestead.

Jeff would be back, though. He would go back to Maryland, tidy up his law practice, dispose of the property and assets he'd acquired in the east, then this year permanently make Paradise Bay home by building on the adjoining property.

Allie had taken a surprising interest in the place. A city girl, she seemed enchanted by the slow pace of the near-ghost town. He had promised her a cottage on the shore, and a life of fiery orange sunsets, the same life he'd known so many years ago. A pleasant and sane place to watch their children grow up.

He had accomplished the coup de grâce. He had taken an unpaid leave of absence, brought his family out here, and begun the job of representing Levi to television shows, radio shows, and recording companies. As if all that wasn't enough, he'd been able to reintroduce his brother to the love of his life. It didn't get any better than that.

Jeff had hired an Internet search company to look for Jenna, and they found her in New York City. She had moved there after the Vietnam War, started a singing career, then married a radio company executive and settled in Manhattan.

Her marriage had produced three children, all of whom were grown now. She told Jeff she was divorced now, that the failure of her marriage was as much her fault as her ex-husband's; he had found someone who hadn't lost the little girl inside, someone spontaneous and fun.

Jeff had asked her if she would be willing to come to L.A. She had agreed, leaning on the excuse that it was high time she came back to visit her oldest daughter anyway.

Jenna had arrived, full of anxiety and questions.

"How can we do this, Jeff? I need some time, and Levi needs

some time. How can I see him without upsetting him? *Can* I see him?"

"Jenna, inside Levi is a twenty-one-year-old. He was one week away from marrying you in Hawaii when the tragedy of the battle in Hue happened. To Levi it isn't thirty years later, it is what he was fighting for in Vietnam. The doctors still don't know why he regained consciousness, or how long it will last. He's in a very fragile state, but his music has you written all over it. I don't know, maybe you're right . . . maybe it's too soon for him to see you."

She paused. Jenna realized that time had been suspended for the man she loved. And she realized time didn't respect people— that he could easily be snatched from her again.

She nodded, her eyes filling with tears. "I've never stopped loving him, you know."

"Listen, I've got an idea. Let me handle the arrangements. I've got some calls to make. You can see him, and he won't even have to know it. Here's two tickets to the show this weekend at the Hollywood Bowl. It's a charity benefit for the veterans, and he's playing as a guest performer."

Things couldn't possibly have turned out better. Jeff smiled now, remembering. The people who needed to be where they were as the whole scenario played out, the paperwork, the marriage license, Chaplain Ringo on leave and in Catalina at the family-owned hotel, and every other detail needed to allow Jeff to arrange the event that should have taken place in 1968, were all easily accomplished. Above all, everyone had been there precisely when Levi was able to handle it.

As if by the hand of God, a timetable unfolded neatly for every new step Levi needed to take.

Jeff smiled as he accelerated the Grand Cherokee and merged onto the Hollywood Freeway. He was becoming a believer.

46

PIANISSIMO

It is now four years since I married Jenna. Moonlit Avalon Bay at Catalina never glistened more, the night sky never offered more luster, more illumination than it did for us on that sacred wedding night forty-eight months ago. I promised to marry her there, back in the summer of '67. Who would have thought it would take this much time to realize our dream?

Now I sit and ponder this cruel twist to our love story. It can't end this way. Better me than Jenna.

I was performing my music at a level I had never known before the long night's sleep of three decades. But when Jenna joined me, became my bride, music poured out of me at a rate and in a way I never could have believed possible. I heard the sounds in my heart, then my head. And until now, they have been melodies inspired by my love for her.

Now I am in fear. More fear than at any time since I dodged bullets in Vietnam. I need her to bring the music back.

There are times when even music ceases and we are left to struggle with the capacities of our minds and hearts without the accompanying pleasant melodies that enrich our time together. I have never been without music, whether at home, traveling, falling asleep, or with Jenna in my arms.

But music is fading from me now as I struggle to see the hand of God in this thing she suffers. Sounds are no longer *forte* but *pianissimo*, soft and so very quiet.

I sit here beside her at St. Francis Hospital, seeking His will, His understanding. But nothing comes. What am I to do if she leaves me? Where will I go? Will I ever write or play music again? Will the child live? If she does, will I be able to care for her without Jenna?

Oh God, what am I to do?

Jack closed the final page of the journal, written just two months ago, a few weeks before Levi's collapse from a stroke and the accompanying cardiac arrest. The fact that Levi had survived the trip back to Veterans' Hospital was no less than a miracle, but his love for Jenna had been the only cement to his fragile existence. Without her, his music was finished. He had been so completely devoted to Jenna and his unborn child that he had worn himself out with worry and had secretly offered a trade with God if their lives could be spared.

Jack went outside, and as he slowly made his way to the café, he recalled what Uncle Jeff had told him about the day Levi fell back into a coma.

It all made sense now.

•   •   •

They had enjoyed just over three full years of blissful married life in Paradise Bay when Jenna came to him with the news after a doctor's visit.

They had found a lump in one breast, which proved to be cancerous. It had been removed successfully, but there was more. She was pregnant, a miracle at fifty-one years of age. They now had two choices: terminate the pregnancy and finish the chemotherapy and radiation treatments, or depend solely on God's help. Trust that His hand, which had been so abundantly manifest in their lives up until now, would bless them with another miracle.

The choice was clear in Jenna's mind, but her friends and family were unanimous regarding the safest course. An abortion, they argued, would buy her some time. If she began treatment immediately, the chances were good. But if she waited nine months . . .

She wanted the chance to bring this soul into the world, though, to create something no one could ever take from them again, no matter what happened.

Levi agonized with her, fighting to believe in a power beyond their own for healing. No one would blame her if she terminated the pregnancy, but she wanted to follow her heart, not her mind, and do what Levi had told her over and over again was the secret to his music.

"The heart speaks softly, the head loudly. The heart is the center of the soul. Trust the heart," he'd say.

They were now seven months into the pregnancy, battling a recurrence of the cancer. The doctors had decided to admit her and take the baby early, then begin emergency treatment on the cancer. Jenna was already exhausted, her immune system weak-

ened, and they couldn't risk losing more time. Levi and Jenna
finally agreed, and decided the baby's name would be Angel.

Jeff was as concerned about Levi's health as Jenna's. He had
noticed the weight loss, the frenzied journal-writing, so he had
insisted on accompanying them to the hospital. Just yesterday,
Levi had complained of dizziness and a pain in the front of his
head.

Jeff had insisted that Levi agree to a checkup, then he called
Chaplain Ringo and asked him to come today and try to convince
Levi to consider what Jenna would want. A healthy father for
their daughter, or a dead one.

Now, Jeff watched the tender scene unfolding from outside
the room. He couldn't interrupt Levi, not yet.

"Jenna, honey. Can you hear me? This is all my fault. I'm so
angry with myself, so confused about why this is happening."

He took her hand as she slumbered. It had been months since
the last chemotherapy, and the baby would be taken by caesarean
tomorrow. Jeff had been coming in to check on them both twice
a day, since Levi refused to leave even long enough to go home
and shower. He argued that there was a bathroom not ten feet
from Jenna's bed, and the hospital cot the staff had brought in
was more than adequate.

"I danced with you in my heart," Levi whispered to her now.
"In my mind, in mansions beyond paradise. A place that was real.
You were there with me. And my body had withered but my
spirit was soaring. We were holding each other in another place,
and we were dancing to a celestial song."

Jenna's eyes flickered open. "Metaphorically, you mean," she
said, her lips barely moving. "You say the sweetest things."

He kissed her tired eyes, her brow. Then he moistened her lips with his, gently, carefully. "No, really. I did dance with you. We were so close—heart to heart—and I remember feeling your warmth, asking God how this could be possible."

"So sweet. You're . . ." She drifted back to sleep.

"Rest now, Jenna," he said. "I need to get my strength back so I can take care of you. The chaplain's coming today, and I know he's going to ask me to take better care of myself. And I will. But I'll be here for you every day—" Levi couldn't go on. He felt dizzy, his chest tight. "Oh, God!" he cried, then fell out of his chair, knocking it over.

Jeff was still standing outside when he heard the crash. He bolted into the room just as Chaplain Ringo was coming around the corner.

"Call the nurse!" Jeff shouted when he saw Ringo in the doorway. Levi's breathing was shallow and labored. Within minutes, he was fighting for his life again, comatose for the second time.

As though preordained, the two lovers were holding vigil for each other, both unwilling to live without the other. They were hospitalized on the same floor, cards and flowers pouring in from thousands of well-wishers as the news spread across the country.

Levi finally stabilized enough for them to risk transporting him across town to the Veterans' Hospital. He lay waiting there now, waiting for Jenna to return from the brink of death.

47

STRANGERS IN PARADISE

I HOPE YOU ACCEPT," JACK SAID.

"I'm not sure. I mean, Levi Harper's condition is . . ."

"Comatose," Jack interrupted.

There was an awkward silence through the phone connection.

"I've never just taken off from work like this," she replied. "I'm not sure I know how."

"Easy. Just do it. Be yourself. Levi will be taken care of. I need to see you, Lin. I need to find out more about him, through your eyes." His voice was gentle but insistent.

"Is that the only reason you are inviting me?"

"No." He paused.

She hesitated. She had a sense of belonging to the Harper family, beginning with intimate ties of friendship that started in the small mountain village in Vietnam so long ago, and continued still with her present vigilance at the bedside of Levi Harper.

"Lin, we need to see each other. We are connected to Levi Harper, his life and dream, whether we asked for it or not. It will do both of us good to be out on the water. We'll learn a little about sailing. Make both our fathers proud. My intentions are strictly honorable. I have hired a captain and we will have separate cabins, if that's what is troubling you."

"I will need an hour or so. Can I call you back?"

"How 'bout if I call you in a couple of hours on your cell phone? Think it over. The boat is already chartered. I hope you will say yes," he ended.

"Thank you. I'll be here at the hospital."

"Talk to you then," Jack ended.

Lin put the cell phone back in her smock pocket and pondered his proposal for the weekend as she made her way to the room where Levi lay. Jenna would be here soon. She had recovered sufficiently from her own cancer treatments and the caesarean, and was surprising the doctors daily with a general recovery. She had asked that Lin be there when she arrived. That might mitigate this decision to go away with Jack Santos for the weekend, Lin decided. Maybe make it easier to say no to Jack.

After all, she had never dated except for a few disasters in college. The night she was assaulted during a med school Christmas party by an intoxicated doctor was more of the same she had come to believe about men. Off the coast of Vietnam, too, there were men, full of evil. Her mother died at their hands, and she had lost everything that was innocent in a child.

Except for her own father and Levi Harper, all men were suspect of wanting one thing in Lin's mind. She wanted to believe, to trust. But the pain was always there. Tran An and Levi Harper: those two men were unique. Saints. Men who had overcome the world's beguiling ways of focus on self to save each other.

Jack was a newcomer to her tidy little world. He had told her to just "be herself." She didn't even know what being herself meant. Lin felt feelings beginning to stir for the man. She had reasoned they were schoolgirl flutters, nothing more.

How could she have anticipated Jack's offer? He was hiring a charter sailboat for the weekend. A professional skipper who taught vacationers the fundamentals of boating in the Channel Islands would command the vessel.

"Think with this," her father would say, pointing to her head. "Trust with this," he would say, pointing to her heart.

Jack turned in the swivel chair and gazed out the picture window to the west. Sky and sea merged in the thin horizon miles away. He hoped Lin would join him there. He was excited at the thought. She wasn't like Claire. Not like the girls that hung around after a jam session with his musician friends. With a mysterious locked-away beauty—apparent on the exterior, hidden inside—she awoke a distant but familiar dream in him, one he had almost abandoned now.

He promised he wouldn't do what his father had done to him—go away, leave him without a real dad to grow up with. He had thought Claire was the woman who would be the mother to his son or daughter. He wanted a family. She wanted to wait. He poured himself into his work. She left.

In today's world, people so often moralized about waiting until you were financially stable, and sure of the person you had married. He felt that marriage and kids should be something that happened naturally. No demands, boundaries, or social expectations set by some elusive set of rules.

Lin stirred him up. He realized that the normal male drive was a powerful motivator, but there was something else going on there. She lingered in his mind like a pleasant melody long after the final note was played. She commanded respect. And she was now an integral part of this new adventure.

A serious health professional, she was probably shy, even awkward in a social sense, but he would put her at ease and be a total gentleman.

He just wanted to know her, get inside her mind and see what she was seeing. The worst case was that he would learn more about Levi Harper and add to his understanding of a legacy he was so suddenly inheriting. But he suspected there was more to it than this.

Like the old song title Levi Harper sang to Jenna on a romantic moonlit night on Catalina long ago, he and Lin were still "strangers in paradise." He wondered if they could ever become more.

48

WATER MUSIC

Calling santa barbara its home port, the small but sturdy sailing craft was manned by a retired investment banker, Gil Gray. A gregarious, happy man, he had created a hobby business, hiring out to vacationers by the day and the week. Jack had arranged for the forty-five-footer to moor in Avalon Harbor this Friday, where Lin would be waiting.

Jack had paid the ship owner in advance and had determined that even if Lin declined he would spend two days out on the water just to clear his mind and think things out, away from Paradise Bay and the journals of Levi Harper.

He was glad she had decided to rendevous with them in Catalina. That made it all the easier to keep this less formal, a friendly cruise, and with Gil constantly there they could find someone to offset any stalled moments or conversation with instructions and tasks on boating.

"As I pull alongside, you hop out and shove me off," Gil called out as they maneuvered into Avalon Harbor. "We're not allowed to tie up at the pier. I'll be out dropping anchor in the bay until you give me a call," he said, holding his cell phone in the air to remind Jack.

"Aye, aye, Captain," Jack shouted back. They were running on the engine as they glided in. Jack jumped safely onto the dock and then, as Gil put the engine in reverse, gently offered a nudge. They would be in Catalina for the night.

Jack suspected Lin An would be on the incoming Catalina Express from Long Beach Harbor about now. He walked up the pier and along the shore to the dock for the passenger line. The last boat had barely disembarked and was now loading passengers for the return trip to Long Beach.

"Hi."

Jack spun around. "Oh. Lin. I didn't recognize you. I guess I expected you to look like a doctor or something." He grinned. "Did I walk past you?"

"Right past." She smiled nervously. "Am I dressed okay for the occasion?"

"You look wonderful," he replied as his eyes inspected her casual shorts and blouse combination. "Here, allow me," he offered, reaching for her backpack.

"I hope we aren't dressing up," she added. "I figured we'd be out in the sun mostly."

"You figured correct," he said, wondering how to begin. They began to walk toward town, which lay a hundred yards from the docks. "I thought, since it's getting late, we'd anchor here in the bay tonight. Have a dinner, take a walk, and then perhaps convince the captain to take us out for a cruise along the shoreline."

"Sounds good," she offered. Shy, not sure of herself, she wondered how much of a disappointment she would end up being for the more worldly and experienced Jack Santos.

"How's Levi?" Jack began. "Any changes?"

"He's steady. No improvement. Jenna is there with him. Tired, she sleeps mostly, then returns to her hotel room nearby at the close of visiting hours. She is so hopeful." Lin was feeling more comfortable now that she was speaking of something she was knowledgeable about.

"I'd love to be able to talk to him. I suppose I will meet Jenna soon," he supplied.

"Yes. I suppose so," Lin replied.

"Say, there's this great little café up along the frontage road. Some shops, too—perhaps we can grab a bite, and then just enjoy the sights for a couple of hours."

"Sure," she replied. Uneasy, not sure how to act interesting, she hoped to find a way to release the tension she sensed building. Perhaps once they were on the boat and out at sea.

"That's the famous Catalina Beach Hotel," Jack pointed. "Heard about it?" he asked.

"No."

"Levi's journals talk about how he and Jenna Bradley came out here. Kind of hard for me to swallow until I realized how much he had always loved her."

"Hard to swallow? I don't understand."

"Well, for one, my name is Santos. I was given my maternal grandparents' surname. It would have been Harper if Levi hadn't left my mother at the altar."

Lin's mind raced to catch up with the story surrounding the lifelong love affair between Jenna and Levi—she only knew bits and pieces of it.

"I suppose it wasn't meant to be," he continued. "I mean, Levi marrying my mother. In any case, what happened in Vietnam would have put me exactly where I am today. Discovering my father for the first time. Can't be bitter. Shouldn't be bitter," he reasoned aloud, talking more to himself than to her.

"Levi Harper saved me. He saved my father. I am still discovering who I am," Lin reassured him.

"For real? I mean, remember when we first met, in the hospital room. You asked about Angel, Levi and Jenna's premature miracle baby?"

"Yes."

"Well, you said, 'heaven sent.' See, I was his child, too. But was I heaven sent? That really hit me. I wondered what it was that made one child more privileged than another. You know, how God chose how and when to send a child into a home. I guess I've felt resentment that I didn't have a father. It has always simmered under the surface. I wandered around my whole life looking for where I fit."

"I understand."

"Really?" he asked with a boyish sincerity.

"Yes. Really," she said, allowing a slight giggle.

"But you are a doctor. You must be very confident to be a doctor. I can't see you not knowing your place in life, in the big universe," Jack answered. He was probing, hoping she would open up.

"I know what I am as a physician. Only if work is everything do I know who I am. My father tried to instill spiritual awareness, that sort of thing, in me, but I am still on the journey, the quest, so to speak."

Jack was silent, pensive. He could talk to her about things that really mattered. That was good. They continued their walk, taking in the sights and sounds of springtime twenty-two miles off the Southern California coast.

Jack pointed. "The Casino Ballroom. Maybe we should check it out after dinner."

"Do you dance? I mean, the old-fashioned slow type of dancing done on formal occasions?" Lin answered.

"I try. I mostly try to not step on my partner's toes." He laughed.

"We'll see." Lin smiled.

"Shall we?" he said, opening the door to the restaurant.

49

CONCERTO FOR THE LIVING

Stop it." she laughed. "i can't take it."

"Just one more," he begged.

"No, please. My makeup is running." She giggled as she wiped at her eyes.

"Okay. I rest my case. Music doesn't have to be all moody to be romantic."

"Where did you learn all those one-liners?" she asked, still grinning from the last joke.

"I'm a piano man. It's what I do—I entertain. Growing up as I did, without a father and needing approval, I went the extra mile, so to speak, to make people smile, see them happy. Between songs, a good one-liner keeps people's attention. What's really cool is to make them laugh one moment, then play a tune and make them cry the next. Music has a powerful effect on the senses."

They had finished the fish, the shrimp basket, and Lin finally
felt at ease in Jack's presence. The casual meal and atmosphere
in the café was made for Jack's exposé on music, lyrics, and
having fun playing the piano.

"I love Levi's music. So much music in so short a time. How
does that happen?" she quizzed, totally relaxed now.

"Levi's waking life has been compressed to under twenty-five
years, but the mind is always at work. Asleep or awake the human brain is active. Music comes from two sources. Here"—he
pointed to his head—"and here," he finished, pointing to his
heart. "Levi always had the ability up here," he said, tapping on
his forehead. "Awakening as he did opened up his heart. Once
the heart is open, music can pour out like a flood. I've felt it
happen now and then. Original compositions, I mean."

"Interesting." She sighed. "Well . . ."

"Shall we take a walk?"

"Certainly." She smiled.

"It's so peaceful this time of year. Cool breezes. Not too many
tourists yet. I'd love to own a boat and spend weeks cruising up
and down the coast, anchoring in small inlets off the islands."

"So much time for fun. What about a job?" she asked.

"That part is something I haven't figured out yet. But I'd still
like a boat."

Jack extended his arm in a gentlemanly manner. Lin, uneasy,
took it, not knowing how to refuse. They walked in silence along
the sidewalk leading to the Casino Ballroom. It looked quiet.
"Closed for the season. Too bad." He sighed. "And I was going
to let you teach me how to dance."

"Don't let that stop you. I took ballroom dance in college. Let
me show you," She held her hands out for him to take. Jack
smiled, moving closer to oblige.

"You are a dancer?" Jack asked. He was entranced by the qualities he would never have seen in Lin had he not asked her to spend this weekend with him.

"Sort of. Actually, it was good for me to break from the heavy routine of chemistry, my major. I was on the ballroom dance team. So, let's begin. One, two, three. One, two, three."

Jack gazed down at the gracefully moving Lin. He was at peace with her. He couldn't wipe the grin from his face as she instructed him in steps he was quite familiar with. He wouldn't let on, though. He wanted to see where Lin would lead him.

His eyes approved of everything about her. Petite, but strong. Quiet, yet with a voice that made sense whenever she spoke. Inwardly sad, but willing to be happy for others. "You are beautiful," he whispered.

She turned her face away, not willing to believe a man could mean those words. "Thank you," she replied in an unsure, almost inaudible tone. "Just a few more steps. One, two, three . . ."

It had been a wonderful evening. Jack made it easy to relax in his presence. The familiar Harper touch, she mused. But she struggled now. She felt restless this first night aboard the small boat anchored in the bay. When she stopped to think about it, she had allowed herself to be captive to two men she had barely met. The tension she felt was reasonable, she reminded herself.

The horror of losing her family had happened at sea. The memories and fears were always near the surface, but she suppressed them by pouring herself into her work. It had been an ample but overcrowded vessel. She had been perhaps ten years old when she was robbed of her mother, brothers, and her personal dignity by pirates preying on the "boat people" off the waters of Vietnam.

That's unfair, she scolded herself. *These men aren't like that.*

But they are men, and you are helpless here. She fought the voices taunting and haunting her for the remainder of the night. With the morning light came the reassuring countenance of Jack Santos. Kind, nonthreatening, and courteous, he put her at ease every time the nightmares from her youth reappeared.

Each night Lin kept her cabin door locked but her heart open. She wanted to be worthy of a man, and wanted the feeling of love that every romance story produced. She did love his smile, his penetrating laugh, the way he put her at ease. He attracted her physically, and the qualities in Levi Harper she had admired for so long lingered around the edges of Jack's manners, his ways with people and things.

The weekend was spent aboard the sailboat with Gil teaching the fundamentals of sailing in the Channel Island waters near Santa Barbara's mountain-lined coast. They anchored in small coves, swam, laughed, and enjoyed the solitude of sea and sky. They talked of life, history, current events, Levi and Jenna, and then shared their dreams. Gil interjected his salty wit and philosophies to round out the evenings. It all ended too soon.

They were coming into Santa Barbara harbor now. Jack would take Lin into the airport and see her off there.

"I hope I've been the gentleman you expected," he said as they docked. He reached for her hand and helped her safely onto the pier.

"You were and more. I don't recall when I enjoyed myself this much. I need to get out of the hospital more often. Thank you," she said.

"I'll take that as a future 'yes' to another date. Of course, with old Gil here as chaperon," he said loudly enough for Gil to hear.

"You come back anytime, Doc," Gil called to Lin.

"See you 'round, skipper." She waved.

"Sorry we didn't make it up to Paradise Bay as promised," Jack said as they walked toward his car. "Sometimes it's just as well to be spontaneous. Take each day as it comes."

She smiled but didn't reply. Jack reached for her hand as they dashed across the street to go for his car, parked up State Street in a long-term parking lot. She continued to allow Jack to hold her hand as they strolled the several blocks into town. Comfortable with small talk now, she found her lips creased in an almost continual smile as they made observations about people, life, and music.

They drove the few miles up Highway 101 to the airport outside of Goleta where a Delta Shuttle flight waited to take Lin south to Los Angeles.

"Mind if I call? You know, to check in on Levi. Just once a day," Jack assured her.

"No, I don't mind at all. I really had a good time. You put me at ease."

A voice called for boarding. Jack had her backpack and felt awkward handing it to her. He wanted to offer something more.

"Well, I'll look forward to your call," Lin smiled.

"Lin?" Jack said as she turned to walk to the passenger gate.

"Yes?"

He came forward and put his arms around her waist, touching her lightly, and bent down to offer a quick but sincere kiss at the corner of her mouth. "Thank you."

Lin's eyes revealed surprise but approval at his sign of affection. "See you," she said, and returned the gesture, cheek to cheek, just enough of a message to assure him that she had accepted this first advance.

This was a first for her. It felt right, good, slow and measured toward something that might develop. But in case she had misunderstood his intentions, her return peck on the cheek wouldn't be taken as a sign of anything more than female courtesy.

Jack backed away as she left to board the plane. He watched until she disappeared inside the cabin. *Back to Paradise Bay*. He sighed. *Life is good*, he thought, his step quickening at the thought of spending more time with Lin.

Now he was going to become the student of Levi Harper, with even more determination. He had learned how devoted Lin was to his newfound father. That, and the fact that his lifelong yearnings for a father-son relationship were being realized in some measure through the journal reading, encouraged him to learn, adopt, and behave according to the convictions of the piano man.

50

SONATA FOR THE AWAKE

Veterans' Hospital, Los Angeles

OVER FOUR WEEKS HAD PASSED. LEVI HAD SHOWN SIGNS OF improvement after a month of the music therapy that Lin An had added to her daily routine, but it had since been determined that he had suffered a massive cardiac arrest. Revived, there simply wasn't much left in him to rescue.

"He's lived an awfully hectic life these past four years," Jack said when she called him in Paradise Bay to report Levi's condition.

"There was improvement, though, until the heart attack last week. I know the music was helping him, but there just isn't a cure for the cardiac and possible brain damage he's suffered. It's going to take a miracle now. But there are times when I feel like he's trying to break out, let us know he's in there."

There was silence on Jack's end of the line. He was trying to come up with an idea that might keep life support going until he could get to L.A. But he also knew the decision wasn't his to make. It was Jenna's, the recipient of a spontaneous healing no one possibly could have predicted. The tables were turned now, and she sat praying by Levi's bedside every day, while her preemie infant Angel grew stronger under the constant attention of the staff at St. Francis, the hospital where she'd been delivered.

"I'm so sorry, Jack," Lin finally said, breaking the silence. "We all wanted him to have another miracle awakening, but we've got to be realistic."

"I understand," he sighed. "I only wish . . ."

"What?" she prodded.

"A lot of things, I guess. That I could hear him say my name, that I could talk to him. His words have stirred up my emotions. I realize that you and I . . . that we have so much to share, and . . ."

"And?" Lin was listening to Dr. Jenkins with one ear, realizing he was giving Jenna information that she needed to pay attention to. But she wanted to hear what Jack had to say. "I hope you'll tell me more about the journals," she went on when he didn't respond. "I need some answers, too."

"I will. I might even have them published. The ideas that came out of his awakening from his thirty years of sleep are so profound that I'm beginning to believe God gave him a second chance, a chance to live a life of innocence again and share it with the world. Does that sound crazy?"

"Not at all. There's nothing wrong with being a believer, Jack. I've always known there was something beyond mere friendship in the bond between our fathers, and I'm also beginning to believe there's a reason for the way I'm starting to feel about . . ."

she hesitated. Now it was Lin's turn to be embarrassed. Part of her wanted Jack there to comfort her, but the other part wanted to remain clinical and aloof. Safe, where no one could hurt her. "Can I call you back?" she asked, noticing that the conversation between Jenna and Dr. Jenkins seemed to be wrapping up.

"Sure," Jack said. "I'm getting ready to head over to the church to relax and play some piano pieces, but I'll be carrying my cell phone."

"Great. I'll call you later." Lin hung up, satisfied with herself, and stepped back into Levi's room from the hallway.

"You don't have to make this decision today, Jenna," Dr. Jenkins was saying.

"Can you predict any improvement at all?"

"I'm afraid not." Jenkins looked up to see Chaplain Ringo coming in with several staff members. "Please come in, everyone."

"Hello, Jenna," Ringo said, taking both of her hands in his. "I can't tell you how deeply sorry I am about all this. You must be under an incredible strain. I have something for you to read. If you'd be more comfortable, I'm sure the others would be happy to step outside for a moment." When Jenna shook her head, Ringo pulled an envelope out of his pocket and handed it to her. "Levi sent this to me," he explained. "A few months ago."

Jenna sat down on the edge of the bed beside Levi and pulled out the letter, unfolding it with trembling hands. Tears flowed as she read it.

Dear Chaplain Ringo,

I want to thank you for all the guidance, the concern, and the care you've given me for the years I've been awake. I can't thank you enough. I do have one more request, though. I feel an urgency to get my journals and a few pieces of music completed.

I know you have a good working relationship with the hospital. If something should happen to me, would you convey to the staff and my dear wife Jenna that I will go peaceably, that I'm not afraid, and that I'll love them all forever? I can't upset Jenna by bringing this up now. She has her own struggles to contend with, and I've made a deal with God that she isn't aware of. I've asked Him to take my life instead of hers, and to give our child a chance.

My waking years have been blessedly full, and I have no regrets. Please do this for me, and if the moment comes to stand beside me one final time, say a prayer.

Oh, and by the way, remember China Beach and Recondo School, when you said you were thinking about becoming a chaplain someday? I knew back then that you were special. Hoo-rah Force Recon! We were twenty years old just yesterday, weren't we? With admiration and belief.

> *Your friend,*
> *Levi Harper*

Jenna's hands trembled. She handed the letter back to Chaplain Ringo, who passed it around for the others to read, then pulled a chair up closer to her and sat down.

"Do what your heart tells you to do, Jenna," he said, as if reading her mind. Unknowingly, he had chosen the exact words Levi had said to her many times in the past.

She looked to Dr. Jenkins, then Lin An, for help. But Jenkins lowered his eyes to the floor; Lin An shook her head and turned

away. Only Chaplain Ringo, no stranger to heartbreak and tragedy, could meet her eyes.

"I should wait for Jeff to get back from his trip to the East
Coast. If I agree to sign this release, can we stipulate that Jeff
gets to say his good-byes before you stop life support?"

Jenkins nodded. "Of course. We'll leave the form here. You
don't have to sign it until Jeff is here and you're ready."

"Okay, fine. I just want what Levi would want," she said, losing the battle for composure.

Chaplain Ringo reached out and took her in his arms. "He
knows that, Jenna," he said as she sobbed.

Lin quietly slipped out of the room, unable to deal with the
intensity of emotion. For all intents and purposes, she knew, Levi
Harper was already dead. She wiped her eyes and headed for the
office, unaware that Chaplain Ringo was now kneeling beside
the bed, offering the final prayer that Levi had requested in his
letter.

51

DIMINUENDO

GOD'S WILL BE DONE," CHAPLAIN RINGO FINISHED.

He was drawn back in time to China Beach, then to the line
of Marine corpses being loaded onto a helicopter during the battle for the city of Hue. He could see Tran An begging for someone to believe that Levi Harper was still alive.

Then, he had examined Levi as they prepared to place him
into a body bag beside Albert Tenny. But he had listened to
Tran's plea, seen tears running from the corners of Levi's eyes,
and finally persuaded the two GIs to take him to the aid station.

"God's will be done, Jenna," he repeated now, embracing her
again.

"I'd like to be alone with him for awhile before Jeff gets here,"
she said, calmer now.

Dr. Jenkins motioned the others out of the room. Chaplain

Ringo followed, then turned back to her from the doorway.

"I'll wait outside. Can I offer you a ride to St. Francis?" he asked.

"I'd appreciate that. Thank you."

He slipped out and closed the door behind him, then stood guard in the hallway.

Jenna smiled down at Levi and stroked his thinning hair, hints of gray along the edges. She had given love to the father of her children, the man she had first married. She had even believed she loved him all those years. But her heart had never released her from the longing she'd felt for Levi Harper since that day he'd come flying down the hill on the silly homemade scooter.

She had been prisoner to the love of a man who'd been dead to her since 1968. But then he'd come back to life, and they'd shared four glorious years of passion and devotion. The diminuendo had begun with her failing health in the third year. If only . . .

At least now something of him would remain.

When she held their daughter, Angel, she'd also be holding him.

"I'm so grateful to have loved you, Levi," she whispered. "I'm praying. We're all praying. And if you can hear me, I want you to know that God granted your wish. I'm getting well, and you're still here. Please come back to me, Levi."

Jenna took the pearls from around her neck, then gently laid them in the palm of his hand.

"These always brought you back to me. Just believe, Levi," she whispered.

"I'm sorry, Jack, but it doesn't look like it'll be much longer." Lin An held the phone in one hand, searching her desk for a CD

with the other. She had gone into her office after leaving Levi's
room to call him and tell him about Jenna's decision.

"I'll come right away," he said.

"No, Jack. There isn't time, and he wouldn't even know you
were here. I'll call you when it's over. I promise."

"Lin, I . . ." He couldn't finish. His heart raced with a confused sense of emotion. Love for a man he learned about from
the journals, and the same emotion for a girl he'd barely met.
"I . . ."

"Yes?"

"I hope to see you soon."

"I will be waiting. Waiting right here. When this is over," she
answered.

Reluctantly, Jack agreed to postpone his trip to L.A. and laid
the phone down quietly.

Lin hung up with a heavy heart. Something about Jack stirred
her. Now mixed with her love for Levi—almost a worship for
the man—she would have thrown herself into his arms had he
been standing in the doorway of her office now.

She caught herself in the reverie and continued her search,
finding the CD she was looking for in the bottom drawer of her
desk. It was her personal copy of the *Believe in Paradise* album.
Levi had recorded the song and several others of his original
compositions with the U.S. Naval Reserve Orchestra and Choir.
Proceeds from the sale of the CD would go to veteran support
groups throughout the state, through a benefit arranged by
Chaplain Ringo that had aired on PBS. Lin hadn't played the
CD yet; she had the video at home, had played it almost every
night over the past few weeks when her worry about Levi's condition kept her from sleep, but this copy of the music was still
shrink-wrapped in the jewel case.

She struggled and finally pulled the case open. Levi had a

right to hear his music again, she reasoned. Her hands were tied with regard to the life-support situation. The only thing she could do now was play his music to him, an appropriate *finale* to his long and tortuous experience. She slipped the CD in her pocket and headed to the nurse's station.

"Tom, I have a special favor to ask," she said to one of the orderlies. "When do you clock out?"

"Not until ten o'clock tonight. Why?"

"Come with me." She led him to Levi's room and pulled the CD out of her pocket, popped it into the CD player on the nightstand, then carefully placed the headset around the dying man's head.

"This is an hour-long CD," she explained. "Your job is to stay here until it's finished and watch Mr. Harper very closely. Write down all of your observations, the smallest details. I want to know if his eyelids move, if a finger jerks, if his lips open even slightly. Understand?"

"Sure. Anything for Mr. Harper. I love this guy." The orderly pushed the play button.

The last of Levi Harper's music began.

52

FINALE

"Are you ready to go now?" Albert asked.

"Yes," Levi replied. "Mission accomplished?"

Albert nodded and motioned for Levi to follow him, a gesture Levi recalled from their Vietnam days. "All clear," he said.

"Ready." Levi rose from his bed, looked down at his comatose body, then turned away to follow his friend. "You've always taken care of me, Albert."

Tenny winked. "That's what I do best." He led Levi out of the room, and they found themselves at the end of the pier in Paradise Bay.

"Where to?" Levi asked.

"One final recon, Button-Fly," Albert grinned. "We're a team again. Look at your clothes."

Levi looked down and laughed in surprise. "Dress blues! What's this all about?"

Albert didn't respond.

"What's that?" Levi had noticed a faint gray object outlined against the white fog out at sea.

"What do you think it is?" Albert asked.

"I know that fishing rig!"

"Yes, you do. All physical objects embody their immaterial equivalent," Albert explained. "Everything that has ever existed exists still. All things that will exist have a birth elsewhere. Like your music."

"That's it!" Levi laughed with sudden comprehension. "That's where the music came from! The notes, the melodies."

It made perfect sense to him now. Creation did not come from emptiness. It simply waited to be organized. The birth of his music had come through his hands, his heart, and his mind, but it had always been there, an immaterial sound, sound waiting for his detection.

"Hear that?" Albert asked, referring to the sounds from town as the ship drew closer.

"Yes." Levi turned to face the white chapel across the street from the wharf. "I'm going to miss this place."

"You need to tell Jack what you're feeling."

"I can do that?"

"Go ahead, Levi," Albert smiled. "I'll be waiting here with the boys."

Levi knew Albert was referring to their friends from the war years, and his heart beat with excitement at the prospect of seeing them again as he walked to the church. He drank in the sights of the ghost town that he'd left instructions about in his trust fund, how it was to be made into a beacon of hope, love, and music to the world. It would be up to Jack, the long-lost son he now felt he had known all his life. It now seemed as if everything he'd ever written, including his music and the journals, had been meant for Jack Santos to find.

He entered the church and walked up to the piano as Jack played for the townspeople in the pews below. He wasn't immediately aware that they had gathered to mourn his death. The experience was all too pleasant, like a wonderful, peaceful dream.

"Hello, son," he whispered into Jack's ear. "You're very good, better than I ever was. Son, I want you to know I love you very much."

Jack didn't notice the emotion stirring inside him until it completely clouded his vision. He couldn't take his hands off the keys, driven to find the perfect melody that he would play as a tribute to Levi Harper when the life support was removed.

"I don't have much time, son," Levi went on, "but I want you to know everything will be all right. Just play the music. Play all the music that's in you. When all is said and done, it's the music we make, the sweet melodies we offer to others, that we're remembered by. I'll come back someday, Jack. Take my name. Care for Jenna and Angel. Go to Lin An and love her with all your heart. You're the piano man now."

Jack stopped abruptly. He felt a strange sensation, like a pleasant breeze wafting by.

Levi bent down and kissed his son's cheek. "Play, son," he whispered, then left as he had come.

Albert inhaled the salty ocean air. "I loved this place," he said to Levi, who was standing beside him again.

Levi stared out at the water, coming to peace with himself.

He wondered if he had loved enough, created enough, been enough of an influence on others in the brief time God had granted him with his awakening.

"Good enough?" he asked.

Albert nodded.

"Who's taking point?" Levi asked.

Albert smiled. "Here they come."

The boat docked, and a small Asian man tied it to the moorings.

As Levi took a few steps forward, they all turned to face him. "Hoo-rah!" they shouted in unison.

Levi flew down to the gangplank. "Tran? Is it really you?"

The Vietnamese fisherman turned and smiled. "I tell you I come back, numba one GI!"

"Tran!" Levi pulled the small man into an embrace. He looked up after a moment to see the entire recon team standing at ease on the deck. But one was missing.

"Who's taking point?" he asked again.

"Tag! You're it!" Cannibal laughed, grabbing him from behind.

"I should've known," Levi grinned.

A flash of understanding came to him then. These men had come to him on the boat that had disappeared when Tran was lost at sea the year before to make him comfortable as they escorted him to the place where he was headed. They had embarked on their last recon mission in Vietnam on a boat, and now it was all right. Everything was all right, the way it should have been.

Levi put a foot on the gangplank to board the craft, then hesitated. "There's no going back if I cross over, is there?"

"No, there isn't," Albert replied.

"Do I have a choice this time?"

Albert put his hands on Levi's shoulders. "Yes, you do, Levi. This is your final test. You have the choice to come with us or stay until your music is finished. Either way, the time is short for those you will leave behind."

"I love you guys. And that body of mine hasn't exactly been a picnic, you know." Levi looked at each one of his fellow Marines, then back at the chapel, struggling with the decision. "Final recon?" he asked.

Cannibal nodded. "If you come with us, it is."

Levi looked at Paulos. He just smiled. Henderson shrugged his shoulders and nodded.

"They need me here. And I still need them. You boys understand, don't you? I mean . . . I owe all of you. And I don't know if I can ever repay you."

"No sweat, GI!" Tran grinned. "Come back for you. Lin okay. You okay. Jack, numba one. Just like you. Go be good piano man." Tran untied the small craft and pulled the plank to the deck as the boat drifted away from the wharf.

"*Semper fi,*" Levi offered with a salute. Albert's voice was faint but he heard him just the same.

"Always," Albert replied.

He fought his way back to consciousness, grateful for the pleasant dream. He could sense someone there, and he tried harder to open his eyes.

Tom moved closer to the bed, thought he had noticed Mr. Harper's eyelids moving. He looked down and saw Levi's fingers rubbing the pearls clasped in his hand.

"Dr. An!" he shouted, running to the door.

Lin An ran down the corridor, a worried look on her face.

•   •   •

Jack had one of those days again. Sleepless, he had gone nearly forty-eight hours now. He was seeing things too, he decided. He went down to Fran's on the wharf, had some of her famous pie, and thought he saw the outline of a fishing boat glide into the afternoon mist.

Tired. He was seeing things because of the story, a worked-up imagination, and exhaustion.

Now he was in the chapel. People had heard the news once he mentioned to Fran that Levi's life support was being removed. Word traveled fast for a town where life was somewhat slower than a snail's pace. The entire population of Paradise Bay, it seemed, had gathered. Even old Bob the hippie had showed up.

Silent reverence had fallen over the people gathered together now. Anticipation and expectation mixed like a heavy mortar. Weighty, the mood was already reminiscent of a memorial service, one that no doubt would take place any day.

Jack Santos's hands had stopped, and he was gazing up at the ceiling as if looking for some answer there. The piano waited for a tune, and the voices in the pews were willing to sing if he could come up with something.

At least Lin An will be there, he told himself, searching for consolation. *At least I have her to look forward to.*

He placed his hands on the tired-looking ivory keys of the antiquated Kimball. Patience, he thought. The vibration of his cellular phone attached to his belt signaled a call.

"This must be it," he mumbled, reaching for it with shaky hands, steeling himself for the news.

"Hello?"

"He's back, Jack!" Lin An said breathlessly. "Your father is awake! We've taken him off life support, and he's looking around the room."

"Are you serious?"

"Yes! He's breathing on his own, and he's alert. Jack, I have to go now. But I love you." The words were out before she could stop them.

"I love you, too, Lin. I've loved you from the first moment I saw you." The line was already dead but he had voiced what he felt to her. He sensed two miracles were happening as he sat stunned by the news.

Jack turned on the piano bench then, remembering the people in the pews before him. He smiled down at them. "He's back!"

Jack then returned to the source of his strength, his music. A new believer, he played. He played his emotions out from his heart and mind, and exulted in his joy at hearing the impossible from Lin, as the townspeople raised their voices to join his.

This was their song, a favorite. The verses of an Oliver Wendell Holmes hymn. Put to music in a special arrangement by a young Levi Harper, they had been added to all the hymnals by his father when Levi returned, wounded, from Vietnam. All who had remained in Paradise Bay had long ago memorized these lines.

> *Thou gracious God, whose mercy lends,*
> *The light of hope, the smile of friends.*
> *Our gathered flock thine arms enfold,*
> *As in the peaceful days of old.*

53

REPRISE

He WAS RESTING PEACEFULLY NOW, TAKING A NAP BETWEEN visits from his loved ones. His speech had been improving, and he was walking unassisted to the recreation hall three times a day. Lin An had come in earlier to check his vital signs. He had thanked her, asked her to bend closer, then planted a gentle kiss on her cheek.

He was showing more of an interest in solid foods again, and his cheery nature belied the depression he had succumbed to during the months when he thought he was going to lose Jenna. The piano man was once again the cause for celebration across the country.

Levi's will to live, to be with Jenna, get to know his son and new daughter must have been the cause, Lin had decided. His words were still slurred, but his hands were already moving effortlessly over the piano keys in the recreation hall. It warmed her heart to know that Levi Harper's love and kindness would continue to influence millions of music lovers for years to come.

"Hello, Lin."

Her breath caught in her throat at the sound of Jack's voice. She turned to find him standing in the doorway, holding a bouquet in one hand and a gift-wrapped box in the other. He closed the door behind him.

"For you." He held the bouquet out to her.

"They're beautiful." She closed her eyes, brought them close, and let the fragrance surround her.

"So are you," Jack added softly. Jack moved to her then, lifting her chin until she opened her eyes to meet his. "I've learned a lot about love these past months."

"What is that?" she ventured, allowing herself to surrender her professional bearing and become, simply, a woman.

"Love is from the heart and not the head. Love is never forgetting that unseen hands guide us. All I know, Lin, is when love knocks, you should open the door. It has knocked hard since I met you."

Lin gazed back at him, desperately wanting to be rescued by him.

He held out the narrow box. "I have something else for you, too," he said. "Open it."

She carefully unwrapped it, laying the bow and paper aside. As she lifted the lid and looked inside, her hand flew to her mouth and tears sprang to her eyes.

Jack took the box from her hand, reached inside, and lifted the delicate pearl necklace out of its case. Lin leaned forward and allowed him to clasp it around her neck.

"Two children once made a pact," he explained, "and they

sealed it with the words, 'Just believe.' " He pulled Lin into his arms and gently kissed her. "I love you, Lin An," he whispered. "I haven't been able to get you out of my mind these past few weeks. And I feel as though Levi's journals led me to you and made me understand what I'm feeling. I am so grateful to feel this way, and for what you have done for Levi."

She didn't know what to say, but she now believed it was possible that her story could include the love that Levi and Jenna shared. She surrendered to him, put her arms around his neck, and buried herself in his embrace.

"I love you, Jack Santos. I've never understood love until now."

"Marry me, Lin," he whispered. "Marry me in Paradise Bay. I'll call Chaplain Ringo. We'll use the old chapel near the wharf. Invite the whole town."

"Yes!" she laughed. Yes!"

He kissed her again, a long, lingering kiss.

"No more than thirty seconds," a weak voice said from behind them.

Six Months Later

Jack paced back and forth in Levi's study, excited but emotional about today. Levi would not only witness his only son wed in the chapel Rex Harper had so faithfully built decades before, but Levi would also be at the piano, and they both would perform a new arrangement composed for the occasion. They had arranged for an extra piano to brought in for the ceremony. Rex

Harper, the grandfather he never knew, would have been proud of the restoration that Jack had so recently completed on the church building. Bringing it back to life seemed to renew the town. Already it was a focus of attention, with nearly every member of the community promising to be there for the ceremony and Sunday services.

Lin was upstairs with Jenna performing last-minute female makeup rituals and adjusting the stunning dress she would wear to the wedding ceremony. Chaplain Ringo could hardly contain his enjoyment of visiting with Levi and reminiscing about the happier moments of their Marine Corps days in the parlor just down the hall. The chaplain would perform the ceremony and then stay for Sunday services, conducting the official rededication of the Paradise Bay Congregational Church.

Now that Lin An had agreed to marry him, the connection between the Harper family, the Santos family, and Tran An had come full circle. The healing balm of love and music was restoring lives to their rightful place in this corner of the universe.

His sense of loss over Claire was still there, but it was no longer painful, and he could see now that they had never been right for each other, that an invisible hand had been at work in all this.

Paradise Bay might have been frozen in the past, but it was magically restoring his lost childhood innocence. He would use this new life and love to create music that might someday make a difference in the world.

Living here with Lin meant he would also get to know a father he had come to love only through journals and music. He would have the family he'd always dreamed of. Together, he and Lin would help Jenna care for Levi, keep him well and happy until his music was finished. God willing, they would have decades together.

In a moment they would head over to the chapel and find the

town had gathered. To top off the miracle of the past six months, his mother had consented to come. Carol, together with the entire family, had enjoyed a quiet meal, compliments of Fran, down at the wharf café last night.

A spirit of warmth and peace accompanied the gathering—a phenomenon known to the givers of mercy, the recipients of forgiveness. The evening ended with sacred embraces, Carol for her childhood friend Jenna, Levi for Carol, and a renewal found in letting go, appropriate for the rekindled life and spirit coming back to Paradise Bay.

Jeffrey, Karen Sue, and their spouses had returned to live in Paradise Bay, and projects such as the Wharf Bed and Breakfast were just one of many that the Harper family, thanks to Jeffrey's astute business sense, had begun, to help shape and revitalize the slumbering seaside town.

Today Levi and Jack would play "Paradise Wedding Suite," one of the first original compositions they had collaborated on for some of Jack's film contacts in Los Angeles. Levi's musical popularity was growing and Jack was a believer in how his new love had unlocked his own creativity.

Jack gazed down at his watch. He couldn't believe minutes could tick by so torturously slowly. He paced in front of the desk where he had discovered the life of a father he had never known, and would not have come to know without his journals.

The last journal lay square on the desktop. He pulled the chair out, sat, and turned to the final page to review how the Harper love story had finally ended.

He looked long and hard at the last page, unsettled and unsure of how he could have missed it. The date was clearly marked in ink at the top, showing it had been written nearly eight months ago—just before Levi had collapsed and almost died.

Jack didn't remember this page, wasn't sure how he could

have missed it. But those few weeks had been so emotionally charged and exhausting for him, all the newness of having a father, meeting Lin An, discovering Paradise Bay—he must have overlooked this page somehow. He began to read.

Love is an incongruous thing, a whimsical attack of the heart and head simultaneously. Although my injuries in Vietnam put me in a catatonic state for three decades, I was never fully aware of my loss. My heart never slept.

Even if I could have forgotten her, like so many other memories that were either faint or nonexistent upon my awakening, I still believe I would have had to face the fact that my feelings for her were etched on my heart. Love did the deed, and I was bound by it.

But I wouldn't have had it any other way. Never should we consider living life free from those chains of love that hold us breathless like a precious sonata until the final note is played.

The sonata of love will have its way to the end. We will play this thing out and, when dying, breathe the words that form the names of those we have loved.

I'm a romantic fool, I know. But when a person you've loved exists in your heart's memory, there's no avoiding where it will lead. Like a strange destiny taking us down paths we may never have chosen to wander, we still would've found a way, somehow, to finally be together.

Was there ever any doubt that this is how our story would end?

CHASE LIBRARY
Route 28
West Harwich, MA 02671

Joyce

Board of Selectmen
Harwich, Mass.

Board of Selectman:

We, the staff and members of the Chase
Library thank you for your support of Article
28, at Town Meeting, on May 5, 2003. We appreciate your recognition of our Library as a
Harwich tradition, and an important service to
our community.

In particular, we send special thanks to
Cyd Zeigler and Donald Howell for their kind
remarks in support of the Chase Library.

Very truly yours,

Ruth A. Hudson, Secretary

HOW TO CONTACT
JAMES MICHAEL PRATT

James Michael Pratt invites correspondence through his Web site and personal mailing address: www.jmpratt.com and P.O. Box 970189, Orem, Utah, 84097. You are invited to join the JMPRATT.COM Bookclub to receive autographed bookplates and bookmarks as well as "Reader's Club" guides for *Paradise Bay* and his other titles. Mr. Pratt visits selected cities across the United States in support of public library and community bookstore events. Contact him directly to request an invitation to your town or city.